C000171562

THE
WIDOW'S
HUSBAND

BOOKS BY LESLEY SANDERSON

THE
WIDOW'S
HUSBAND

LESLEY SANDERSON

bookouture

Published by Bookouture in 2022

An imprint of Storyfire Ltd.
Carmelite House
50 Victoria Embankment
London EC4Y 0DZ
United Kingdom

www.bookouture.com

Copyright © Lesley Sanderson, 2022

Lesley Sanderson has asserted her right to be identified as the author of this work.

All rights reserved. No part of this publication may be reproduced, stored in any retrieval system, or transmitted, in any form or by any means, electronic, mechanical, photocopying, recording or otherwise, without the prior written permission of the publishers.

ISBN: 978-1-80314-065-0
eBook ISBN: 978-1-80314-064-3

This book is a work of fiction. Names, characters, businesses, organizations, places and events other than those clearly in the public domain, are either the product of the author's imagination or are used fictitiously. Any resemblance to actual persons, living or dead, events or locales is entirely coincidental.

To Louise, for supporting me and my writing and making it fun.

PROLOGUE

She would go mad if she knew what he'd done. He had to manage the situation carefully, extract himself from his knotty predicament and slip away before she found out about it. All he had to do was get through this afternoon – hopefully it wouldn't even turn out to be a whole afternoon if everything went to plan. If he was found out now, he risked losing everything.

He knew his own weaknesses; if he saw her again, he might change his mind – she had that power over him, despite everything. Weakness was what had got him involved with her in the first place. He'd come to logical conclusions after a lot of soul searching; he'd even got as far as preparing a speech and getting the words clear in his head, exactly how he planned to say them. He was determined not to drink, to harden himself to her charms. He needed to – take that last time he'd been so determined to leave her, and all it had taken was a look from those eyes, a brush of her red lips against his cheek, a word whispered in his ear, and he'd been ripping her clothes off, his earlier resolve discarded on the floor along with her dress.

But he'd made the right decision about the will. She couldn't take that away from him – nobody could.

He went over his resolve as he locked the car, his feet crunching gravel as he strode towards the house, steeling his determination with each step. Two steps up, the farmhouse not quite what he expected, the low female voice telling him to wait a moment, a sultry voice, the door opening and her perfume wafting out, a soft hand on his wrist. Maybe one last time, he thought as she reached for his tie, deftly ripping it from his neck along with the resolve from his mind.

As long as you don't tell her what you've done.

One last time before you leave without saying goodbye.

ONE

RACHEL

Lara is in her favourite position – on the sofa, legs hanging over the armrest, phone glued to her hand, half watching a game show on the television. Rachel wishes she was in her place, that it was three hours later, the children up in their bedrooms, builders departed and a glass of gin and tonic at her side. Instead, she is at the kitchen island, chopping garlic and mushrooms to make a risotto for dinner. She spends a lot of her life wishing she were doing something else, but if she didn't cook, the kids wouldn't eat and... She switches off that familiar train of thought. Her sigh is so loud that Lara looks up from her phone.

'All right, Mum?'

'Of course, love.' She smiles at her daughter's compassion. Such a thoughtful child; if only the girls in her year could see Lara through her eyes.

Now, if it were Emma who was asking, Rachel would pour out her frustration at the lack of privacy with the building work, the noise of constant drilling and banging, the workmen stomping up and down the stairs in their heavy boots, wishing she could afford to live elsewhere while the work is going on. Her sister is like a walking gratitude list, always there to remind her of what is good about her life – and she's right. She has a home and two healthy children. Some evenings, when the builders have departed for the day, she even wanders around the empty space admiring their work, thrilled that her grandmother's kindness has enabled her to extend the house, to make it her own and erase the memories of the past. She understands what Emma is intending: by pointing out her blessings, the loss of Rachel's husband will feel less overwhelming – they've survived, haven't they? Emma puts her right on her worries about her introverted daughter too – Lara is almost a teenager. She reminds her what they themselves were like at that age, spotty and moody – Emma stressing about her too curly hair and Rachel wishing her own wasn't so straight – and no wonder, with their bodies sprouting in uncomfortable directions and that weird desire for attention from boys. The fascination with the opposite sex gripped the whole class somewhere in the middle of Year 8 and never seemed to stop. 'Speak for yourself,' Rachel tells her.

It makes Rachel think about Tom and what might have been. Seven years on from his disappearance, she still marvels at how every thought is like a tributary, streaming back to the same river. *What happened to him?* Emma assures her these musings will fade with time, but she can't imagine how. Unfinished business has a way of rearing its ugly head.

'They've found that woman, Mum.' The game show has finished, and the local news is on. 'A woman jogging in the park stumbled over her. Can you imagine? That's horrible.'

The newsreader is going over the recent headline-hitting story: a university student who disappeared a few months ago without a trace on her way to a lecture. Lara has been following the story avidly, making comparisons with their own situation, which is understandable. Rachel watches the end of the bulletin with her.

'It's so sad, Mum.' Lara tugs at her blue beanie hat she's taken to wearing 24/7.

'I know. Try not to upset yourself. Why don't you give Holly a ring? You could invite her over. You haven't mentioned her for ages.'

'She's busy.'

'You don't know that.'

'Yes I do, she's got her cousin staying. What time is Josh back?' Lara switches off the television and turns her attention to her phone.

Rachel must be one of the few mothers who wishes her child were using her phone to contact her friends; instead, Lara mostly uses it to play games on, losing herself in childish worlds where animals are collected and aliens are friendly. At least Rachel doesn't have to worry about online predators. Some of the anecdotes her friends tell her make her want to lock her children away forever. Which goes completely against her desire for Lara to be more sociable... The way her mind works reminds her of a scrambled pair of headphones, the wires taking forever to untangle.

'Mum?'

Rachel looks at the clock. 'About six thirty, Emma said. We'll eat as soon as he gets in.'

Lara perks up. 'Is Auntie Emma staying for dinner?'

'No, she's out somewhere this evening.' Lara slumps back onto the sofa. 'I'll get her to come over another night; you know she loves seeing you.'

Emma drops Josh off just before six.

'Thanks so much for picking him up. I know how busy you

are.' Emma's life is a social whirl. She always makes time to help when she can, but she's also always in a hurry.

'Can't stop, I'm due at Slimming World in ten minutes,' she says, giving Lara a hug before she drives off too fast down the street. Rachel smiles ruefully, wishing her sister would stop worrying about her weight. Impossible to imagine.

The head builder, Pete, calls her upstairs to show her the work they have done today. His assistant, Danny, is packing up their tools and tidying away the pots of paint and other paraphernalia before folding his ladder. All Rachel's conversations to do with the building work have been conducted through Pete. Danny is friendly enough, but a man of very few words. He's extremely good-looking – enough to make her daughter blush when she first met him, despite being so much older. Rachel collects their used cups from the windowsill.

'Not long to go now,' Pete says.

The work on the loft extension started seven weeks ago; already it's taken longer than the promised six weeks, due to a delay in the delivery of building materials. It's by no means a luxury renovation, given Rachel's limited budget; it represents a lifestyle makeover. Her grandmother would have wanted her to be happy after everything they've been through. The money is enough to cover the landscaping of the garden too. Sometimes she wonders whether they'd have been better off moving out of this house, with its resident ghost lurking around, but the children are dead against moving, and in particular she doesn't want to upset Lara. She looks around the empty room.

'We've put the windows in today,' Pete says. 'Great view you've got there.' She crosses to the window and looks out over the fields, where sheep are dotted about like blobs of cotton wool. That's another reason why she'd be reluctant to move away from here: the beautiful countryside on their doorstep. Sometimes over the past seven years she's needed a moment taking in that view to compose herself, to calm her racing mind and get herself into a meditative state.

'Exactly,' she says. 'Why do you think this is going to be my bedroom?'

Pete laughs. 'It shouldn't take us long to finish up here – just another week or so – then we'll leave you in peace.'

'Great,' she says. 'Not that I want to get rid of you or anything.'

Josh lets her know he is starving – another constant – and she marvels at his endless pit of a stomach. No matter how much he puts away, it doesn't make any difference to his bony frame. She packed a more than adequate snack for him to take with him.

'How was drama club?' she asks as she ladles risotto onto their plates and pours them each a glass of water.

Josh can't get his words out fast enough. 'It was ace. We had to be part of a street gang and I had to grab this lady's bag and run away really fast. I had to do it three times because one of the boys kept saying his words wrong. Sophie said I was really good.'

'Well done.' Praise from Sophie, the drama club teacher, is not easily earned. 'Did she say what time rehearsal is next week?'

'Hmm.' Josh screws up his face. 'Can't remember. I'll ask Toby.' He reaches for his phone.

'Not now. Wait until after dinner.'

He keeps them entertained with more anecdotes from his evening. He eats at the same rate as he speaks, and his plate is soon empty. Rachel and Lara have barely started theirs. 'Can I go and learn my lines now, Mum?'

'Haven't you got any homework to do?'

'No.'

'Are you sure? I don't need to look at your homework book?'

'No, I promise. We didn't have a proper lesson this afternoon. It was only art.'

'*Only* art,' Lara says. 'That and English are the only lessons worth going to school for. And swimming, obviously.'

With neither of her children being academically inclined, Rachel imagines they will follow a more creative path in life. Josh is set on being an actor at the moment. Lara has inherited her father's talent for swimming. Rachel herself wanted to be an air hostess at that age; nowadays the thought of being stuck in an aeroplane high up in the sky holds no appeal for her.

'OK, off you go.'

Josh takes his plate over to the sink, then runs upstairs, his feet heavy on the wooden floorboards.

'I need you to help me with my Spanish, Mum,' Lara says. 'I tried to do it earlier, but it's a bit complicated.'

'Have you finished your meal?'

Lara has left some food on her plate. Unlike her brother, she has to be encouraged to eat, but Rachel doesn't chide her about it today.

'I'll wash up and then we can have a look at it. Not sure how much help I'll be, though, *amigo*. Doesn't Holly help you any more?'

'She's too busy. And it's *amiga*, I think, as it's feminine.'

'See – you know more than me already, but I'll do my best.'

Rachel washes up and tidies the kitchen, relieved that the end of the building work is in sight and she'll be able to begin the part of the project she's been looking forward to – decorating and furnishing the extension rooms. She's been gathering samples and creating mood boards, getting some great ideas for using reclaimed items and upcycling what she already has to make the most of her budget, but she hasn't quite finalised exactly how she wants the rooms to look. What might seem like a frivolous pastime to others has great meaning for her – it's to reward herself for getting through the past few years amidst such uncertainty.

She can't believe that the seven-year period is almost over and that finally they will be able to put it all behind them. Declaring her missing husband dead is not a task she relishes, but it will bring this chapter to a close. The money from her grandmother has enabled her to change the house, so that if Tom were to walk back in – something she finds it impossible to rule out, even now – he would no longer recognise the home they once shared. It's a way of giving herself a new start. Without the promise of the imminent life insurance payout, she wouldn't have taken such a risk; she'd have saved the inheritance money, she'd have needed it. But now, finally, the end is in sight. She glances at the calendar, where a cross marks each day off as the deadline creeps closer. Sometimes it feels like forever away.

Lara appears in the doorway.

'Nearly ready, love.'

'This came for you, Mum.' She hands her a white envelope, *RACHEL* written on the front in capital letters.

'Where did you find this?'

'It was on the doormat just now. It wasn't there when I went upstairs so it's only just arrived.'

Rachel turns the envelope over for a clue as to who might have sent it. Her first thought is Freddie. Their relationship – *friendship*, she corrects herself – is in its early stages, and he likes to spring little surprises on her, like the meal out at the new Italian last weekend. But this isn't his neat slanted writing. The flamboyance of the lettering sends a shock wave through her. She rushes to the front door and opens it, looking up and down the street. The pavements are empty, no sign of anyone around.

As she stares at the envelope, her gut tells her this isn't going to be good. She sits down, unseals it and pulls out a single sheet of paper. She angles it away from Lara, who is watching with interest, just in case. She hopes she is wrong, but her gut is usually reliable.

The paper is thin, the message in blue biro, one sentence. She gasps. She'd know that writing anywhere.

'Mum?'

'It's nothing, just business – a note from my solicitor. He must have had it delivered by a courier.' It's the first thing that enters her head.

Lara frowns, shrugs and goes back to the living room.

Rachel's hands are shaking as she reads the message from her ex-husband, who left home one morning six years and ten months ago and disappeared without trace. Who she loved and missed and mourned. Who she is about to declare dead.

I want to come back to you.

TWO

Lara is back, fidgeting in the doorway. 'We need to do my Spanish, Mum.'

'OK. I'm coming.' Rachel shoves the letter into her back pocket. Somehow she manages to turn her mind to her rudimentary knowledge of Spanish and help Lara answer the questions on the conjugation and basic differences of the verbs *ser* and *estar*. It was something she could never quite grasp herself, but trying to grapple with the meaning now helps turn her mind away from Tom's note.

Temporarily.

Of course it's bogus.

Is he alive?

Do I want him to be?

Lara goes up to her room when she's finished her homework, and for once Rachel doesn't fret about her spending so much time on her own. She sits out in the garden and allows herself to go over the details of that fateful day six years, ten months and seventeen days ago when Tom vanished. Every moment is engraved onto her brain – she went over and over it for weeks until there came a point when she'd had to stop or she'd have driven herself mad, and she had two small children to take care of.

What if the note is from him?

He wants to come back to me?

The local press relished the opportunity for lurid headlines once they found that the missing local businessman had left his wife for a younger model a few months prior to his vanishing act. Rachel pleaded for privacy, begged them to respect the family's right to process what was happening without reporters haranguing her from all sides, reminding them there were two small children involved. That didn't stop them splashing lurid details of their acrimonious split across the front pages, prodding at an open wound. Heidi was *so* photogenic, and Tom was a high-profile citizen, having won a prestigious award the year before his disappearance. Besides, in this small town, any departure from garden fetes and petty vandalism had the journalists of the *Tribune* slavering for a story.

The memory of the day he vanished without trace is still fresh in her mind, as if it were yesterday. Breakfast that morning was strained. Josh had kept her up most of the night; since Tom had left the family home and moved in with his mistress, he'd gone from being a trouble-free child to one who was constantly demanding attention. From the moment he was born he'd developed a special bond with his father, to the point where on occasion Rachel had felt a twinge of jealousy. Josh was a daddy's boy, and Tom was the one who used to get up at night to appease him when he needed it, which wasn't often back then. Until his father was gone, and Rachel's life underwent a huge change. If it hadn't been for her mother and sister, she's not sure how she would have managed.

At the time of his disappearance, Tom had been living with Heidi for eight months. Rachel had had to accept the situation, and they'd come to an arrangement whereby he had the children Tuesday to Friday, and the rest of the week they were with her. It meant she got to spend weekends with them, though occasionally they'd go off with Tom if he had something he particularly wanted to do with them. She'd missed them desperately at first, and it had taken six months before she'd started to appreciate having time to spend on her own. Josh was too young to understand what was going on, and Lara insisted everything was fine but was quieter than she had been. She'd insisted on keeping her door open at night so that the hall light prevented her from being in complete darkness.

The last day anyone saw Tom was a Monday. He and Heidi had taken the children to the zoo that weekend, and he'd dropped them back home early on Sunday evening. He'd waved from the garden gate, avoiding any mention of the previous weekend, much to Rachel's frustration, and driven off before she had a chance to speak to him. That night she had spent mulling over what exactly she wanted to say to him and how she was going to pin him down.

She'd snatched two hours' sleep before the alarm went off. She woke Lara first, allowing Josh to stay asleep until the noise of their movements around the house roused him. Breakfast was messy, and she left the table covered in spilt milk and Coco Pops to deal with when she got back from dropping Lara off at school. Her mother was taking Josh today – Rachel had sent an SOS message when she woke up asking her to have him so that she could catch up on her housework.

Her mum offered to stay and help her tidy up, but Rachel declined the offer, wanting to get on with her chores. She was finally appreciating making better use of her time away from the children. She used to spend hours just sitting and reflecting on what had happened, on why Tom had left her for Heidi.

She was younger of course, Heidi, barely twenty-four, never appearing without her hair styled and make-up carefully applied. Botoxed and beautiful, as Emma described her, but lacking in substance. None of them could imagine her relationship with Tom would last. What on earth did they talk about? I doubt they spend much time talking, Rachel couldn't help thinking.

She cleaned the house from top to bottom, ate a sandwich, then crashed out for two blissful hours, setting her alarm to wake her in time to fetch Lara. After her mum had brought Josh back and made them all tea, she put the children to bed. She had just left, at around nine, when Rachel received the call. *Heidi* flashed up on her mobile. She stared at her name, transfixed. Tom had insisted on giving her Heidi's number in case of any emergency when they had the children, but Rachel had never wanted it; she'd seen it as some kind of toxic element disturbing the balance of her phone. Now she took so long considering whether to answer that the ringing stopped, then started again immediately. She figured Heidi wouldn't call her without good reason. Tom must have told her about last weekend, she thought, panic seizing her. She was going to have it out with her. Hope mixed in with alarm. She breathed deeply and accepted the call.

Had she seen Tom?

The question confused her. Was it a trick one? *Did* Heidi know? Maybe she didn't. Besides, it had happened a week ago, and surely if she was going to find out, she would have done so by now.

Heidi repeated the question, elaborating, and Rachel composed herself. No, not today, she told her; not since yesterday, when he'd dropped the children back home. *Home.* Their real home, with her, not the fake set-up she refused to believe would last.

She tried to sound normal, calm.

Was it only nine days ago?

The events of the weekend before last had been on her mind every day since. She couldn't make sense of it no matter how much she went over it in her mind, and she daren't mention it to anyone else. If she were a vindictive person, she'd have crowed about it to Heidi – could do so now, in fact – but Heidi was asking her again if she'd seen Tom, and this time Rachel picked up on the anxiety in her voice and felt a responding twinge, wishing she didn't still care.

Heidi hadn't seen Tom since that morning. He'd gone to work as normal, phoned her at lunchtime to remind her he had a meeting that afternoon and would be home early. She was very apologetic about having to disturb Rachel, the last thing she wanted to do – Rachel knew that was certainly true – but it was getting late and she'd called his colleagues and friends, anyone she could think of, and nobody had seen him since he'd left for the meeting, and... Then she'd dissolved into tears. None of his colleagues knew what meeting he was talking about, though he organised his own appointments, so that wasn't necessarily anything to worry about.

'But I *am* worried,' she said.

And so was Rachel, but she didn't say anything. Her stomach was churning, and she thought back to the events of last weekend; how different Tom had been in the months since he'd left her and how last Saturday he'd been the old Tom from the minute he'd entered the house. At first she couldn't work out what had changed, but he hadn't had that stiff, defensive posture he'd adopted since meeting Heidi, guilt stamped all over him for what he'd done to his wife. He'd asked if they could talk, and they had, for hours. They were still talking when the sky had darkened and she'd switched on the lamps and the outside light. They'd sat on the terrace with a bottle of wine, and with his hunched shoulders and beaten air, she could see how sorry he was, how conflicted. She'd just put her hand on his to comfort him, because she still loved him despite everything and couldn't bear to see him in pain, and he'd leant towards her...

It had been natural to kiss and embrace and tear at each

other's clothes like they used to do, but then afterwards he'd dressed quickly, that anxious look back, saying *what have I done?*, and the spell was broken and she was back to being Rachel alone with their children in the house while he returned to the woman he'd left her for. To Heidi.

Did Heidi know?

Rachel had to assume she didn't, because otherwise she'd be screaming at Rachel, full of recriminations, as was usually her style. She wasn't known for holding back on her thoughts.

Guilt from that weekend enabled Rachel to push aside her personal feelings, and she tried to calm Heidi down. No, they hadn't had a row, Heidi said, everything had been normal and she didn't know what else to do. She'd called him and texted but his phone was off, and Tom never turned his phone off, she didn't have to tell Rachel that. She agreed to wait until morning, and if he hadn't returned by then, she was going to call the police.

'Let me know what happens,' Rachel said.

Once Heidi had hung up, Rachel allowed her own worries to surface. It was so out of character for Tom to go out of circulation; he was normally a kind and considerate man. She could hear her sister's scorn at this – *after the way he treated you?* – but she knew what he was really like. Tom was decent, a good sort, as long as he wasn't driven by lust. Her anxiety was based on what had happened last weekend, why Tom had slept with her. Unlike Heidi, he'd admitted there were problems in the relationship: she was possessive, demanding and extremely high maintenance. That was what had given Rachel hope.

Would Tom really leave Heidi? She'd seen a fragile side to him when he'd dressed after taking her to bed, face riddled with guilt, barely able to speak to her. Despite everything, she sensed that he still loved her, and it stirred up feelings she had finally started to forget. Had it all become too much for him and he just couldn't face her that evening?

Now she takes the envelope from her back pocket and smooths out the piece of paper. Tom's looping handwriting has a unique style. She envied it when she first saw it, teased him about having such flair; previous boyfriends had without exception had terrible handwriting. Her own isn't too bad, legible at least. Heidi's is round and girlish; Rachel remembers how four-year-old Lara tried to copy it, even though she could barely write, much to Rachel's irritation.

I want to come back to you.
  To you.

Definitely Tom's writing. Her stomach is churning, butterflies and terror all at once. If he is alive, after leaving them all without word, would she even *want* to see him again?

Yes, for her own peace of mind she'd prefer to know. Could she forgive him? She stares into her glass as if the answer lurks at the bottom. Does she want to?

She allows herself to imagine that the note *is* from Tom, that he's alive as she has always believed and he wants to come back to her. Would she have him back? Does she still love him? It's hard to get past the swell of rage that engulfs her just thinking about what she and the children have been put through these last years. The initial horror, the police investigation, and above all, the lack of a conclusion. If Tom ran away from his life, she can't forgive him, especially when he'd got her hopes up after that weekend. Love him? Yes or no? The question is too complicated for a one-word answer.

'Mummy!' Josh's voice rings out from the house, and she sighs as she heads indoors. Whatever this note means, one thing is clear. Her children matter in this, nothing else. She won't let anything upset them, not even their father.

THREE

RACHEL

Heidi's call had been on Rachel's mind all day. Not in an excessive, dominant way; the question it had posed was rumbling along in the background as she purchased items from her list in the supermarket, spoke to her mother – or rather listened to her latest saga with her troublesome neighbours – and cooked a meal for the children. She had been thinking about Tom all week as she battled the realisation that she was still in love with him, still desired him, but was still furious. She needed answers. Did he feel the same? Had he taken some time out from Heidi to think about it? Maybe he found it difficult to look her in the eye after what had passed between him and Rachel. Despite these thoughts, she also wanted confirmation that he was OK. When she sank into the sofa later that evening, she gave in to the impulse she'd been fighting all day.

Any news? she texted Heidi.

The reply was as fast as the return of serve in a tennis match.

Nothing. I've called the police and they're looking into it.

Rachel hesitated, typed, retyped, changed her mind and then started again.

Good idea. Please keep me posted.

She hesitated over texting Tom. What if he *was* in trouble? She'd never forgive herself if she didn't try.

Everything OK? Heidi is worried about you. So am I. Give me a call.

Her finger hovered for a while before pressing send. She used WhatsApp, so she could see whether he'd read the message. The single tick taunted her. Maybe he was offline. But where? And why? The questions continued.

She hadn't slept well that night. Josh had been fretful, and for once she was grateful for the distraction of having something to do while the hours stretched like an endless tunnel. Attending to her children's needs validated her existence, given the drop in confidence that Tom's betrayal had caused. *And you're considering taking him back? Seriously?*

Eventually she'd fallen asleep, but grabbed her phone as soon as she woke. There was no message from either Heidi or Tom. The single tick remained. Why wasn't he picking up messages? She worried at a loose piece of skin on her finger.

She waited until the children were at school before

contacting Heidi. This time she phoned her. Heidi picked up immediately, and Rachel's stomach dropped. It wasn't good news.

'The police sent someone round. The officer pointed out that Tom is a grown man, said he's most likely forgotten to call. Utter crap. He's not turned up at work today.'

Rachel called Freddie, Tom's close friend and colleague. Not so close since Tom's affair with Heidi, though. He'd known Rachel since she and Tom had started dating, and had made his feelings quite clear to Tom when he'd left his family and moved into Heidi's flat. He picked up immediately too, as if everyone was waiting for news. Not a good sign; he must be concerned.

'Have you heard from him?' he asked.

Rachel sighed. 'No, I was hoping you had.'

Freddie had been away the previous week, so couldn't comment on Tom's recent behaviour; prior to that, he said, he hadn't been any different from usual. 'Apart from the obvious; we hadn't been getting on so well, as you probably know. But he's an old mate and we have a business together – who am I to tell him how to run his life. Everyone makes mistakes; I just wish it hadn't meant hurting you and the kids.'

They agreed to speak again that evening.

The police turned up later that morning, and then it began. The slow realisation that Tom had vanished.

A Detective Sergeant Mortimer was in charge of the case. The first interview was conducted by a pair of younger police constables, one male, one female, the woman asking the questions and scribbling in her notebook while the man wandered around looking at photos and making Rachel nervous. What was he looking for?

'How do you feel about your husband leaving you for another woman?' the male officer asked. He was still standing, towering over her, and Rachel wished she was on her feet too.

He didn't look old enough to be doing such a responsible job. The woman stared at her notebook, waiting for her response.

'It hasn't been easy.' She chose her words carefully, not liking his accusatory tone. He's playing bad cop, she reminded herself, hating the indignity of having to share her personal life with these strangers. They were doing their job, looking for Tom, that was what mattered. 'I have two children, and their needs come first. We've sorted out a childcare arrangement between us, and he has them some weekends if he wants to take them out. We've been getting on better lately.' She swept her hair behind her ears as she said this, hoping they wouldn't notice her blush.

'What do you think has happened to him?' the officer asked.

'I really can't imagine. Last time I saw him, he was more like his old self, and I wondered if he was having regrets, though that may be wishful thinking.'

Both officers watched her, and she blinked hard, suddenly emotional.

'We'll be in touch.'

After that, DS Mortimer took over the case, as days dragged by and it became clear Tom had gone missing. Rachel saw him rather more often than she would have liked. At first, she welcomed every scrap of information, until it became clear from the line of questioning and the frequency of it that she was one of the police's primary suspects, along with Heidi. Her mother had had to move in to take care of the children while she was being grilled by the police. She'd existed in a state of terror, seeing the disbelief in the eyes of the officers at the answers to their questions, the desperate fear that she appeared guilty of something she hadn't done, and the inability to convince them she had nothing to do with this. Couldn't they see she was in bits? She'd imagined herself a balloon, with the air slowly filtering out until there was nothing left of her.

Her last moments with Tom were raked over and she gave them some of the details, omitting the part where they'd slept together, merely revealing how they were getting on better than at any time since the brutal split. That was how the detective described it – brutal. Rachel wanted to believe that Tom had chosen to take himself out of the situation because it was too stressful, but it soon became clear that the police, the media and the wider public were still open to the possibility that something terrible had happened to him.

DS Mortimer was very choosy about what he revealed to Rachel. An affable older man, he had a kindly face with a comically large moustache, and when he was being nice, she believed the case was in the most capable hands possible. But he had a steely side, reminding her to be careful. Not that she had anything to hide – well, not about the disappearance anyway – but she was a suspect and was terrified of being wrongly accused. He was very discreet, and refused to give away details no matter how many times she begged him.

The local media picked up the case and ran with it; after all, not too much happened in this unprepossessing town. Burglaries and car chases were about as thrilling as it got around here, and this was a bona fide mystery. An adult male going missing was a story, but throw in a bitter wife, two young children and a photogenic girlfriend, and it became front-page news. Rachel read every word written about the case, desperate to know whether Heidi was a suspect too. Heidi poured out her story to the press.

Police investigating the disappearance of local businessman Tom Webb spoke yesterday to Heidi Ingram, 24, the woman he was living with after splitting from his wife. In recent weeks her partner had appeared to have something on his mind. On the morning he was last seen, he left for work as normal and phoned Heidi at lunchtime as was his habit. He mentioned he was going to a meeting that afternoon and would be home early, but he never arrived. The last person to see him that day was colleague and partner at Webb Designs, Freddie Davis, 35. Mr Davis was unavailable for comment at the time of writing this article.

Ms Ingram mentioned the strain of leaving his wife and young children, wondering if the pressure had become too much for him. 'We're all very worried,' she said. 'He made a huge sacrifice when he left his family. We love each other desperately and I thought he was strong enough to deal with it. Now I'm not so sure.'

Every article was accompanied by photos of Heidi, along with the same one of Rachel and the children, the only one she made available, with the children's faces blurred. She didn't want to be recognised in the street, hated the way everyone knew their business. She took the children and they went to stay with her mother until she could face being in the house again.

CCTV was found of Tom leaving his office at lunchtime and walking down the high street. His car was picked up driving out of town, but there the trail went cold. The surrounding countryside was vast, and it was as if he had completely vanished. Rachel knew those closest to the missing person always fell under suspicion, and at first she'd worried that she had no alibi as she'd been home alone for most of the day before leaving to collect Lara from school. Shortly after that, her mother had arrived to watch a film with her, but phone signals picked up her mobile at the house, and she'd replied to Heidi's texts. Her car had stayed in the driveway all night. Nowadays, cameras spotted most things. Rachel was grateful for this. Things were bad enough without her being accused of something she hadn't done.

The police asked about Tom's finances, whether that been a

cause for concern, given that it couldn't have been easy managing two households and he'd just put a deposit down on a new house. It also transpired that he'd withdrawn a large amount of money from his bank account shortly before his disappearance. Rachel hoped she'd hidden her shock at hearing this piece of news, shrugging whilst gripping the seat hard. He hadn't mentioned a new house. It didn't fit in with the hope she had that they might get back together after his change of heart. *Ask Heidi* was her constant refrain. She hated the reminders that she wasn't Tom's confidante any more. He was bound to be struggling with money, but it wasn't her problem to worry about. He no longer shared those practical details with her, unless it concerned the children.

The darkest time was when the police questioned her over Tom's mental state, asking whether she thought he was capable of taking his own life. She was filled with horror at the very idea; her mind refused to go there. Tom adored his children and would never leave them in that way. He might have acted out of character in the last year, but he enjoyed life too much, and he'd never suffered from depression or any other kind of mental illness. He was under stress, yes, they all were – even Heidi, she grudgingly admitted to herself. The idea that Tom could have been so unhappy was devastating, and she longed to know where he was, to be able to talk to him and make him see that no matter how desperate the situation seemed, there would be a way out of it.

DS Mortimer eventually informed her that the conclusion of the police investigation was that Tom had chosen to start again somewhere new, and that decision had to be accepted. That fitted with her own view – not for a minute had she believed he was dead. Her gut told her otherwise. Even so, she hated waking up each morning and feeling sick as soon as she remembered what had happened, wondering what new horrors that day would bring.

Rachel didn't want excitement, she wanted stability. She wanted the endless scrutiny to stop, and above all, she wanted Tom back, or at least to know what had happened to him. Without closure, she felt as if she was trapped in an open book, turning the pages slowly, unable to reach the end.

FOUR

RACHEL

Later that evening, Rachel gives Freddie a ring. Her skin tingles with anticipation as she waits for him to answer. Their friendship has taken her by surprise, so much so that she hasn't even told Emma yet. She doesn't want to jinx it. Freddie is Tom's oldest friend, though the twinge of guilt she sometimes feels is entirely unwarranted. Tom has gone now, and until the letter arrived she'd put him firmly in the past. Reconfiguring the house was a physical manifestation of this, but emotionally she was taking a while to catch up and accept the fact that she will never see him again. Now, the letter had thrown all that up into the air and she doesn't know what to think.

'Hey, you,' Freddie says in his deep voice, and his affectionate tone relaxes her.

'Hi.'

'I was just thinking about you.'

'Oh yes? Good thoughts, I hope?'

'Of course. It was lovely the other night.'

'Until I went and ruined it.'

'No you didn't. The only thing that mattered was that we didn't arrange when we're meeting up again.'

'I know. Sorry I had to run off like that. One of the hazards of having children.' They'd met for a drink and the babysitter had rung; Josh was running a temperature and Rachel had to rush home. If Freddie had been harbouring any romantic feelings towards her, she was convinced that would have put him off.

'It's not a problem. If you'd *like* to see me again...' He's teasing her.

'I would like that. Actually, do you mind if I stop by the office tomorrow? There's something I need to show you. Nothing to do with the other evening,' she adds hastily.

'I'm intrigued. Are you sure about coming here? To the office, I mean. You haven't been back since... We could go to a café if you prefer?'

'No, it's fine. It's about time I faced up to it.'

'OK. Come by mid morning, does that work?'

'Perfect, thanks.'

Freddie was at university with Tom; he'd known him longer than Rachel had. After graduating, Tom set up his web design business. He was one of those much-documented young people who started a business from a bedroom that went on to have huge success. He dedicated hours to making it work, eventually doing well enough to rent an office space in town and taking on two other members of staff. As the business became more successful, he invited Freddie to buy shares and come and work with him. He retained overall control, but Freddie looked after the day-to-day operations. Rachel still had control over Tom's share of the business, which she'd be able to inherit once the seven years were up.

Freddie was her rock when Tom disappeared; she wasn't sure she'd have got through the immediate aftermath without him. He took over the business and has been running it ever since. He also went out of his way to support her in dealing with the many practicalities of her husband's disappearance. They lost touch after a couple of years, until he surprised her with a phone call six months ago, suggesting they go for a drink. They've always had a strong connection, but this time Rachel admitted to herself that she found him attractive. In the early aftermath of the disappearance, Tom was a presence between them, his absence the reason for them becoming close. Now things feel different, though she wonders why Freddie got in touch after all this time. She hates her suspicious mind, but when your husband vanishes, you get into the habit of questioning everything. Going to the offices for the first time won't be easy, but seeing Freddie will help her through it.

Before heading off to school the next morning, Rachel knocks next door to ask her neighbour, Deborah, if she noticed anybody delivering something the day before, pretending a gift arrived without a name. But Deborah was out at the time. Rachel has driven herself mad wondering during the night: if the note wasn't from Tom, then who sent it? The answer evaded her, as did sleep.

After she drops Josh off at school, she heads into town. It's market day, the sun is out and the marketplace is bustling already. Elderly people sit on benches and chat. Rachel wishes she were relaxed enough to do the same – to take in the sun and not have so much pressing on her mind. Instead, she heads off to Tom's office – Freddie's office, she reminds herself.

A young man she hasn't met before is on reception and calls Freddie. He comes bounding down the stairs, lanky and full of energy.

'Rachel,' he says, kissing her on both cheeks, hands on her arms, giving her a supportive squeeze. Immediately her face feels hot. The instant physical attraction takes her by surprise every time. They've only been out a few times, and Freddie has made no move beyond friendly affection; she senses he's interested in her, but she's so out of practice she's terrified of getting it wrong and scaring him off, so is hoping he will move first. For now, she's happy with what they have, and crawling along at tortoise pace suits her fine.

'Let's go upstairs. Coffee?'

'Yes please.'

He shows her to a seating area in his office, plush leather chairs and an abstract painting, walls painted a tasteful grey. He busies himself at the coffee machine in the corner of the room.

'White, one sugar?'

'You've got a good memory.'

He shrugs, smiling. 'As if I'd forget.'

Rachel looks around the office, so different from how she remembers it. 'The place looks great, Freddie. It's been completely done up. You must be doing well.'

He hesitates before replying. 'Yes, we are.'

'I don't know what I'd have done without you. I hadn't a clue about the business. I've got no idea what I'd have done if you hadn't wanted to take it on. At least I'll be able to make a decision about Tom's share soon, hopefully.'

'Anyone would have done the same. I'd invested a lot of time into it too. It's so good to see you.'

'You too.'

He sits down and places the coffee in front of them. 'Is everything OK?' he says, the tone of his voice telling Rachel he means it, it's not the usual niceties of conversation.

'I'm OK.' She sips her coffee.

'Sure?'

She puts the cup down. 'You know me too well. It's *so* nice to see you. I mean that. I shouldn't disturb you at work when I have a problem, but... well, something's happened.' She takes a deep breath. 'Have you heard from Tom in the last few days?'

Freddie is about to drink from his coffee, but at her question, he lowers his cup, shakes his head, his pale blue eyes serious.

'No, I'd have told you immediately.'

'Of course you would.'

'Have you?'

She sighs, pulling the note from her bag. It's crumpled from the number of times she's looked at it. 'I received this yesterday. Hand-delivered. Lara found it on the doormat. I looked outside but couldn't see anyone who might have left it. What do you think?'

'Gosh.' Freddie runs his hands through his hair, making it stick up even more than usual. 'May I?' He takes the paper and scrutinises it. 'It's Tom's writing, or a bloody good copy. But who would do that?'

Rachel shakes her head. 'God, Freddie. Just when I thought we were over the worst. You know it's almost seven years, and I was psyching myself up to declare him officially... gone.' She can't bring herself to say the word *dead*. 'But what if this really is from him?'

Freddie hands the note back to her. 'I bet it's to do with that documentary. Somebody will have seen it and decided to stir up trouble.'

'I hadn't thought of that.' A documentary reviewing several missing persons cases, including Tom's, aired last week. Lara in particular was affected by it.

'Have you shown this to the police?'

'No. Do you think I should?'

'I would.'

Rachel thinks of DS Mortimer, the pity she used to read in his eyes. He hated not getting her the answers she so desperately wanted. She couldn't bear to rake it all up for him again.

'What about Heidi?' The words fizz in the air. Freddie

knows better than anyone how she feels about Heidi. They've managed to avoid mentioning her so far.

She shakes her head. 'I really don't want to go there.'

The phone on his desk buzzes.

'Excuse me, I have to get this.' He turns slightly away from her. 'Yes? OK, give me five minutes.' He covers the handset with his hand. 'I'm so sorry, Rachel, I've been expecting this call and I have to take it. Why don't we go for a drink tonight, or dinner?'

'I'd like that, but I can't, Lara has swimming. How about Friday? I could get Mum to babysit.'

'Ah, Fiona. I'd love to see her.'

'I'm sure she'd love to see you too. I'll tell her you were asking after her. She always had a bit of a soft spot for you.'

'The feeling is mutual. Friday is perfect. I'll have a think about where we can go. But I'll call you to confirm. Try not to worry.'

Seeing Freddie has buoyed Rachel up a little, and her anxiety has lessened. Better to talk it through with him before doing anything rash like contacting the police. She hasn't heard from DS Mortimer in years; he may have even retired by now – police retire earlier than most professions. She isn't sure of his exact age, though he always struck her as the grandfatherly type, and that was more than six years ago. She'll ring her sister when she has a chance, get her take on the letter, but for now, she tries to put it out of her mind, telling herself it's been sent by a time-waster. Back when Tom vanished, she had so many horrible messages and attention-seekers wasting her time by contacting the police or leaving messages on the Facebook page Freddie had set up for her. He took over managing it in the end, to spare her seeing anything upsetting. DS Mortimer told her it was normal for people to contact the police in any missing persons case and lead them down false trails. 'It comes with the territory, unfortunately,' he said, 'folk wanting their chance to be in the limelight. It wastes hours of our time, and we're stretched as it is what with staff being cut further and further...' It helped to know it wasn't just happening to her, and she tried to develop a thicker skin.

After Lara's swimming practice, and a quick meal, Josh goes up to his bedroom and Lara goes into the living room. The sound of the news soon drifts across the open-plan room. Rachel clears the table and washes the dishes. She's just wondering whether to treat herself to a cold glass of white wine when Lara appears in the kitchen chewing her finger, the TV remote control in her other hand. This habit has taken over from sucking her thumb, and Rachel can't forget how long it took her to stop that. She notices how forlorn Lara looks, as she did when she was little and used to wander downstairs unable to sleep, appearing in the doorway like a little ghost in her nightie.

'What's up, love?' When she looks closely at her daughter, she notices that she seems pale, her eyes anxious. 'I know something's bothering you. You've been a bit jittery lately. Is it school? Have you fallen out with Holly?'

'No,' Lara says, almost snapping. 'Why do you always think everything is about Holly?' She hovers in the doorway. 'It's Dad,' she says at last, her voice catching on the word that rarely gets mentioned in this house. 'I can't stop thinking about him.'

'What's brought this on?'

'It's ever since that documentary was on last week. I was watching that discussion programme just now, and they showed a clip. Come and see.'

Rachel dries her hands on a tea towel and follows Lara into the living room. Tom's picture is frozen on the television screen, giving him a slightly startled air, lips parted as if he's about to tell her something – anything would do, just one clue as to what happened to him all those years ago. Without taking her eyes off the screen, she takes the remote control from Lara and turns it off, putting her arm around her daughter's shoulders. Lara is trembling like a baby bird, and she squeezes her tight, trying to reassure her when she feels no reassurance herself.

'I don't need to see it. What are you so worried about, love?'

Lara chews on her finger, frowning.

'You can tell me anything, you know that.'

'I get scared that somebody will find Dad's body. That we'll find out something terrible happened to him.'

Rachel strokes Lara's hair, inhaling the delicate scent of apples from the only shampoo she will use. At least she's taken that beanie off.

'It's so hard, isn't it, not knowing. Yes, that's a possibility, although my gut feeling has always been that your father chose to walk out of his life. But if anything was found that the police think could be relevant to the case, they would warn me before it broke in the news. That's what happens. They look after families much better these days. Dad barely featured in that documentary, he wasn't the focus; it wasn't about finding new evidence. It was more about the presenter understanding her own situation.'

'I liked her,' Lara says. 'She's lost a parent like I have. Maybe blogging about it would help me to find out more about what happened.'

'I don't think so, love, it will only make you more anxious.'

'You can't stop me looking online.'

'I'd be surprised if you haven't already.'

Lara shrugs, a wry smile on her face.

'All the publicity about the missing university student is focusing your mind on our situation, which doesn't help. You'd be better off channelling your energy elsewhere. What about a family tree?'

'Mum, that's so boring. History at school is bad enough. There's no way I'm choosing it at GCSE. I can't wait to drop it.'

'You and Josh are so different.'

'He's just annoying.'

'No he isn't, he's just lively. Drama club is good for him, in the same way swimming is for you.'

Rachel hopes she's hidden the anxiety that she can't help feel at the idea of Lara dredging up the past, just when she's finally looking forward.

'If you do find out anything more about Dad, you will tell me, won't you? I'm not a baby any more.'

'I will, love. But like I said, we'd have heard from DS Mortimer if something new had come to light.'

An image of Lara handing her the letter flashes into her mind, and she shuts down the possibility that it could somehow really be from her husband. It has to be unimportant.

Lara's face is riddled with a mixture of confusion, anxiety, hope. Rachel knows that if she were to look into a mirror, she'd see exactly the same mixture of emotions written on her own.

FIVE

The following morning Freddie texts to confirm the meal out on Friday. Rachel accepts, wondering if she'll get time to fit in a session at the gym before then. Exercise is a good way of relieving her stress, but the reality is that her gym bag has lived in her car boot for months now without seeing daylight.

Once Lara has left to get the bus for school and she's dropped Josh off, Rachel makes herself a black coffee instead of her usual milky latte and eats a piece of toast and peanut butter. She's barely slept since the letter arrived. Despite persuading herself last night that it didn't need to be taken seriously, she can't help but be nervous. Is there a little hope in there too?

The timing of the note has to be deliberate – just when Rachel has finally got together with someone she can see a future with. That's only possible because the anger that consumed her is receding, slowly, although some days it takes her by surprise and she has to practise being mindful, as her therapist taught her. But she's getting there, and Freddie is part of that. No longer is she fearful of Tom walking through the door and the tsunami of feelings that would evoke. Getting involved emotionally again is a huge step forward; finally she's allowing herself to believe that she can make a life for herself.

This year is significant. She's been counting the days until September, until the day when she can officially declare Tom deceased. The thought makes her shiver every time she has it, but it has to be done for practical purposes. When Tom disappeared, she was still his wife; she was living in their house and she found herself at an impasse in many of her financial affairs. He had inherited the house from his parents, which meant she had no mortgage to worry about, yet she still had to cover all the bills and family expenses. His money was in a separate account, which initially she was unable to access. Having stopped work when she had the children, the last years haven't been easy.

After Tom had been missing for ninety days, she was able to take advantage of the recent Guardianship Act, and applied to be guardian of his affairs, which gave her some legal rights. Heidi challenged her for the guardianship, but although she had been living with Tom at the time of his disappearance, whatever promises he may have made her proved legally to be empty ones. Once Rachel was successful in court, she assumed declaring him deceased would be straightforward. Although the guardianship had given her some control over Tom's share of the business, inheriting his full share would give her the freedom to sell it to Freddie if she wanted to. Declaring Tom dead would also enable her to access the life insurance and give her the financial independence she craved. She had to do this; it would help her to move on, mentally if nothing else.

Tom contacting her now would put a stop to all that; this note could be the undoing of all her plans. She'd never have spent her grandmother's money on the extension if she had thought for a moment she'd need it to live on. And if it wasn't Tom who'd sent it, then somebody has a really sick mind to try this now, just when she is finally emerging from the darkest period of her life. She can't imagine who would do this to her.

The conversation with Lara has got her thinking about the documentary again. Seeing Tom's face on the screen last night gave her a shock – it always does when she's not expecting it, especially as she's tried so hard to forget him.

The documentary was shown a week ago. She planned to watch it on her own, but Lara had seen the trailer and insisted they watch it together. It had taken her by surprise. About a year ago, she'd had a call from a producer who suggested she might be interested in being involved in a documentary, but as soon as she'd mentioned the subject matter, Rachel had stopped her and put the phone down. Maybe she should have done a little digging, but she'd not heard from the woman again and had pushed it into the compartment in her mind where she stored anything she wanted to forget. Even if Lara hadn't alerted her to the screening, she'd have known anyway, as her phone had buzzed with messages from her mother, her sister, her friends. She'd tried to contact DS Mortimer to ask him if there was anything she should know about, but she'd been unable to reach him. Josh hadn't been aware it was on as far as she knew, and anyway he was at Scouts that evening. Rachel doubted he would be interested, even if he did hear about it.

Unable to stop worrying about the note, she decides to watch the documentary again, to see if she's missed anything. At the time, she was so conscious of Lara and how she might be affected, she didn't give it her full attention. She locates the recording and switches it on.

A warning is given at the beginning, alerting viewers to sensitive content. Most programmes these days carry some sort of alert; violence against women is rightly very much at the forefront of the news, and the current case of the missing university student is on everyone's minds.

The documentary is narrated by a young woman, Stephanie, whose mother walked out on her family when she was twelve years old and was never seen again. The police officer in charge of the case, now retired, talks about his gut feeling that she deliberately left home and, for whatever reason, created a new identity.

Five similar cases follow, all where parents have left young families behind and disappeared. Tom is the final missing person to feature. A clip is shown of the news at the time, detailing his unusual family situation. Seeing herself on screen is always a shock for Rachel, and revisiting these clips has her scrutinising her appearance. She was a lot slimmer then, and it's hard to see beyond the dated clothes. Ironic, given that as soon as she'd found out about Heidi, she'd embarked on a diet, without much effect, but the minute Tom disappeared in such mysterious circumstances, the pounds fell off her without trying. Even now, she squirms at hearing her own story, the humiliation of Tom leaving her still painful. She hates being branded the vengeful ex-wife. If only people knew about that last weekend with him, how she had hopes for a future with him. If only she could forgive him for letting her down a second time.

Heidi is on the screen now, the camera close-up on her face, and Rachel feels the same stab of complex emotions she felt the first time she found out what her husband's mistress looked like. Delicate features in a heart-shaped face, blemish-free skin and glossy hair. The camera pans out to reveal her standing outside the flat she shared with Tom, alongside a group of spectators drawn by the cameras and the story unveiling in their street. The shot widens to take in the scene, and Rachel spots a familiar figure. She grabs the remote and rewinds the image, stopping at the man in such close proximity to Heidi. She crouches in front of the television to make sure. It's Freddie.

Freddie has never tried to hide the fact that he dislikes Heidi, and it strikes Rachel as odd that he should be there amongst the onlookers. He's bound to have an explanation, though, and she has enough to worry about as it is without creating unnecessary dramas.

She switches the television off. Nothing in the programme has convinced her that Tom's inclusion is of any consequence – any number of cases could have been used. It's the note that has made her pay attention; she's worrying unnecessarily, not only about that, but about Lara's renewed interest in her father's disappearance too. She jots down the name of the therapist involved in the programme, wondering if that might be helpful for her daughter.

That evening, Lara picks at her meal.

'You're still worrying about Dad, aren't you?' Rachel has always encouraged the children to talk about Tom, even though they have few memories of that time, but lately she's wondered if she was wise to do so.

Lara shrugs, pushing peas around her plate. 'I wish I could remember him more.' She lays down her cutlery, giving up any pretence of eating.

'You were only five,' Rachel says. 'I can't remember anything much from when I was that age.' She puts down her own fork.

'Would you mind if I had a look?'

'At what, darling?'

'At seeing what happened to him. I've often wondered whether I should, but now, seeing how it helped that presenter, Stephanie, I think it might be good for me. I was thinking about starting an online story about it.'

'As long as you don't expect to find any answers.' Lara gives her a look. 'I didn't mean it like that. I hope you do. But I did the same and had to give it up in the end. It was upsetting and difficult.'

Rachel can't imagine what Lara will search for – other than newspaper reports from the time.

'The library might have old local papers you can look at.'

'Mum, you're so prehistoric. I can get all that stuff online.'

She smiles; she hasn't seen her daughter this animated in a long time. If only it were a different subject that was piquing her interest.

'Do you think you'll ever marry again?'

Where did that come from? Lara has never asked anything like this before. Maybe Rachel hasn't been as discreet with Freddie as she'd have liked. Introducing a partner into the family for the first time isn't something to take on lightly.

'How would you feel about me dating?'

'I'd like it, I think, as long as he was nice.'

'Well obviously. Actually, I'm going out on Friday, with Freddie.'

'See, I knew it! You *are* dating. You went out with him last week.'

Rachel can't help smiling. 'Do you approve?'

Lara nods. 'He looks nice. I don't really remember him, though. How come you suddenly met him again? Did you bump into him?'

'No. He contacted me out of the blue.'

'That's weird.'

'Not really. He was very good to me when Dad disappeared. He used to come around a lot at the time.'

Freddie started seeing someone else shortly after and his visits gradually petered out. Rachel remembers how she herself dropped all her friends when she met Tom, swept up in the ecstasy of being in love. Things would be different this time round, with her life revolving around the children. Her love life would come second, and she was sure Freddie would understand.

. . .

Later that evening, her sister rings. Rachel is in her pyjamas, and settles in for a long chat.

'How's the romance with the lovely Freddie going?'

She stretches out like a cat. 'I told you it's not a romance – yet.'

'Ha! I knew it.'

'He's taking me out for a meal on Friday.'

'It's all very civilised.'

'We're getting to know one another. It's a weird situation. I told Lara.'

'Does she approve?'

'Yes. I wasn't sure how she would take it, but she said it was about time I started dating, Says I don't go out enough.'

'Which is exactly what you always say about her. I felt terrible not being able to stay the other day. It was obvious she wanted me to.'

Rachel sighs. 'I can't help worrying about her. At her age she shouldn't be looking to her aunt for company. She's a bit preoccupied with that documentary.'

'I thought you said she found it helpful.'

'She did, she could relate to that presenter. But now she's decided she's going to do some sleuthing of her own.'

'She's such a little Miss Marple. How has she been lately?'

'OK, though she's never going to find school easy, I've accepted that now, I just wish she could make friends. She says she doesn't want to, but I think that's just bravado. I worry she's lonely.'

'Has Holly been round lately?'

'No, and Lara bites my head off whenever I ask about her.'

'They've probably fallen out. You know what teenage girls are like. It will be the biggest tragedy in the world. Then they'll be best mates again next week and forget all about it. Remember me and Tania?'

'You were just a drama queen about everything.' Lara isn't

like that at all. She's never been one for big demonstrations of emotion; she keeps her feelings locked inside. 'Thank goodness the documentary wasn't much to do with Tom really. Even now, it doesn't get any easier seeing his photo on screen, that picture of him and Heidi.'

'Bloody Heidi. Do you ever see her?'

'No, not for years. She still lives around here apparently.'

'I've never got over her challenging you in court, all that drama she created over the guardianship. She had no chance of getting it. She'd only been with him for five minutes compared to you.'

'They were living together for several months, and who knows how long they'd been seeing each other behind my back.'

'I thought you'd stopped worrying about that. You have to let go.'

'I know, but...'

'Has something happened?'

'Yes, but you mustn't tell anyone. I don't want the children to know – especially now, what with Lara fixating on her dad. It's probably nothing, only...' Rachel tells her sister about the note being posted through the door.

'It's a hoax, has to be,' Emma says. 'Are you worried?'

'It's just a bit weird: first the documentary last week, and now this. I watched the documentary again this morning, just to make sure I hadn't missed anything significant. But there's nothing. If anything, it confirmed that the police did everything they could to find him. DS Mortimer was so kind to me. He went out of his way to keep me up to date, no matter what time of day it was. It meant a lot.'

'Why would Tom turn up now, though? If he's still alive – and I know we both think he is – what possible excuse can he have for putting you through this torment? *I'd* kill him if you didn't. Leaving you for that woman was unforgivable enough.

He couldn't possibly expect that you'd want him back, could he?'

Rachel imagines opening the front door to Tom, the rage and anguish that would burst out of her. Not only did he leave her for Heidi, he left her for a second time when he walked out of his life. She imagines pummelling him with her fists until he fell to the ground.

'You're right. I just can't believe this is happening as I'm finally moving forward, making the house better for all of us, getting closer to Freddie. No way would I allow Tom back in my life.'

She bites her lip. The truth is, she's not one hundred per cent sure what she'd do, how she would feel. Emma knows nothing of the last weekend she spent with Tom; she's never told a soul what happened that night, not even the police. A rush of guilt at the thought takes her over. If *she* lied about something so momentous, how can she ever trust anyone else?

SIX

It takes Rachel a while to find her make-up bag – it's been that long since she last wanted to make an effort with her appearance. Eventually she locates it, and as she dabs foundation and concealer onto her face, she examines her reflection in the mirror. She's aged in the years since Tom left home; lack of sleep and months of angst in the immediate aftermath stripped weight from her body and furrowed worry lines onto her face that no amount of expensive creams will eliminate. Her foundation promises to 'rejuvenate and re-energise' – she's not sure that's quite the result she gets, but she looks brighter when she's added a stroke of eyeliner and mascara and slipped into a silk shirt and smart trousers. She scrutinises her face. The mid-length bob she has worn for the last years suits her, the fringe making her look youthful, even more like her daughter. She plucks out a lone grey hair from the brown before coating her lips with nude lipstick. Getting dressed up invigorates her.

'You look nice, Mum,' Lara says, looking up from her laptop. She's been spending more time on it in the last couple of days, whereas she always used to be engrossed in a book. Her latest read lies untouched by her bed.

Freddie has booked a table at a cosy bistro. Walking into town, Rachel can't remember how long it is since she last went out for a meal. She has a small circle of friends who meet up for drinks or cinema, and there's her book group, but she hasn't been in much of a reading mood lately, and this month's book is gathering dust on the shelf. She prefers to spend her evenings with Lara, where she can keep an eye on her.

Freddie gets to his feet when he sees her approaching the table he is already seated at, tucked in the corner of the restaurant. He's still in his work suit, and Rachel wonders whether she's made too much effort. Since his surprise call six months ago, they've been out for drinks and seen a couple of films together, plus enjoyed long walks in the country followed by a pub lunch. So far they've kept it safe, sticking to conversations around the children, common interests, the extension she's having done. She's deliberately not invited him to the house for fear of unsettling Lara and Josh, not wanting to take this step until she's more sure of the relationship. Nor does she want him to think she's only interested in him for his connection with Tom. Both Tom and the business have stayed off limits, but telling Lara and going to the office mark a significant change. The note has served the purpose of delivering Tom into the relationship, putting him back between them. This time she's determined not to let him take centre stage. Better to address it, get the issue out of the way, make sure this is all about her and Freddie.

'It was strange to go back to the office the other day,' she says. 'I still can't believe he would have left all that behind.' This is something they must have discussed hundreds of times in the weeks after Tom went missing. He was so proud of the company he'd created.

Freddie nods. 'Without knowing what exactly happened, we're always going to be wondering, aren't we? I must admit, keeping the business going wasn't easy. There were many times I thought of jacking it all in.'

'It was doing so well when he left, and he would be pleased with what you've done, the success you've made of it without him.'

'Who knows what would have happened,' Freddie says, looking away from her. He pauses. 'Rachel, there's something I didn't tell you at the time because I thought you had enough going on. I hope you won't be angry with me for only telling you now, but the truth is, I didn't want you to have anything else to worry about.'

'What do you mean?' Rachel feels a cold sensation inside.

Freddie sighs and runs his hands through his hair. 'You're right, the business was doing well back then, but Tom wasn't. Financially, I mean. I didn't find this out until afterwards. When I went through the accounts, I discovered he had been taking large sums of money and billing them to non-existent clients.'

Rachel gasps. 'No.' She covers her mouth with her hands, feeling strangely off-balance. Not Tom. Whatever he might have done to her, she can't believe he was capable of this. 'But it was his own business.'

'Exactly. It was so confusing, especially not being able to ask him what the hell was going on.'

'What was going on was he was trying to support two households. I was determined to stay in the family home, and he reassured me that wasn't a problem for him. He always implied he had plenty of money – that's why I assumed the business was doing well. Is that why the police concluded he chose to leave? Because for a while they were convinced it was murder, and right now, that almost feels preferable.'

'You don't mean that.'

'No, I don't. But you should have told me this at the time. I had a right to know.'

'I didn't find out immediately, and I kept the police out of it. Tom was my friend – had been my friend before he met Heidi and ruined his life.'

'I had no idea you were struggling with this. You're doing OK now, aren't you – with the business, I mean?'

'We're managing OK.' He pours some more wine. 'Hard to believe the seven years is almost up, isn't it? I remember us talking about that back then, and it seemed so far in the future, but time has flown since then. Maybe not for you, though.'

'No, it hasn't, but I'm glad it's almost here. I'm going to apply to have his death officially registered. Finally.'

'That must feel like reaching a milestone.'

'Definitely. It enables me to draw a line under it all. Financially, I mean. I've had to live within certain parameters, and the limitations on my freedom have stopped me putting the life we shared behind me. The insurance payout will make a huge difference. Declaring him dead without knowing for sure is horrible, but it's the only way I can move on.' Their eyes meet, and she feels a frisson of hope-filled desire.

'Will you need to involve Heidi in the registering of the death?'

'No, or at least I hope not. And I hope she isn't going to resurrect her unfounded claim about a will.'

At the same time Heidi contested Rachel's claim to guardianship, she also insisted Tom had made a will leaving everything to her. Rachel knew for a fact he hadn't; it was one of the things he'd confided to her that last weekend. He had told Heidi he was going to change his will just to stop the pressure she was putting on him to do it, but he'd kept putting it off.

'Tom told me he hadn't got round to changing it, but I didn't have any concrete proof of that; it was just hearsay as far as Heidi was concerned. I tried to appease her by reminding her that I couldn't declare him dead for seven years, and obviously we'd have to wait until then to have any will read. She thought he'd move her into the house eventually, that's what it was all about for her.'

'And kick you and the kids out – that was never going to happen.'

'She was so young and immature, although I can understand her being upset at losing the house they were planning on buying.'

Tom's disappearance meant that Heidi had to pull out of the house purchase; she couldn't afford the mortgage on her own.

'That hardly compares to losing her partner.'

'You don't know Heidi. She was furious.'

Freddie changes the subject. 'Did Lara watch the documentary?'

'Yes, it was interesting to see her reaction. I told her I was having dinner with you, actually.' Rachel grabs her drink to hide her blushing cheeks.

He looks pleased. 'How did she take it?'

'Let's just say she practically pushed me out of the door this evening. Told me I didn't get out enough. She doesn't remember much about you, though.'

'You'll have to invite me over then. I'd love to meet her. She was five when I last saw her, such a tiny little thing.'

'Not so little now. She's twelve, almost a teenager – Year 8 at school. She's fine, but I do worry about her.'

'If she seems happy, I wouldn't worry. What did you mean about her reaction to the TV programme?'

'She found it interesting, said she could relate to Stephanie, the narrator. Afterwards, she asked me if I minded if she made her own enquiries. I don't, to a point, as long as she doesn't upset herself. It's more to do with finding her own identity, I think. She's at that age. I haven't told her about the note; it's unsettling enough for me, let alone her. Expecting her father to suddenly turn up could blow her mind. Imagine it *is* from him –

I just can't even go there. It's made me question whether I should have agreed to her setting up this blog or whatever it is she wants to do, though it's good to see her taking an interest in *something* at last, even if it is this.'

They finish their food and the waiter clears the table, leaving them with dessert menus.

'Do you want anything else?' Freddie asks. 'This is my treat, by the way.'

'No, Freddie—'

'Don't even try and stop me, I want to, OK? I'm enjoying myself, I love being with you. It's a rare treat for me, spending time in a woman's company. I'm sorry we lost touch back then; we always got on so well. Jen was a bit possessive, and our friendship made her uneasy despite what you were going through. I should have known then it was never going to work out.' He puts down his menu. 'Dessert for you?'

'No thanks, but coffee would be nice.'

'Great idea.'

He orders the coffees and stretches back in his chair.

'Do you have the note with you? I'd like to have another look if that's all right.'

Rachel finds the note in her bag and gives it to him.

'It's either genuine, or a really good forgery,' he says, passing it back to her after a few moments. 'But why send it now? I don't think you should ignore it. Just in case...'

'Just in case it's from him.' She nods. 'I feel the same. If there's the slightest chance he's alive, I have to follow it through. It sounds far-fetched, but what if he's being kept prisoner somewhere? I know it's normally women who are the victims of those kinds of scenarios, but...'

'It could happen to anybody. Such dark things are going on out in the world – like modern slavery. You know my younger brother's a police officer now; some of the stories he tells me you wouldn't believe.'

'I probably would.' Rachel spent months looking into stories of missing people turning up, incredible stories from all over the world. 'What do you think I should do? Contact DS Mortimer?'

'Maybe, but first... You might not like this idea...' He is interrupted by the waiter arriving with the coffee. They wait until he's left the table.

'Tell me,' Rachel says, breaking a small packet of sugar into her cappuccino, watching the creamy swirls as she stirs the leaf pattern away. She doesn't want to spoil the evening with difficult conversation, but she trusts Freddie's advice.

'I think you should show it to Heidi and see if she's heard from Tom too.'

Rachel decided once the guardianship battle was over that she'd have nothing more to do with Heidi, but every now and then she can't resist a peek at her Facebook page to see what she's up to. She's heard that she's still in the area, still living in the flat she shared with Tom. Rachel hoped she would move away after Tom disappeared, far away where there was no chance of bumping into her. In truth, though, she didn't know the woman at all. She might even have liked her if they'd met in different circumstances.

'Have you kept in touch with her?' Freddie asks.

'God, no. How could you think that?'

'In a business sense, that's what I meant. I know you wouldn't choose to.'

'That reminds me – I thought I saw you in one of the shots in the documentary.'

'No! What shot?'

She describes the scene, watches him closely for a reaction. He frowns, his generous eyebrows coming together, then jerks his head up.

'I remember, there was one time I traced Tom's route from the office to his flat. The whole thing was so perplexing, I wanted to walk in his shoes, as it were, see if it would give me any clue as to where he might have gone. A pack of photographers were outside the gate. That must be it.'

Freddie made it quite clear to Rachel at the time that he thought Tom was making a mistake, that he didn't think the relationship would last. 'Classic mid-life crisis,' he said, although Tom wasn't remotely middle-aged. 'Tom's always seemed old beyond his years. When we were students, the rest of us lads were out drinking and chatting up women, and he was saving for the deposit on a house. He doesn't have anything in common with Heidi, not enough to sustain a long-term relationship. And the way he's upset the children, that doesn't sit easy with him no matter how much he tries to brazen it out.'

Outside the restaurant, Rachel shivers, despite the warm evening they step into.

'Would you rather I approached her?' Freddie asks.

'No, I need to do this myself.' She's not entirely convinced by his reaction to the photo. 'But thanks for offering.'

'Are you driving?' he says.

She shakes her head. 'On foot.'

'I'll drop you off.'

It's warm in the car, and the inside is pristine, unlike her own vehicle, which is full of random items and discarded sweet wrappers. It's mostly stuff left by Josh, but she's used to it and likes to be reminded of his presence when he's not with her – unlike his bedroom, the state of which perpetually drives her mad. Freddie's breath smells of coffee as he leans towards her to look over his shoulder, reversing out of a space. She hasn't felt this comfortable with a man since Tom. None of her brief dalliances over the years have amounted to anything much, because she's still a married woman with a missing husband. Freddie is different somehow, because he knows the reality of her situation. He's just a good friend, she reminds herself, but when he pulls up outside her house, she doesn't want the evening to end, to go back into her usual existence.

'Want to come in?' she asks him.

Light falls onto his face from the street lamp, and his brown eyes shine.

'I can't, annoyingly. I've stupidly arranged to meet a friend for a run early tomorrow morning, but I'd love to do this again, very soon.'

She nods. 'Me too.'

She is no longer feeling cold as she watches him drive off, but warm and fuzzy inside, more balanced, hopeful. No matter what happens with Tom, she needn't be so alone.

The garden gate scrapes the ground with a horrible screech, and she reminds herself to mention it to Pete, the builder. The noise sets her nerves jangling – how quickly her emotions can change – and the sound of footsteps causes her to turn around. A woman is crossing the road, walking quickly along the pavement where trees cut out the light. As Rachel watches her, understanding the undercurrent of anxiety that accompanies every step of a woman hurrying home on a badly lit street at night, she notices a car parked on the opposite side of the road, lights on, engine purring. Willing the woman to reach the corner, where the bright high street awaits her, she grips her phone in her pocket. Even as her eyes adjust to the darkness, she can't quite make out if the driver is male or female. What she can see, without a doubt, is that their gaze is focused on her.

SEVEN

TOM

He's beginning to recognise the pattern on the ceiling, the way the street light slips through the blind and casts stripes there. Every night this week he's fallen into sleep like a stone in water, only to find himself wide awake at three o'clock, thoughts whirring like the second hand on a clock. Round and round, chasing the answer as elusive as time.

It's been happening ever since he met her.

Don't be so stupid. You'll ruin everything. Rachel shifts next to him, mumbles in her sleep, and he rests his hand on her arm to reassure himself as much as her. She doesn't know she needs to be reassured. Heaven forbid. Sweat pools on his back at the thought of her knowing what treacherous thoughts he's been having, and he closes his eyes, blocking out the light but not the anxiety.

A cry breaks into the silence and he opens his eyes. Josh. He lies still, in case it's a false alarm, but Josh, like his father, has a night-time routine. The cry becomes a whimper, quiet at first, and Tom swings his legs out of bed, not wanting to wake Rachel.

'Is it Josh?' she says, her voice thick with sleep.

'Go back to sleep,' he whispers. 'I've got this.' At least this is something he can do right.

Josh's room is past Lara's; her door is ajar and he pauses for a moment to watch her. She's asleep on her back, hair spread over the pillow. She never wakes, no matter how much noise Josh makes. Josh's cries are getting more indignant now, and Tom whips him out of his bed and clasps him to his shoulder, his small body warm against his bare skin, rocking him gently up and down. Josh's eyes are closed already, and Tom wipes the tears from his face with his sleeve. He walks around the room in circles, slow, steady steps, his eyes prickly with fatigue. When he's satisfied Josh is asleep, he puts him back into his bed and lies down on the floor next to him.

Being a father has overwhelmed him in a way he could never have imagined. Josh being his second child, he's that bit more confident, and somehow having a son makes him want to burst with pride. It seemed natural to him to get up and attend to his cries before all this started, encouraging Rachel to trust him, to allow her more sleep, which she desperately needed. It was only a month ago that Tom would fall asleep no problem too, his mind filled with work and family instead of troublesome thoughts about *her*.

Heidi.

He wishes he'd never taken the call, never met her, never set this obsession in motion. For it *is* an obsession: he can't get her face out of his head. And it so nearly never happened. The call came through to Freddie's desk – it's random as to how they allocate their clients – and if Freddie hadn't been making coffee in the kitchen, he would have taken the call and picked up the commission. Instead, Tom intercepted it and took down the details of the job – a basic website for a small clothing boutique.

He agreed to meet a Ms Ingram, who was acting on behalf of the shop owner, and they set up a meeting the next day at a local coffee shop.

He arrived early, waiting for his client to arrive before he ordered drinks. He was taking out his iPad when a young woman appeared in front of him.

'Mr Webb?'

'Tom, please. You must be...'

'Heidi.' She pulled out the chair and sat opposite him. Her hair was pale blonde, worn long, and she had a heart-shaped face and arresting green eyes. He met them with his own and then looked away, lest she thought he was staring, but they were the kind of eyes poets write lines about getting lost in. Her smile was friendly and he felt instantly at ease.

'I haven't ordered yet. What can I get you?'

'A latte please, almond milk, no sugar.'

She's already sweet enough.

He wishes he'd known then, when he was having corny out-of-character thoughts, that he should have passed the job on to Freddie, but the woman was so friendly and they had an instant rapport, so much so that he ordered a second round of coffees. They were in the café for two hours before he tore himself away. The attraction was mutual; he could tell by the way she looked at him and let her fingers brush against his arm when he left to go to the bathroom. In the Gents, he splashed cold water on his face and stared at his flushed reflection in the mirror, knowing he was standing on a precipice. He thought of Rachel, Lara and little Josh, the family he thought the world of, and straightened his tie, composed himself and told his mirror image not to be so ridiculous. But back in her presence, his resolve melted away when she looked at him with those piercing green eyes, and he wanted to rip her clothes off there and then.

Which he did on their second meeting. He's been seeing her ever since, and despite knowing it is wrong, that he doesn't love Rachel any less, Heidi is like a drug. No matter how many times he resolves to put an end to it, the minute he speaks to her, or gets a text, or her face flashes into his mind, his resolve dissolves and he makes a new arrangement to see her. Night-time is when his self-hatred kicks in, and sleep eludes him, as does a resolution.

Rachel wakes him in the morning, Josh in her arms, a bottle in his mouth.

'You fell asleep in here again. It must be so uncomfortable. Why didn't you come back to bed?'

'It wasn't intentional. I wanted to make sure he was really asleep and I must have dropped off.' Lying to Rachel cuts into him every time, and he knows he can't keep this up for much longer. Make a decision, choose between them; he knows already that's what it will come to. His feelings for Heidi are too powerful and cannot be ignored.

If he chooses Heidi, his actions will upend his life and that of his family. And if he goes the other way and chooses his wife, he'll have to confess to the affair, because he can't live like this any longer, and Rachel may not allow him to stay. Whatever he chooses, life is not going to continue as it is, and the cloud of dread he lives under is about to burst.

Heidi is on his mind and he fears he will take the more treacherous path.

But he has so much to lose.

EIGHT

RACHEL

Rachel opens Heidi's Instagram page. Shiny Heidi, glossy hair, possibly airbrushed – probably not. Her photos are clean, almost clinical, featuring strategically placed plants. They are all images of her; she doesn't appear to have a partner, although it's likely she wants this to be all about her. One posted from last month shows her posing in front of a white Fiat 500. Rachel stares at her number, wishing she didn't have to do this. She presses the call button.

'Hello.' Heidi sounds breathless. Rachel imagines interrupting her at the gym, sleek in her carefully coordinated gym clothes, sweat glistening on her tanned shoulders, weight raised above her head. 'Rachel, is that you?'

Rachel is taken aback that she's kept her number. Her tone is friendly. Nerves?

'Excuse the heavy breathing; I'm just running around trying to do a million things at once. Is everything OK? This is... unusual.' There's a thump, as if Heidi has sat down on a padded chair.

'Yes. I'm sorry to bother you.'

'It's fine, don't be so formal. Has something happened? Is it the children, has something happened to one of them?' Heidi sounds alarmed.

'No, they're fine, it's nothing like that.'

'Josh must be eight now, right, and Lara...'

'She's twelve. Look, I'm sorry to bother you, but I have to ask you this – and it's going to sound strange. Have you heard from Tom?'

Heidi gasps. 'No. You mean...'

'I don't know what I mean exactly. It's most likely a prank, but I've had a note supposedly from him.'

'What?'

'I know. It can't be from him, can it?'

There's a pause of a few seconds before Heidi speaks again.

'It's been such a long time. At least five years.'

'It's six years and ten months.' *How don't you know this?*

'Wow. Time goes so fast. I'm in my thirties now, I still can't get over that. I was so young when I met Tom – sorry, you don't want to hear that. I'm in shock, I guess. I'm all over the place. What kind of note – I mean, how did you get it? Was it posted to you? Was it letters cut out of a newspaper?'

She's making this sound like some kind of Agatha Christie plot, and put like that, Rachel thinks it's ridiculous and she shouldn't be paying any attention to it, or making this call. Needlessly opening up a channel of communication with Heidi. But...

'Slipped through the door one evening. No stamp, it didn't come via the post.'

'Typed?'

'No, that's the thing. It's in Tom's handwriting.'

'That's impossible. You remember his writing, right?'

'Of course I remember his writing.' She practically spits the words out. 'It's distinctive.'

'It has to be copied; criminals can turn their hand to anything these days.'

Criminals?

Rachel shudders, visualising Tom holding the pen in his left hand, slightly awkward, as if apologising. His father didn't like him being left-handed. His father didn't like a lot of things. *Your writing has flair*, she used to say to him. She thought it made him special.

'You don't think he's alive?' Heidi asks.

'He can't be. Do you?' Rachel realises they've never had this conversation before. They weren't able to get past their emotions back then. She had to read Heidi's theories about Tom's disappearance in the local paper, and who knows if she was telling the truth. Now she *needs* to know.

Heidi lets out an exaggerated sigh. 'I want to think he's alive, obviously. I've been over and over this trying to work out what might have happened, but I keep coming back to the children. He adored them. I can't see him ever willingly abandoning them. Which means he must be dead. I hate that, I don't want to believe it. But after all this time, it's the most likely scenario.'

'You haven't had a note like this then?'

'No, I'd have said.' Heidi sounds irked. 'Have you shown it to the police?'

'Not yet. If it's a joke, I don't want to waste their time. It feels a bit trivial.'

'Not if he's alive it isn't.' She hesitates, taking a breath. 'Do *you* want him to be alive?'

Rachel has no idea what the answer to that question is.

'Forget I asked. It's none of my business. Besides, I don't even know how *I* feel about it. Would I want him back if it turns out that he had chosen to abandon me like that? Oh gosh, there my mouth goes again.'

'It's OK. Raking it all up again, it's the last thing I wanted.'

'I don't suppose you want to meet, do you?'

Rachel gets up and paces around. Before this call, she'd have cut the suggestion dead, but now... She's interested in what theories Heidi might have. Freddie was right to push her into this.

'It might help, that's all. We could try and put it all behind us. I've often wanted to talk to you about it. It's a unique experience that we went through, and you're the only person who could possibly know what it's like. We both went through hell.'

Rachel feels an unexpected pang of affection for Heidi.

'Yes, we could do that.' It might help to thrash it out with her. And she has Freddie to discuss it with afterwards. They arrange to meet for a coffee the following afternoon.

Rachel is in the kitchen with Lara, who is at the table, plugged into her laptop. Pete comes in, his heavy boots alerting them to his arrival. He addresses Rachel.

'Danny's fixing the front gate now. It just needed a new hinge. Otherwise, we're finished for the day.'

'That's great, thanks, Pete.'

'See you tomorrow. Don't work too hard, Lara.'

Lara smiles shyly.

Once Pete has gone, Rachel looks over her daughter's shoulder, hands resting on her arms.

'What are you watching?'

Lara pulls out her earbuds. 'I'm listening to Stephanie's podcast. You know, the girl from the programme the other day? I've gone right back to the beginning to see how she started out trying to find her mother. She talks about meeting up with this girl whose mother had gone missing too, but when she tracked her down she said she'd left the family deliberately because she didn't want that life any more. She turned her own daughter away. Can you imagine?'

'No. I can't imagine leaving you and Josh, ever. I must admit I didn't think your dad would leave us the way he did, but our situation was different then – when he left us for Heidi, I mean. He always hated missing any part of your development when you were growing up, like when he'd get back late from work and you'd already gone to bed. He used to love reading you stories.'

'I wish I could remember more.'

'You used to insist on him reading the same book every night – *Mr Pumpkin*, I think it was called. He hated that book with a passion. He'd threaten to hide it but could never deprive you when it came to it. I wouldn't have let him anyway. But you need to be careful. I don't want you getting hurt. There are so many stories about adopted people trying to find their birth parents. Everybody's circumstances are so different and you don't know what you are going to find when you try and re-enter somebody's life. Many people will have moved on, or have reasons for not making contact. Their current family may not be aware, that kind of thing.'

'You're talking as if I might find him but he won't want to know, that he'd hate the idea of his daughter rocking up now. Do you know something? If he's alive, you have to tell me. Josh might be too young, but I'm old enough.'

Lara's voice has risen, and Rachel squeezes her shoulder, hiding her alarm. Has she somehow seen the note? She can't have.

'No, of course I don't know anything. I'd tell you if I did.'

She doesn't want to concern Lara with the letter, not until she's checked it out for herself. She's ninety-nine per cent sure it's going to be a hoax, and she won't upset her family for that – just look how jittery this discussion is making her. 'I promise if I find out anything about Dad's whereabouts, I will tell you.'

'OK.'

'I've got to pop out for a while before we eat,' Rachel says.

'You and Josh will be all right, won't you? Deborah from next door is going to come over.'

'Does she have to? I'm old enough to stay on my own. Where are you going anyway?'

'I'm meeting a friend for coffee; she's having a crisis.'

'What friend?'

'Kim. You don't know her.'

'Where's she from?'

'That art class I used to go to.'

'That was ages ago.'

'Yes, and that's why you don't remember her. I was surprised to hear from her actually.'

The doorbell rings. 'That will be Deborah. I won't be long.'

But it isn't Deborah.

NINE

The envelope lies on the doormat amongst bits of mud and twigs from Josh's football boots, which are abandoned beside the mat. She opens the door in case Deborah is on the other side, but the garden is empty, her neighbour's front door closed. Cold wind blows Rachel's hair into her eyes as she scans the street. Not a soul in sight. She doesn't want to pick up the envelope, because until she does, it could be entirely innocent; Tom's distinctive writing won't be on the front of it. But the churning in her stomach tells her it will be. She walks down the path and looks along the street. A cat stares wide-eyed before scuttling under a car. The gate closes without a noise; Danny must have fixed it.

A door slams and Deborah emerges from next door. 'Am I late?'

'No, I thought I heard a knock.' Rachel leaves the door open, sweeping the note up from the mat, checking the front, where the familiar writing confirms her fears. She shoves it in the pocket of her coat, which is hanging in the hall, willing her hand to stop shaking. 'Thanks for coming at such short notice.'

'No worries. I wasn't doing anything much.'

'I'll be two hours, tops.' She takes her jacket from a peg, deliberately leaving the coat with the offending white square inside. Seeing Heidi is enough of an ordeal without the added pressure of whatever is in the envelope. 'Help yourself to anything.'

It was her idea to meet Heidi in the café. She certainly didn't want her to come to the house. Heidi suggested her own place, but that was way too intimate for Rachel. She's not even sure this is a good plan now that it's happening, despite Freddie's encouragement. The conversation with Heidi was unexpected in its nature; instead of full-blown hostility like they used to experience, it was as if they were acknowledging each other for the first time as independent people who'd both been through the same ordeal, united in their grief. Although Heidi having to ask how long it had been since Tom disappeared surprised Rachel; surely the date must be ingrained in her brain like it is in her own? Despite their telephone conversation being fairly amicable, she also can't help mulling over Freddie's revelation about the money. If it hadn't been for Heidi and her demands, that situation might never have arisen. However, she's aware that it's easier to blame Heidi, given Tom's absence.

A white Fiat 500 is parked outside the café and Heidi is inside, seated on a bench looking out of the window, a glass of something red in front of her. Rachel was anticipating a mug of tea, somehow more appropriate to the situation.

'They do cocktails after five,' Heidi says, grinning.

Now that she's here, faced with Heidi's smiling face, her long tanned limbs and shiny hair, Rachel feels frumpy in comparison. She hasn't changed, and she's acutely aware of the coffee stain on her sleeve from earlier in the day. In an attempt to relax, she orders a glass of wine and steers Heidi to a small table on the far side of the café.

'I wasn't sure you'd come,' Heidi says, flicking her fringe out of her eyes, a movement she repeats constantly, her chirpy demeanour clearly a cover-up. Rachel is relieved to know she's feeling the awkwardness of the situation too. 'Last time we met, it was horrible. I want to apologise. The guardianship not going my way meant I lost the house we were planning to buy, and I was going around in a permanent cloud of anger.'

'It was a horrid time.' Rachel pictures Heidi standing outside the solicitor's office, shouting at her lawyer, who was doing his best to appease her. Rachel herself was just glad it was all over. Heidi had questioned her right to be the one to take charge of Tom's affairs, and on top of not knowing what had happened to him, she had felt as if she was drowning. On the day of the verdict, the sky was dark, and waiting outside for the outcome, Rachel paced up and down, imagining what would happen if she were to lose the house. She'd have wanted the sky to burst over her and pummel her into the ground, all traces of her disappearing into the pavement cracks – like Tom, no sign of him anywhere to be found. She hated him now for causing this instability, this sensation of having nowhere solid to put her feet. He'd hurt her.

But the worst didn't happen. Heidi lost and Rachel survived.

'About the note,' she says.

Heidi frowns at the sudden change in direction. 'Yes,' she says, taking her bag from the back of her chair. 'I've had one too.'

Rachel places her wine glass back down on the table, not trusting her wobbling hands.

'You've had one too?'

Heidi nods. 'It arrived late this afternoon. Posted through

the letter box. I'd half expected it ever since your call. I've been so convinced he was dead, but this is just the kind of messed-up thing he'd do.' She looks around in an exaggerated way. 'He could be here now, watching us...'

'Tom isn't like that. Can I see it?'

'You show me yours...' Heidi raises her eyebrows, a glint in her eye, but Rachel doesn't respond. This is no time for jokes. 'Did you bring it with you?'

'Just the envelope.' Rachel takes out the plastic bag she's put it in and hands it to her.

'Oh. Why not the letter?'

'It might be evidence. Lara has already handled the envelope, so I figured it was OK to bring it.'

'I wish you'd brought the letter.'

Rachel wishes she could forget the second note, burning a hole in her pocket.

'I told you what it said.'

'Whatever. Here's mine, anyway.' Heidi lays it on the table between them.

I want to come home.

Rachel's insides crumble. If Tom wrote this, then her own note is meaningless. Sadness turns to fury.

'I don't believe he wrote these,' she says. 'I did at first, but I've changed my mind now.'

'Why?'

'Too much time has passed. Anyway, he wouldn't write to both of us.'

'What if he's messing with us?' Heidi says. 'Maybe we should put our differences aside and work to beat him.'

'I don't think it's him. As I said, he's not like that.'

'Maybe we should go to the police.'

'I doubt they'd take it seriously,' Rachel says. 'They made it quite clear they believed he had left of his own accord, running away from his debts. They didn't find anything to suggest otherwise, and as they ruled out foul play, I accepted their expertise. That's why when I got the note I thought it was genuine. Do you?'

She stares at the table, feeling disorientated as she often does when she thinks about Tom and Heidi. *What is she even doing here?*

'I shouldn't have come.' She gestures with her hands. 'I don't know what this is. I'm not sure it was a good idea for us to meet.' She sighs. 'I guess what I'm trying to say is I don't know what the rules are.'

'There aren't any rules. I wanted to see the note for myself, look at the writing. But when mine came, it made me wonder. If we think it's forged, we should involve the police. They can test that kind of stuff.'

'What if something terrible happened to him?' Rachel says. Up until now, her gut has told her the opposite, but her doubts about the note are getting too strong. Who else could have sent it, though? A disgruntled colleague? Freddie? She shivers.

'I doubt that. I reckon he's more likely to have a whole new family and he wants something from us. But he could have had a family with me... Maybe he just couldn't face telling me he didn't want to be with me any more.' Heidi stares into the distance.

'I've never wanted to believe he was dead,' Rachel says.

'Why?'

'Just a feeling I have. I'd know, I'm sure. My gut tells me he's alive. But obviously you were closer to him then.' She can say this dispassionately now. Just about. She finishes her drink, using the moment to formulate her thoughts.

'You last saw him the day before, didn't you?' Heidi asks. 'When he dropped off the kids?'

'Yes, but only briefly.'

'What about the weekend before that? How did he seem then?'

'Same as ever. Slightly awkward, as it always was, usually we both treated it as a transaction, tried to get it over with as quickly as possible. But he did come in that time, which was different. He asked for a cup of tea, and we had a chat. I told the police.'

That was all she told the police. She's never told anybody about the rest of it and she hopes she isn't going to blush now.

'What did you talk about?'

'How guilty he felt. It was the first time he'd opened up about it. I was still angry with him. I couldn't forgive him for what he'd done. To Lara in particular. She was devastated when he left home, and it changed her.'

'In what way?'

'She became much quieter, keeping things to herself. She used to chatter about everything to me before then – to both of us. That was the problem. She enjoyed our different ways of being with her. It was never the same after he left. And now she hardly remembers him.'

'Remind me what the note said exactly.'

'"I want to come back."' Rachel looks at Heidi when she says this, holding her gaze to hide the lie, wanting to appear truthful. The omission of *to you* is deliberate. 'The same as yours. It doesn't make any sense. He could come back if he wanted to, nobody is stopping him. But would he really expect either of us to take him back now?'

'Too right,' Heidi says. 'He'd have to face all the people he's angered by disappearing, the children too. He's missed their childhoods and nothing can undo that. Unless he thinks he'd be charged with wasting police time, and hopes to persuade us not to go to them.' She stirs her drink with a straw. 'It must be a hoax.'

'Let's not go to the police. If he was alive, it would be easy to prove – he could speak to one of us so we knew for sure it was him. There are so many ways of doing it. FaceTime, whatever. It's so easy to make contact these days. The more I think about it, the more ridiculous it is. I agree with you now. I reckon this is an imposter. Somebody's idea of a sick joke.'

'But who? Who would want to do this to us, and why?'

TEN

As soon as she gets home, she rips the second envelope open, pulls the single piece of paper out. This note is longer.

You know why I want to come back to you, don't you? I can't forget that moment we had together, the weekend before I left, what happened. You felt it too, I know you did. I made a terrible mistake and I should never have abandoned you. Leaving was unforgivable, but when you know the real reason, you'll understand. Hear me out, give me this one final chance.

Rachel can't take her eyes from the paper. It has to be from Tom; only the two of them know about that night. She leans back against the wall, taking a deep breath.

'Mum.'

She jumps, presses her hand to her chest. 'Lara, you startled me.'

'Are you OK? You look as if you've just seen a ghost.'

Rachel fakes a laugh. 'Of course I'm all right.' She scrunches the note into her pocket. 'Where's Deborah?'

'Here.' Deborah comes downstairs, drying her hands against her trousers. 'Have fun?' She frowns. 'You look a bit pale.'

'It was cold out, that's all. Everything OK?'

'Fine, we've just been watching TV.'

'Thanks so much for coming.'

'Any time.'

It has started to rain, and Deborah runs down the path. Lara goes upstairs and Rachel goes to the kitchen, spreading the crumpled note out on the table. Does this mean Tom is alive? After thrashing it out with Heidi, is she changing her mind again? Rain patters on the window, the wind blowing the spray towards it at an angle. The sound mesmerises her, and a beat of rage begins inside her. Tom wants to come back after abandoning her, and is just assuming he can waltz back into her life?

How dare he?

Freddie phones that evening, and she tells him about the second note, omitting the details of its contents.

'Heidi's had one too. She brought it with her.'

'Did you show her yours?'

'I showed her the envelope. I didn't want her to see what he'd written.'

'Why?'

'Because he specifically said he wanted to come back *to me*. I didn't want to antagonise her.'

'Would it still matter to her?'

'I have no idea, but given our past relationship, I didn't want to risk it.'

'She can be pretty volatile.'

'How do you know that?'

'From what Tom used to say about her, and the court hearings. Plus the way she presented herself in the press.'

'Exactly. Given that we've been forced into this situation, I think it went pretty well. She suggested going to the police, but I'm not sure there's much they could do.'

'Did it help? Seeing her?'

'Yes. And we managed to keep it civil.'

'I have so much admiration for the way you've dealt with this.'

Rachel's face heats with pleasure, pleasantly surprised. She's just about muddled through the last few years.

'Look at you, how you've raised two kids despite the adverse circumstances...'

'That's what any mother would do.'

'Maybe. I guess I'm comparing you to myself.'

'In what way?'

'The business. We're still not doing as well as I'd like.'

'Really?' Rachel thinks of the plush offices, the professional atmosphere of the space she visited the other day. 'It doesn't show.'

'I'm good at maintaining a facade.'

'Is it because of Tom?'

'Yes. Aside from him taking the sums I told you about, he had let his work slide on account of his personal problems. When I delved into his records, his work was behind and we were owed money from clients that it was his job to chase. I had no idea any of this was going on. If he'd only told me, we could have addressed it together – you know what good friends we were. Or at least, I thought we were.'

'Don't forget he wasn't with me for the last few months, so he mentioned nothing of this to me. I'm shocked. He'd always worked really hard, so I just assumed everything was ticking along fine. Even when we were together, he didn't discuss how the business was doing, not after the early days. He had you for that.' Rachel can still picture the time before Heidi as if it were yesterday: Tom arriving home after a day at work, dressed in his smart chinos and navy linen jacket, sweeping Josh up into his arms and carrying him through to the kitchen.

'Good day?' she always asked, but did she really listen to the answer? Mostly she was so preoccupied as a mother, she'd regale him with tales of her day and what the children had been up to, and he'd only talk about work if something memorable had happened, like he'd taken on a new client or had had a particularly successful meeting. Not talking about work didn't necessarily mean it wasn't going well, and she took it to mean the opposite.

'Did he continue paying for household bills and the children as well as contributing to his accommodation with Heidi?'

'I don't know what their arrangement was for sure, but he was definitely still paying money to me. I couldn't have managed otherwise, and neither of us wanted to disrupt the children by selling the house. Heidi rented her flat, so I imagine he contributed. They were making plans to buy a house; he wouldn't have done that if he was struggling to get by. The only thing the police mentioned was that he'd applied for a personal loan and his application was rejected.'

'He might not have told Heidi about it, given that their relationship was quite new. It may have been projecting about the future that worried him, that financially he might not have been able to cope.'

'I'd have thought he might have confided in you,' Rachel says.

'That all changed after he left you; he wouldn't have wanted me to think his personal life could reflect upon his work and the business. I know he was helping you when he could.'

'We wanted life to carry on as normal for the children – as much as it could do. Which was hard, because I was so angry with him and Heidi. I hated it when the children spent time with her. I know she was trying to take my place; Tom kept going on about how much she wanted a family. I wasn't letting her have mine, that was for sure.'

'Going back to your chat with her, what did she think about the note?'

'She thinks it must be a hoax. Her theory is that Tom chose to leave and take up a new identity because he couldn't cope with his life. I'm inclined to agree with her. In my heart, I believe he's still alive, and that's the conclusion the police drew. There was no evidence of foul play, plus he'd drawn out quite a bit of money before he left and then stopped using his bank account. I don't think any of us knew what was really going on with him. But... there was something else...' She hesitates, unsure how much to tell him about her last weekend with Tom.

'Yes?'

Once it's out there, she can't undo it. She trusts Freddie, but she'd rather not have this conversation over the phone.

'Nothing. You know, Heidi didn't mention that there's anyone else in her life now, but I doubt she would want him back.'

'And would you?'

Rachel pictures Tom appearing in front of her, his face still so familiar, as if it were only yesterday that she last set eyes on him. The dust from the fallout has only recently begun to settle, and she feels a hot flash of fury. She'd never wish him dead, but that would have been easier to accept. If he were to turn up now, she would want *him* to want her back, to validate the belief she'd clung to that he still loved her. He'd need a bloody good reason for his absence though.

'Not to take him back, but I'd give anything to tell him what I think of him.'

ELEVEN

TOM

Of course, nothing went to plan. Tom didn't act on his thoughts, and seven months on, he was still seeing Heidi and cheating on his wife. Still in love with two women at the same time. He'd almost confided in Freddie one night, blurted everything out after the third pint, when Freddie's smile was blurring a little and Tom was glowing with warmth towards his friend. But Freddie and Rachel were good friends too, and the thought of him taking Rachel's side stopped him. Tom was the Cowardly Lion in *The Wizard of Oz*, only no wizard was doling out courage here and he couldn't make himself step over that line and tell Rachel what he was doing.

She didn't appear to suspect a thing, which was what stopped him telling her, wanting her to have a few more days living as they were before he put a bomb under everything. He was afraid of her reaction, unable to bear upsetting her in this way. And there were the children, too, Josh toddling about, following his daddy wherever he went in the house, his little mate who he loved in a way he hadn't thought possible. He appreciated what his dad had done for him more now as well; finally he got why it mattered, given the sacrifices his father had made for him when he was young. Supporting him in his swimming career, up at a ridiculous hour to drive him to training at the pool in the next town, there to pick him up without fail at the end of the session. Sacrificing holidays in order to pay for his expenses, back when they all believed he was going to make it big. Their unspoken goal was the Olympics, a dream that never materialised because of the car accident that forced him to abandon his dreams.

It was such a simple thing that upended everything. He'd told Rachel he was having dinner with a client – 'might be a late one' – going to a restaurant in town instead of driving to a nearby village. Careless. He'd been holding hands with Heidi across the table when he'd sensed somebody watching him and glanced over her shoulder into the eyes of Tanya, one of Rachel's book group friends. The glare on her face had struck fear into his heart. Despite Heidi's assurances that Tanya wouldn't tell – it was the sort of dilemma people wrote to agony aunts about, not wanting to be the one to upset a marriage or devastate a friend – he'd left the restaurant early, unable to eat the food that had looked so delicious when it had arrived. His stomach churning, he'd driven around for hours, afraid to go home, trying to look normal when he went into the house.

Tanya hadn't wasted any time. Despite the late hour, the living room light was on. Rachel was there, a half-empty bottle of wine on the table. She had barely drunk since Josh was born. Telltale blobs of mascara flecked her cheeks, and her neck was flushed as it always was when she was agitated.

He didn't try to hide anything. Told her the exact truth: that it had been going on for seven months and it wasn't a fling; he didn't love Rachel any less but he loved Heidi too. 'Heidi – what sort of a name is that?' she'd said, before bursting into tears and throwing a glass at him. Josh had woken at the noise and started screaming, and Lara had appeared at the top of the stairs and asked why Mummy and Daddy were shouting. It was so unusual, he realised afterwards – they rarely argued – but then nothing was very usual after that.

They attempted for a while to keep the marriage going; he slept in Josh's room while they tried to work out how to move forward. He agreed he wouldn't see Heidi any more – at the moment when he was confronted with Rachel's distress, he'd have agreed to anything to stop her from hurting, plus she'd reminded him that as a stay-at-home mother she would be bound to get full custody of the children should she wish to pursue that route. He backtracked, agreed to ditch Heidi and focus on their family one hundred per cent. It only lasted three days, three days of ignoring Heidi's calls and texts, working from home instead of the office, avoiding going out. That wasn't living. On the fourth day, he went back to work and she was waiting outside for him. One look at her and he was back in the nightmare of being torn between two women.

That evening he packed a bag and told both of them he was going to a hotel for two days to think about his future. He deliberately chose a basic bed-and-breakfast, with few fripperies to distract him, where he lay on the lumpy bed staring at the damp-stained walls with a pack of beer and decided what to do. He was going to leave Rachel for Heidi. But when he pulled up outside the house he'd shared with her for the past seven years, their marital home, he found his bags already packed in the hall. The choice had been made for him. 'The fact that you had a decision to make, that someone else meant as much to you as I do, is all I needed to know,' she told him. 'I thought our love meant more to you than that.' She'd changed her mind about the children, though; she wanted their father to figure in their lives no matter what had happened between the two of them. Her reaction surprised him, and he respected her even more for it.

Heidi took him in her arms when he turned up on her

doorstep, squeezed him to her and promised that they'd get through this. From the start, she understood how important Lara and Josh were to him – after all, he knew she hoped to have her own children one day – and she told him they were welcome at the flat any time. He loved her even more after that and knew he'd made the right decision. Not being able to see Josh and Lara every day, though, to read them stories, help them clean their teeth and reassure them in the night when they couldn't sleep – that was a physical pain lodged in his chest that even Heidi couldn't smooth away.

He was sure he and Rachel would be able to come to an arrangement that enabled them to have the children on an equal basis, especially as Heidi was being so cooperative. Rachel was scornful about Heidi's willingness to take them on – 'She'll say anything to get you away from me' – but he could see she was hurting and that it was the grief talking, not his normally rational wife. Mostly he avoided mentioning Heidi to Rachel, whereas Heidi wanted to be involved in every decision, know everything Rachel said so she could keep one step ahead. Both approaches he could understand.

Freddie was the person he had most difficulty with. Tom took him out for lunch and told him the situation, explained why he was no longer living at home. 'Josh is still a toddler,' Freddie said, and Tom felt his heart swell at the thought of the little boy who was so special to him. He tried to explain how falling in love had just happened to him, but he could see Freddie didn't get it – he'd never experienced mad passion himself, he'd confided to Tom once; he loved his current girl-friend, but it wasn't the stuff people wrote songs about. He said the right things, made the right noises, but there was a wall between them after that, Freddie behind it, almost within reach but not quite. It was only later that Tom found out how much time Freddie had spent helping Rachel, providing the solid support he himself had once enjoyed from his friend.

That he was willing to endure all this convinced Tom he was making the right choice. He wished he hadn't fallen in love with Heidi, but it had happened and he would never go back now. They would all make this work. The irony was he hadn't even done it then, taken the step that would really set Freddie against him. He'd merely thought about it. The first time had been shortly after that.

TWELVE

RACHEL

Present day

Rachel stashes the notes in the back of her underwear drawer. Neither of her children would ever look in there. She should probably just chuck them away, but something makes her hang on to them for now. A small doubt, in the back of her mind, especially since Heidi got one too. She'll keep them just in case.

Downstairs, Lara is sitting at the kitchen table, frowning over her maths homework. She drops her pen on her book when Rachel enters the kitchen.

'I hate maths, Mum. Why do we get so much homework? I've got two pages of these equations to do and I can't even get one right.'

Rachel pulls up a chair. 'Let me have a look.'

'You won't be much help. You're always telling me how rubbish you are at maths.'

'Thanks for rubbing it in. I have a GCSE, an average grade, and it's been adequate in my life so far. But you're right, it isn't my strong point.'

'Holly's sister does hers for her. It's so unfair. The teacher has no idea. My stupid brother is no good for anything.'

'Poor little Josh. He keeps you entertained, doesn't he? Here, let me have a look.'

Rachel pulls Lara's exercise book over and reads through the example she did in class, and then the worksheet.

'Would you like me to arrange some extra lessons for you?'

'I'm not spending any more time at school than I do already, if that's what you mean.'

'I was thinking more along the lines of a private tutor who could come to the house.'

Lara pulls a face. 'Do I have to?'

Rachel sighs and the doorbell rings.

'Who's that at this hour? Are you expecting anyone?' she asks Lara.

'Yeah, like who? I've not exactly got friends beating the door down, have I?'

Rachel wishes she could take the words back. 'I didn't mean... I'll go and see who it is.'

'You're no use to me here, Mum. I just want this homework to be finished.' Lara sighs and picks up her pen, chewing the end as she stares at the figures on the page.

'Oh,' Rachel says as she opens the door to find Heidi standing there.

Heidi grins, her wide smile showing her neat teeth. Anyone would think they were friends.

'Did I leave something behind?' Rachel asks, although their meeting was yesterday and surely Heidi would have let her know by now.

'No, I was just passing and thought I'd stop by on the off chance that you were in.'

Rachel is gripping the side of the door, holding it ajar. She glances back over her shoulder.

'Lara is home. I don't want to disturb her.'

'Oh, I'd love to see her. She was such a sweet little girl. So lively.'

'She's calmed down a lot since then.' Rachel keeps her voice low, not wanting Lara to hear their conversation. 'And she's very sensitive.'

'Mum?' Lara appears in the hallway. 'Oh,' she says. 'Are you Heidi?'

Rachel does a double-take; she didn't expect Lara to recognise this distant figure from her past.

Heidi smiles at her. 'Yes! Do you remember me?'

'Kind of, a bit. Not really, actually. Only from the television the other day.'

'Of course you don't.' Heidi's smile falters a little.

'Lara is doing her homework,' Rachel says. 'We should get back to it.'

'Ah, the horrors of homework, I remember it well.'

'I'm giving up, Mum,' Lara says. 'I can't do it and you can't either.'

'Giving up is not an option. When's it due in?'

'Tomorrow.'

Heidi perks up. 'Anything I can help with?'

'Maths,' says Lara, enunciating the word as if she has something painful on her tongue.

'Aha. One of the few academic subjects I happen to be good at,' says Heidi. Rachel stares, not believing her. 'Would you like me to have a look?'

Lara nods eagerly. Rachel reluctantly lets go of the door so that it swings open, and Heidi follows Lara through into the kitchen. Lara shows her the worksheet and Heidi reads it through.

'This is no problem. Do you mind, Rachel, if I stay and help Lara?'

'Of course not,' Rachel says. She does. But how can she

refuse when it will benefit Lara? 'Can I get you a coffee or anything?'

'Coffee would be great. Do you have almond milk? I'm a vegan.'

Of course you are. She doesn't remember Tom mentioning this. She can't imagine him wanting to go without meat for even a day. Maybe that was why he disappeared.

'Soya, that's the best I can do.'

'That's fine.'

As Rachel makes the coffee, she realises that that is the first time she has been able to joke to herself about her husband's disappearance. She hears murmured conversation, and then Lara laughs, and a weight lifts from her soul. Her daughter rarely laughs nowadays; maybe it's the stress of struggling in some of her subjects at school that is dragging her down, and all she needs is a little confidence. If Heidi can offer that, then she won't turn her away. It's not as if Lara remembers her, and she no longer constitutes a threat in that area. Unlike back then, when Rachel used to lie awake worrying that Tom and Heidi would plot to get full custody of her children.

The homework takes no time at all once Heidi has worked through some examples with Lara, showing great patience.

'Thanks so much,' Lara says. 'Can I go upstairs now, Mum?'

'Course you can. You don't have to ask.'

'Thanks again,' Lara says, 'and I'm sorry I don't remember you.'

Heidi waves her concerns away. 'I wouldn't expect you to. I certainly remember you and little Josh. You used to come to my house every weekend for a while.'

Lara hovers awkwardly in the doorway.

'Off you go,' Rachel says.

'She's so well behaved,' Heidi says. 'I was a terror at that age.' They listen to Lara's footsteps as she walks up the stairs. 'Does that mean she doesn't remember her dad either?'

Rachel nods. 'Barely. She has a couple of vague memories that she describes as flashes of moments. It's a shame in one way, but then given what happened, it's probably best. She's such a quiet girl, and I try to encourage her to make more friends, but she rarely hangs out with people her age.'

'Shame,' Heidi says, 'although it must make it easier for you. You don't want her falling in with the wrong crowd, disappearing and getting up to all sorts.'

Rachel raises an eyebrow. 'Is that based on your own experience?'

Heidi laughs. 'God, yes. I was such a horror as a teenager. My mum used to threaten to put me in a home. I'd be out until all hours with my mates – older mates my mum didn't approve of – and I got kicked out of school when I was fifteen. Believe me, you're lucky with Lara. Where's Joshie?'

'Josh,' Rachel says sharply. Nobody calls him that any more.

'Sorry.' Heidi looks put out.

'He's at a friend's for tea. Josh has too many friends. I can't keep up with his social life. It's way more exciting than mine.'

'This is great coffee,' Heidi says.

'Thanks.' If that's a hint that she'd like another, Rachel ignores it. 'I haven't thanked you for sorting out Lara's homework. Honestly, it's embarrassing, I haven't a clue how to help her. I even asked the neighbour once if her son could have a go, but he was as clueless as me.'

'She just needed showing the right method. It's easy once you know what you're doing. By the end, she was working the answers out by herself.'

'It's such a relief,' Rachel says. 'Some weeks she ends up in tears. She gets so frustrated at herself when she can't work out how to do it. I was wondering earlier about hiring a private tutor.'

'I'd do it,' Heidi says, her face animated. 'I'd love to help her. It was so satisfying. Maths was my favourite subject at school. It was the one thing I was any good at. Whereas French...'

'Lara does Spanish, which is lucky seeing as I took it at school. History is my favourite to help her with.' Rachel is gabbling as she mulls over Heidi's suggestion. It would make perfect sense, but does she really want the woman in her house? Should she be inviting her into their lives?

She gathers the cups together and puts them in the dishwasher. She pictures Lara's face when she went upstairs.

'I'll give it some thought,' she says.

Rachel knocks on Lara's bedroom door later that evening. She likes to check in on her to make sure she has put away her phone and her laptop and is actually going to sleep. The light under the door gives away that she is still up; Rachel hopes she isn't going to be difficult. She's been moody lately, and she hopes it isn't a foreshadowing of worse to come.

Lara is sitting with her back against the headboard, looking at her laptop.

'Maths?' Rachel smiles.

'Yeah, right, Mum. I finished that hours ago.'

'Was Heidi helpful?'

Lara's face splits into a smile. 'Super helpful. And she explained it much better than Mr Graham. I told you he was rubbish.'

'I'm sure he isn't rubbish, but he obviously isn't helping you. Teachers have different styles, that's all. It's unfortunate that you're in his class. I'm planning on discussing this at the next parents' evening.'

'Can Heidi come and help me again?'

Rachel frowns. 'It's awkward.'

'I know you don't like her because of what happened with Dad. I bet you hate her.'

Rachel sits down on the edge of the bed. 'She isn't my favourite person, that's true. But... well, that all happened a long time ago now, and people move on. I saw a different side to her tonight. She's certainly very patient. I'll think about it, but only if you go to bed when I tell you. Like now.'

'Mum.' Lara rolls her eyes.

'Seriously, though, it's lights-out time. What's so interesting on there anyway?'

'I'm finding out what happened to Dad.' Lara closes her laptop and Rachel takes it and leaves it on the desk.

'Oh darling, if only you could. We all tried, believe me.'

'Don't try and stop me. I'm putting all the information together, like for a project. I want to know all about it, Mum – you never want to talk about it.'

'That's not true.' But Rachel hears the lack of conviction behind her words. 'I don't want you to be upset, that's all.'

'I might find something out that would be helpful. Stephanie uncovered lots of things in her situation. I've been chatting to her online. She's really friendly.'

'You must be careful when you're talking to people online that you don't know, no matter how friendly they seem.'

'You saw Stephanie on television. Of course she's who she says he is.'

'Promise me something, though. If you do see Heidi again, don't bother her with the stuff about your dad. It's a very delicate situation.'

'You will think about the maths thing, though?'

Rachel nods. 'But don't get your hopes up. Night night, sleep well.'

'Night, Mum.'

THIRTEEN

Rachel lies in bed pondering the events of the evening. Has she done the right thing by letting Heidi into her house? For the first time in ages, Lara had some energy about her, and her happiness and stability is more important than anything else. If she can finally get to grips with her maths, that will be a huge help, as it's been bringing her mood down for a while, but inviting Heidi in is a huge step.

If Lara had been older when her dad disappeared and had formed a bond with Heidi, there's no way Rachel would have allowed them to reconnect. But she doesn't even remember her, and Heidi genuinely seems to want to help. If she has a gift for maths, then maybe it's meant to be. Rachel is a great believer in fate.

Before she goes to sleep, she finds herself wondering about the question Freddie asked her: whether she would want Tom to be alive. At the time of his disappearance, she was caught in a state of limbo. Since he'd left her that weekend, fresh from her bed, she'd been in turmoil. On the one hand, she didn't regret what had happened; on the other, it had set her back.

It had taken her months to get over his affair, his leaving

home, setting up with Heidi, a gorgeous younger woman – every wife's worst nightmare coming true. The next few months were almost like the aftermath of bereavement, in that she'd had to go through the various stages of grief and loss.

Denial was the immediate reaction; when she was finally able to assess what had happened, she refused to believe the evidence before her eyes. Pain and guilt followed, and that was the worst part, or so she thought at the time, as she went over all the memories they'd created together, the promises they'd made and the work they'd put into their relationship. These thoughts produced a stabbing pain in her chest that wouldn't go away, a constriction in her throat that made it impossible to swallow, the whole time trying to put on a brave front for the children and get through each harrowing day.

The next stage was anger and bargaining – desperate conversations with Tom where she let out all the anguish, hurled venomous threats at him, knowing exactly where to hurt, seeing from his recoil that she was driving him further away, but unable to stop herself. She wanted to see him hurt as much as she was, yet she knew he was going back to the nubile blonde who would wrap her tanned limbs around him and make him forget everything else that had happened. The anger coincided with and was fuelled by the uncertainty over the house, worrying that he might try and take it from her, or force her to sell up and move somewhere smaller, uproot the kids and cause them further suffering. Fear-filled rage consumed her for months.

In hindsight, the next cycle was worse: depression, reflection and loneliness. She had to accept that he was serious – that he had left her and the children and was actively pursuing a new life. He was moving on and away with a future in front of him, whereas she had to navigate her present life, under which a bomb had exploded. Having the children saved her; protecting them was her priority and she had to make sure Tom didn't try and take them away from her. The upward turn was the stage she had finally reached just before he vanished – she'd established a new routine, realised there were some positives about her new unexpected life, and was finally accepting that Tom was part of her past.

And then that weekend happened. One evening of deep conversation, connecting again in the way they always had, and she remembered why she had fallen in love with him in the first place. She had tried so hard to fight those feelings from getting a hold of her again. The unexpected passionate encounter that followed was the kind of sex where you have such a deep understanding and love for one another that it just feels *right* and that you were meant to be together. It was a Saturday night, which posed a question in itself: why wasn't he out on a date with his glamorous young girlfriend? It was almost compulsory for young people to go out on a Saturday night: she wasn't too old to remember that phase of her life. If she didn't have the children, she'd doubtless be the same.

That night, she lay awake wondering what it meant. Did she dare believe that he had lost interest in Heidi? Perhaps the brief passion was fizzling out in the way she had suspected it would, the age gap and lack of similarities too much to overcome. Maybe the children were coming between them; they were having to adjust their plans to accommodate Lara and Josh in their lives. Undoubtedly not what Heidi had signed up for. She reminded herself of the anguished look on his face when he'd got dressed and left, leaving her on the warm sheets where he had writhed just moments before, gazing into her eyes and telling her he still loved her. Could she take him back after what he'd done? She could already hear her sister's outrage just for having that thought.

That weekend left her on a precipice, unsure of her next move, scared to take a step in case she fell too hard. When the phone call came with the news that Tom had gone missing, that was when she first asked herself the question she's asked herself thousands of times since: would Tom really leave Heidi, abandon her *and* his children and take himself off, never to contact them again?

Her conclusion at the time was that he had left because he couldn't cope with his situation. Either the prospect of ditching Heidi was too awful, or he genuinely didn't know what to do. He hadn't spoken much about his feelings for Heidi that night, and she hadn't wanted to spoil it by bringing her into the room with them. It could have been one almighty argument that had driven him into Rachel's arms, getting his own back on Heidi – she wasn't stupid. Only deep down she didn't believe that was the case. His words and actions had been genuine, and she sensed that he regretted leaving her but hadn't been able to put his feelings into words. He was standing on a cliff, not knowing whether to jump or step back from the edge. He'd done neither, she believed – had simply slunk away into the darkness, too cowardly to face either of them or make a decision.

But now? She can't deny that when the note arrived the other day, seeing Tom's handwriting on the envelope, she had a jolt of hope. *He's alive.* She's never stopped loving him, because there has never been a conclusion. She can admit that to herself now.

That week – Tom's last before he disappeared, after they had slept together again, almost seven years ago now – she fluctuated between daring to want him back and being furious with herself for allowing him back into her life and reigniting the uncertainty inside her. She'd worked so hard to get to the place she had been in; she couldn't let one night of passion undo all that.

After he vanished, her conclusion was that he was a coward, that he couldn't face this awful dilemma of his own making and had run away. No, she doesn't want him back now, but she'd like to tell him exactly what damage he's caused by his spineless abandonment of his life. She falls asleep thinking it's a positive thing that Heidi is back in their lives; it's about time they opened up to each other with the truth about Tom. And now that she has Freddie, the ally she wasn't ready for at the time, maybe together they can find out what was really going on inside Tom's head, and what had happened to him.

Lara nags Rachel on the issue of maths lessons with Heidi.

'You wanted me to get tuition, Mum, it makes sense. That stuff with Dad happened a long time ago now. You need to move on. That's what I'm trying to do with my blog.'

'When did you get so wise?' Lara definitely seems more upbeat lately, so Rachel gives in.

Heidi sounds happy to accept the offer to give Lara another lesson.

'Shall we try it for a couple of weeks, see how you get on?' Rachel doesn't want to commit to having her in their lives indefinitely.

'She can come to my place if you like,' Heidi suggests, 'or we could meet in a café.'

'No,' Rachel says, rather too quickly. 'Here is fine. If you come at around four, the builders will be finishing up by then. And I'll pay you the going rate.'

'No, you—'

'Yes. I insist.'

Heidi arrives early the next day.

'Oh.' Rachel answers the door, a tea towel in her hand. 'I was just clearing up after the builders. They've almost finished.'

Danny comes into the kitchen. He looks ill at ease, hovering in the doorway in his paint-splattered overalls. Pete is usually the one to brief her at the end of the day.

'Hi,' says Heidi.

Danny nods at her, embarrassed. Rachel can never equate his shyness with his burly build. He's good-looking, and clearly works out to get such huge muscles.

'Pete says to tell you we're done. The floor should be finished tomorrow.'

'That's good news,' Rachel says. 'And thanks for fixing the squeaky gate. See you tomorrow.'

'What are you having done exactly?' Heidi asks as Danny leaves. 'I've seen the scaffolding, so it must be a pretty big job.'

Expensive, she means.

'My grandmother left me some money and the house needed work doing. I'm having a loft extension and the garden is being landscaped.'

'It sounds wonderful.' Heidi laughs. 'I'm a bit addicted to property programmes.'

'How long have you lived in this area?' Apart from the fact that she stole her husband, Rachel knows very little about this woman.

'All my life. I was born here, so I know it well. Any chance I could have a little tour of the house?'

Rachel has to believe that Heidi has never set foot here before. To have done so would have been a betrayal too far. From her body language, the way she looks with interest at everything, Rachel tends to think she hasn't. She wishes she didn't keep trying to second-guess everything Heidi does – if she's allowing this woman into her home on Lara's behalf, then she has to accept her and stop scrutinising her every move. Heidi isn't assessing the value and making comparisons – Tom is in the past now, and she too has no doubt done her best to move on, with no less of a battle than Rachel has had. Rachel admits that last point grudgingly to herself.

'Sure,' she says, deliberately sounding upbeat. 'Let's start upstairs.'

She walks Heidi around the new loft extension, which is going to be her bedroom. It has an en suite shower room, which she is particularly thrilled with, and pleased with the finish she hopes to be able to achieve with her limited budget, showing Heidi a photo of the finished look.

'This is gorgeous,' Heidi says. 'Did you design it yourself?'

'I'd like to say I did, but I just gathered some pictures and ideas of what I would like and worked with the builder. He has a good eye, plus his rates are very competitive.'

'It helps when you know someone,' Heidi says. 'You'll have to give me his number.'

'Oh, are you thinking of having some work done?'

'Only on my face.' Heidi grins. 'No, not at the moment, but it's always good to have a few names stashed – should the time come when I get some money together.'

'Let's go downstairs.' Rachel leads her down to the next level, where the three bedrooms are. 'I won't show you Lara's because she's very private, but Josh won't mind, although you might be horrified by the mess. I certainly am.'

'Oh, I don't mind messy kids; it shows character, I think. I don't like everything being too uncluttered – it makes it clinical somehow.'

Rachel can't work out whether Heidi is making a dig at her, or whether she's just being honest.

Josh's room is painted sky blue and has a feature wall of coloured dinosaur paper. Sure enough, there are piles of toys and books on the floor and a heap of clothes at the bottom of the bed. His rucksack is open and stuff is spilling out.

'Honestly, this boy will be the death of me,' Rachel says, picking up a few items of dirty clothing and sticking them in Josh's washing basket. 'This bag hasn't been properly unpacked since his weekend away camping with the Scouts. He promised me he'd done it.'

'I see he loves his dinosaurs,' Heidi says. 'How old is he now?'

'He's eight. Yes, he's had a thing about dinosaurs for ages. I'm sure he'll grow out of it soon and will insist on redecorating his room.'

'Why not do it while the builders are in?'

'I wish. I have a finite amount of money and it's all accounted for to the last penny. I'm sort of project-managing the build to save costs. Josh painted his own room last time with his best friend – with close supervision, of course. But he's got a lot on at the moment with all his social activities.'

Rachel holds the door to her own bedroom open, giving just a brief glimpse of what Heidi will doubtless think of as clinical grey walls, her current paperback at the side of the bed with her reading glasses. Everything else is stored away, but the window has a nice aspect looking out over the fields, sheep dotted on green hills in the distance.

'Not much to see in there,' she says, feeling a sudden desire to close the door firmly, not let the woman see further into her private space. 'Let's go down to the kitchen and have a coffee, and I can talk you through what I'm thinking of doing in the garden.'

'I wish I had a garden,' Heidi says. 'All I have is a tiny little yard. I've tried making it pretty with some trellises and flowers, but there's only so much I can do. I'd give anything for a space with some sunshine.' She rubs her arms. 'I do like a bit of colour, but mostly I have to make do with fake.'

Rachel looks at her own pale skin. Faking a tan is something she does occasionally if she's going away and doesn't want to look like an ice cream on the beach against all the glorious golden limbs sunning themselves.

She's making coffee when there's a noise at the front door and Josh bursts in.

'Hi, Mum,' he yells, dropping his school bag to the floor. He stops short when he sees Heidi. 'Oh, hello, who are you?'

'Josh, manners, please.' Rachel raises her eyebrows at Heidi.

'I'm Heidi, and you must be Josh.'

'Do you know me?' he asks. 'I don't think I know you – do I, Mum?'

'No,' Rachel says, getting in before Heidi. She hopes the other woman understands that she doesn't want to make any allusions to the past. Josh is far too inquisitive and unguarded as it is.

'I can't wait for tomorrow, Mum. We're doing our first full rehearsal on the big stage at drama club.' He opens the fridge and extracts a carton of orange juice, pouring some into a glass.

'I'm impressed,' Heidi says. 'My younger brother used to drink juice straight from the carton – utterly gross. I can see you have good manners, Josh.'

'And I won't have to do science as we're leaving school early. I hate science.' He addresses the last part to Heidi.

'It wasn't my favourite subject either,' Heidi says, 'but it can be very useful in life.'

'Maybe. Mum, are you picking me up?'

'Toby's mum will be collecting you. I'll be making sure you don't miss out on anything at school. That's not what doing this is about.'

'I'm gonna text Toby right now, see if he knows his lines yet.' Josh glances from Heidi to Rachel. 'Can I go?'

'Of course you can.'

He runs off upstairs.

'What a lovely boy. That sounds really exciting – putting on a play.'

'He's a natural, even if I say so myself. He goes to a drama school on Saturdays and one evening a week. His teacher reckons he could do well, and he loves it. He likes attention, as you've probably realised. Pretty much the opposite of Lara.'

'Yes, he's a right little character. It must be great fun.

Talking of drama, Lara mentioned she recognised me from the documentary. What did you think of it?'

'I'm relieved it wasn't focusing on Tom, not now the seven years is nearly up. Did they consult you about it? I wasn't even aware that it was on until I saw a trailer. Lara was very interested to watch it. I'm not sure how I feel about that.'

'She's at that age, I suppose. Curious about everything, especially about her background. And yes, I was contacted about the programme but told them I wasn't interested. I can't help wondering if it's linked to the notes we received.'

Rachel sighs. 'Same here. I thought there might be some new information being revealed on the show, but there was nothing.'

'Would you have liked there to be?'

'Well of course, wouldn't you?

Rachel watches Heidi's face, keen to see her reaction – can only see genuine eagerness as Heidi nods her head vigorously.

'It's the not knowing I can't stand. What I think happened is that the coward couldn't cope and took himself off – most likely somewhere sunny – and is living a glorious life under a different name, probably with a younger model, because I'm not in my twenties any more, am I? Even *I* would be too old for him now – I mean, look at these wrinkles.' She points to her eyes, but Rachel sees only smooth skin. 'And if I knew where he was, I'd be straight over there to have it out with him for putting you and the children through this. It's unforgivable.'

Rachel is astounded by Heidi's hypocrisy, although her slightly frivolous take on what to her is a heavy drama is refreshing, and she should learn from this attitude. 'Where do you think he might have gone?'

'It could be anywhere really. He loved travelling. Somewhere hot.'

She tries to visualise Tom on a beach, relaxed, renewed. 'I don't see it. I agree he's more likely to have run away from something, made a fresh start with someone new. After all he's got form.'

'He could be in the next town,' Heidi says, 'but it's pointless guessing – he could be anywhere.' The clock ticks as they both sit with their thoughts for a moment. 'Did you try and find him yourself?'

Rachel nods. 'For years. I still do occasionally. And I follow crime reports – you know, if ever any remains are found, I always imagine the worst, live in dread for a few days, until enough time has passed that I know the police would have called if it was him.'

'Same here. I don't think I'll ever stop looking. You know, I never thought I'd say this, but it helps talking to you about this. Nobody else gets it.'

'How could they?'

Lara arrives for her lesson and Rachel sits in the living area, grateful that the open-plan arrangement enables her to keep an eye on them. She wouldn't admit this to Heidi, but she finds talking about Tom therapeutic too, the same as it is with Freddie; somehow it makes her feel less lonely. It's good to be able to speak frankly with someone who understands. Heidi too will have had those moments of bewilderment, the what-ifs, the whys, the way the not knowing puts an obstacle in your path that it's impossible to surmount, a boulder too heavy to push. Perhaps now that it's shifting a little, the two of them can push it away, clear the path for a way out of this.

Enough time has passed for her no longer to hate the very mention of Heidi. She has new priorities now. Freddie, for a start. He's creeping into her thoughts more and more, and once again she wonders if they could possibly have a future. She feels warm inside at this thought, like an arm is around her, holding her – that someone is looking out for her needs. She's going to forget the notes, push forward with declaring Tom dead as soon as possible. It's time for her to move on with her life.

FOURTEEN

Freddie's text arrives first thing. She smiles at his keenness.

Fancy eating out tonight?

She spends a moment looking at his profile photo, sunglasses hiding his brown eyes, and the crooked grin that makes her want to smile too. Hint of stubble on his chin. The sea is in the background and she wishes she was there with him now.

I'd love to.

No exclamation marks, no kisses, keep it simple.

I'll choose somewhere and let you know details later?

Great.

She crosses that out. She doesn't want to over-enthuse.

OK.

Her body feels light this morning, as if she is floating. It's funny how having given herself permission to act on the desire she has refused to acknowledge for so long, it feels as if a weight has been lifted. She's always felt the weight of her past like a stone in her stomach, assuming it to be the situation with Tom, which wasn't about to go away any time soon. That situation intensified with the anonymous letters, but everything has changed now that she knows she has a future and is looking forward to it. She's realistic enough to know that this situation with Freddie may not work out, could fizzle out before it's even got going, but she's about to step onto the stage and play her part, instead of hiding away and letting the understudy take over.

Once the children have set off for school, she runs upstairs to check the builders' progress. Light pours in through the dormer window of the room that will soon be her bedroom. How soon is what she wants to find out. Last time she checked, only one wall had been painted; today, the whole room looks as if it's been given at least one coat. Pete told her that once the painting is finished, the job will be more or less complete. She stands in the middle of the room and marvels at the space she will soon have to call her own. The room is twice the size of her current bedroom, and she hopes to make new memories in this one. She's never been able to forget that her current sleeping place is the one she shared with Tom. She hugs herself, sending thanks to her grandmother for making this possible. Could a new start really be on the horizon – and possibly a new relationship?

She checks the bathroom before she goes back downstairs, to see whether that room has been painted too. Grey tiles cover half of the wall space, so there isn't much to do in here. The new shower cubicle is fresh and shiny, and the huge shower head promises a satisfying experience. She turns to check the wall behind her, where a large mirror has been placed above the neat round sink. She grabs hold of the basin when she sees the mirror. Red writing covers it, huge letters spelling: *GET OUT*.

Her body shakes as if she's in shock. A juddering runs right through her. She grips the sink tight and tries to make sense of what is in front of her. She touches the red G with a shaking finger, recognising the texture of lipstick. Heidi flashes into her mind; she was here last night, but Rachel was with her the whole time. She wants it to be Heidi, because that she could deal with, but logically she knows it can't have been her. This means someone has been in her house, someone uninvited. And why do they want her to leave? What does this mean?

She goes next door to see if Deborah is in, not caring what her neighbour thinks of her sudden interest in her CCTV. She's not there, and reluctantly Rachel heads back to her own house. The builders aren't coming today. She takes a photograph of the mirror but leaves it untouched, unsure exactly what to do about it. Should she report it to the police?

Freddie has booked a table at Nero's. It's normally one of her favourite Italian restaurants, but tonight a ball of anxiety sits in her throat and she's unsure if she'll be able to eat. She spent the day cleaning the house, eventually going back upstairs to wipe the mirror. She doesn't want the children to see it. It takes her ages to get ready, trying on dresses she hasn't worn in ages, surprised to see she has lost weight, which narrows down her choice. There is only one that doesn't make her look like a sack of potatoes. It fits perfectly around the waist, whereas before it was a little too snug, so this is the first time she's worn it.

She and Freddie arrive at the same time. He kisses her cheek and they follow the waiter to their table. They decide on a wine and put in their order. Ordinarily conversation flits between them with the steady rhythm of an equal tennis match, reminding Rachel how it used to be in the early days with Tom, when they had so much to say to each other and not enough time. Tonight she forces herself to focus. Freddie is wearing a beautifully cut white linen shirt, with straight trousers and grey lace-up brogues. Long-forgotten desire surprises her, and she drinks from her wine glass to hide the sudden flare in her cheeks.

The waiter delivers their meals while Freddie is telling her a funny story about his day. Rachel looks at the plate of risotto in front of her and picks up her fork, swallowing hard. Freddie stops talking.

'Are you OK?'

She puts her fork down. 'I'm so sorry, I can't concentrate.' She tells him about the writing in the bathroom and shows him the photograph.

'When do you think it happened?'

'No idea. The builders were in yesterday for most of the day, but they're on a different job today. Presumably it was fine when they left, which was around four.'

'And the children, have you asked them?'

She shakes her head. 'Not yet. I don't want to worry them. Josh is tied up with the play he's doing at his drama club – he's really into it at the moment.' She touches the table. 'He's a happy little boy most of the time and I don't want to unsettle him. And as for Lara, well, she has enough to worry about. She's been stressed about her maths, and...'

She blushes and curses her body as she has thousands of times before. She's grateful she left her silk scarf on to cover the pink blotches on her neck that appear whenever she's in the slightest discomfort.

'I've possibly done something stupid. Last night somebody was in our house helping Lara with her maths. The thing is...'

She fiddles with her hair. 'You're going to be surprised, but it's Heidi.'

'Heidi!' Freddie almost spits his wine out. 'How did that come about?'

Rachel explains. 'I gave her a tour of the house, which I wasn't exactly comfortable about, but she was with me the whole time. She had no opportunity to nip upstairs and vandalise the mirror. She didn't go to the bathroom, and I didn't leave the room.'

'It can't have been her, then, although it's a bit of a coincidence, you have to admit.'

Rachel nods. 'She's really helping Lara, and Lara likes her. It's making a real difference to her mood.'

'Does she remember her?'

'Not at all. She knows who she is, but has no memories of that time whatsoever. In a funny way, I think it makes her feel closer to her dad, as she doesn't remember much about him either and I know she wishes she did. She keeps his photo by her bed, and we talk about him, though not often, because it isn't easy for me either. I just feel it's important to answer any questions she may have.'

'Aren't you worried she might ask Heidi questions when you're not around? You won't have any control over what she tells her.'

'I'm always there with them. I wouldn't let Lara see her alone, or outside of the house. It's all under control. Besides, it's not a regular arrangement. Lara would like it to be, but I'm stalling.'

Freddie is frowning. 'I still think you should be careful.'

'I get that, but Tom isn't coming back, Heidi and I both know that, and we both feel cheated by the not knowing. We talked about it and it helped, actually. I can't help thinking that we might even be able to find out where he is if we work together.'

'Seriously? I don't want to be patronising, but if the police didn't get anywhere...'

'I thought you'd be on my side.'

'I am.' He sighs. 'I just don't want you to get your hopes up by stirring it all up. And I'm worried about the vandalism.' He takes her hand. 'I know you don't want to hear this, but the chances are he's no longer alive.'

She pulls away, as if stung. 'I've never believed that.'

'I get it, but it's a possibility; you know it's what the police thought at first. Even if they didn't spell it out to you, they certainly did to me. I'm worried about you. I don't want you to get hurt. And how much do we really know about Heidi? Just be careful, that's all I'm saying. And if you are going to embark on an investigation, then I want to be in on it.'

'It's hardly an investigation. And it's not because I want him back, it's just to know what happened. I want you to understand that. And thanks, that means a lot.'

'You mean a lot to me, Rachel, you must know that by now.'

She stops herself from smiling too broadly. He's put her hopes into words. She has sensed he feels the same about her, but when she's away from him, she begins to doubt. She has so much baggage, after all. He takes her hand again, and this time she lets him, and her skin tingles.

After a moment, she eases away. 'There's something I have to tell you,' she says. 'About Tom. I can trust you, can't I?'

'Of course. I've known you for years.' But he hasn't, not really. Her sister is always telling her she's too trusting.

She is just about to speak when the waiter appears with the dessert menu. She's barely touched her meal. She shakes her head absent-mindedly.

'Coffee?' Freddie asks. 'I'm having one.'

'OK.' Maybe it's best to hold off from telling him about her reconciliation with Tom for now. She has no idea how Freddie will react, and she doesn't want to drive him away.

'What did you want to tell me about Tom?'

'It's not so much about Tom, more about you really. I just wanted to say that it must have been hard for you to keep the business going – and you've done so well. I feel bad for not knowing what a hard time you were having. Especially as I've taken over Tom's share. You were so kind to me.'

'It wasn't the easiest time. I had to invest more money in the business, but I figured it was worth it. We'd put so much into it by then, and not knowing what had happened to Tom made the decision even harder. I had nothing else to fall back on and it kept me busy. Gave me something to focus on.'

'I wish you'd told me.'

'I was trying to protect you.'

'That makes me sound pathetic.'

'Don't be so hard on yourself. You've done well too – look at your amazing children. I've always admired you. That's why I found it hard to condone Tom's behaviour. Throwing away such a wonderful woman.'

'Stop it.' Rachel can't help smiling.

'Two coffees.' The waiter serves the coffee along with the bill.

Outside the restaurant, Freddie takes Rachel's hand as they walk. He sees her into her car and she winds down the window.

'You'll have to come for dinner at the house sometime,' she says. 'Meet the children. Although I have to warn you, Lara is already trying to matchmake us.'

He laughs. 'I knew that girl had taste. I'd love to.'

'It won't be for a while, though. I'd rather wait until the builders are out of the way.'

He walks away and then turns back. 'Be careful,' he says.

'About the builders?'

'No – well, I guess you should always be careful. You might want to think about strengthening the security on your house. Do you have a burglar alarm?'

'No.'

'Give it some thought. I actually meant be careful about Heidi.'

'I will.'

'She might have an agenda, worming herself into your life.'

'Heidi's OK. It was me who contacted her, remember.'

She watches him cross to his car before she drives off. His words are making her wonder. Heidi isn't the only one who suddenly came back into her life. Freddie's call came out of nowhere. It thrilled her at the time, but *is* she too trusting of him? After all, he was the closest person to Tom aside from the two women in his life. Cold air blows in through the open window.

FIFTEEN

When Rachel returns from shopping the following afternoon, she hears the sound of her daughter laughing as she lets herself into the house, and her heart lifts. Josh is at football – his friend's mum is bringing him home later – so Lara must have brought a friend home from school. At last.

'Hello,' she calls, eager to get into the kitchen and check her out. She's assuming it's a girl, but there's no reason it couldn't be a boy. She's not sure how she feels about that. Lara is only twelve, after all. But when she enters the room, she stops dead.

'Oh, hello, Heidi.' She drops her shopping bag onto the counter. 'I'm confused. We haven't arranged a maths lesson today, have we?' The way their heads were bent together, almost touching as they looked at something on Lara's laptop screen, makes her feels as if she's interrupting. How dare Heidi turn up without her permission.

'No, Lara called me and I was in the neighbourhood so thought I'd drop by.'

'Oh, I didn't know she had your number.'

'I gave it to her in case she had any problems with her home-work after I left. Can I help you with your shopping?'

'No. Thanks. It's only a few bits.' Rachel frowns, irritated by Heidi's offhand attitude. 'Did you need extra help with your maths, Lara?' There are no books on the table.

'No. I don't have to see Heidi just for maths.' Lara sounds defensive. 'Actually, I asked her to help me with my project.'

'What project?'

'My investigation into what happened to Dad.'

'Oh.' Rachel hides her irritation that Lara is going against her request not to discuss this in front of Heidi. Added to this, Freddie's suspicions from last night are fresh in Rachel's mind. She's perfectly capable of making up her own mind about Heidi, but Lara is a child still, and young for her age. Thanks goodness she came home when she did.

'Have you been here long?' she asks Heidi.

'About half an hour.'

'Would you like a drink, Heidi?' Lara asks. 'Coffee? Tea?'

'Peppermint tea would be great.'

'That sounds nice. I'll have one of those too.'

'Really? I didn't think you liked it.' Lara is filling the kettle and Rachel can't think of a way of stopping this without being rude. Heidi shouldn't be here without an invite from her, and that rankles.

'You don't know everything about me.'

Rachel pretends not to notice that Lara is playing up in front of Heidi. The hint of bolshiness she's displaying today is new. It could just be the start of the teenage years, which she hasn't been looking forward to. Her own teenage years were a time of great insecurity, trying to work out how she fitted into the world and the sort of person she wanted to be.

Lara carries two mugs of tea to the kitchen table.

'So what have you been talking about?' Rachel asks.

Lara closes her laptop. 'The documentary mostly. How it made me feel. Heidi's really good to talk to.' She smiles at Heidi, who smiles back. Again Rachel feels excluded.

'Any time. There's more to me than maths. As long as your mum doesn't mind – you don't, do you?'

Rachel dismisses her question with a shake of her head, arranges her face to conceal the discomfort she feels about this. There's something a little worshipful in the way Lara is watching Heidi, nodding vigorously at her every comment. She doesn't want to alienate her daughter – far from it – but she needs to find out exactly what is going on here.

'Can I have a moment alone with Heidi, please, love?'

Lara pulls a face. 'I haven't even started my tea.'

'It's very hot, and it won't take a second. Why don't you pop up to your room, and I'll call you down when we're done. Your tea will have cooled down by then.'

Lara pushes her chair back so that the legs make a screeching noise on the floor.

'Careful. You'll scratch the wood,' Rachel says.

Lara throws Heidi a look, but Heidi's face remains impassive.

'Why don't you fetch those photos you were telling me about? From when you were little,' she says.

'Good idea.' The suggestion perks Lara up, and she makes for the door.

'Lara...'

'What?'

Rachel hesitates, sensing Heidi watching her. 'Never mind.'

'I hope you don't think I'm imposing,' Heidi says once Lara has left the room. 'Only Lara invited me, and like I said, I was just passing. She mentioned that she doesn't have many friends. She seems a little lonely. I had no plans, so...'

'Look, Heidi,' Rachel says. 'I can see she enjoys your company, but you can't just turn up here without an invitation from me.'

'But Lara—'

'Lara's a child. If she asks you again, tell her you need to run it by me first. Surely you must understand?'

'Of course,' Heidi says, her mouth pinched.

Having got that off her chest, Rachel's unsure how to phrase what she wants to ask. She lowers her voice. 'Has Lara been asking you about Tom? It's just that I'm a little concerned about her since the documentary. She's been showing more interest in him than she ever has before.'

'She's curious about him, that's for sure. She's been asking about the times she stayed at my flat. She doesn't remember me at all, and that puzzles her. I think she hopes that talking to me might trigger a memory of her dad, because she has very few. Who remembers being five? I certainly don't.'

'It must be strange for you.'

'What?'

'Being here, seeing Lara so grown up now. And I must admit, you being here in this house, that's weird in itself.' Rachel takes a deep breath. 'Walking in just now and seeing you here, it gave me a shock.'

'I get that, and I'm sorry. Lara was quite insistent I should come in.' Heidi pauses. 'It's amazing that we can talk civilly now. I thought you hated me.'

'I did, for years. But that's in the past now, and I want to forget it. It's time to move on.'

'I appreciate the way you've responded to me. I'm grateful, you know, that you're letting me help Lara. It makes me feel as if I'm making amends for what I did back then. I'm ashamed when I recall it now; ripping a family apart is a wicked thing to do.'

Rachel hasn't considered it in that way. Does Heidi owe her?

'I wouldn't worry about Lara, though,' Heidi goes on. 'It's natural for her to think about her father; she's at the age where she wants to get to know herself and how she fits into the world.'

Lara comes back into the room. 'I can't find the box I keep my stuff in. I'll show them to you another time. See you for maths tomorrow?'

'Tomorrow? I don't remember agreeing to another date,' Rachel says.

'I asked Heidi, Mum.'

'We need to check with your mum first, Lara. Only if it's all right with you, Rachel. I didn't realise she hadn't asked you first.'

'It's fine,' Rachel says.

'I must go now,' Heidi says, although she's scarcely touched her tea. 'I need to get home for a delivery. Thanks for the tea.'

Rachel sees her out, Lara behind her.

'She's really cool, Mum. I like her so much. She's easy to talk to, even though she's so much older than me.'

'She's not a friend, Lara; you shouldn't be contacting her. I prefer to deal with her myself, given the situation. I don't want you getting too attached to her. Remember Ms Cotton?'

Ms Cotton was Lara's teaching assistant in Year 7, when Lara had difficulty transitioning to secondary school. Initially resistant to help from anyone but her mother, she became incredibly attached to the young woman, refusing to let go of her hand or let her out of her sight, to the point where Rachel was called in and they all agreed it would be better if she were moved to a different class. Helping her untie the connection took a lot of time and effort, and she needed help from school professionals to forget the attachment.

'Shut up, Mum.'

'Lara!'

'Why do you always have to spoil everything? You should be pleased I've found someone I can relate to.'

'I just wish you'd spend more time with people your own age. You haven't mentioned Holly much lately; why don't you give her a ring?'

'Why won't you ever take me seriously? It drives me mad. And stop going on about Holly.'

Lara runs up the stairs and slams her bedroom door. Rachel closes the front door and wonders whether inviting Heidi into her home was a terrible mistake.

SIXTEEN

'What are you doing?' Rachel looks at Danny, who is just about to climb the stairs into the loft. As she arrived on the landing, he was emerging from her bedroom. If she'd been a few seconds later, she'd have missed him.

He glances at her. 'Sorry, my bad. I was looking for the toilet.' He disappears up the stairs.

Rachel stares after him. He's been working here for weeks now. She makes a mental note to ask Pete about him. She's never been entirely comfortable with his presence, but he could just be shy. Could he have something to do with the writing on the mirror? And the notes? *Don't be ridiculous.* Getting an alarm system for the house seems an increasingly good idea.

Heidi is due to see Lara later. Rachel is relieved it's a Wednesday, as Lara will have to go to her swimming club straight after they finish with the maths. Since unexpectedly finding Heidi in her kitchen yesterday, she's determined to make any future arrangements herself.

. . .

The maths session goes without a hitch, and Rachel makes sure she is present the whole time. When they're done, Lara chats to Heidi about swimming. She's been swimming since she was little – she showed signs of emulating her dad's talent as soon as she encountered the water. Then the doorbell rings – the neighbour who's giving her a lift to the pool – and a look of annoyance crosses her face.

'Have you got everything?' Rachel asks at the front door.

Lara looks mutinous. 'Do I have to go?'

Rachel puts her arm around her daughter's shoulders. 'Yes, you do. You'll enjoy it when you get there.' She rests her hand on her back and eases her out. Normally Lara loves going to swimming club.

'Bye, Heidi,' Lara calls. She looks back before she leaves.

'Bye. See you next time.'

Heidi is standing in the kitchen.

'Do you have plans for this evening?' she asks Rachel.

'Not on a school night. Normally I have to drop Lara at swimming and collect her later, so that's my evening gone. For once, I get the house to myself for a couple of hours. How about you?'

'Microwave meal for one, as per.'

Rachel makes a snap decision. Heidi may have the answers to her worries about Lara, or she may have an ulterior motive. Either way, she needs to know.

'Why don't you stay for a drink?'

'Are you sure?'

'Yes. Is wine OK? I've got red or white.'

'Red, please.'

Heidi sits back down at the table while Rachel opens the wine and pours them each a generous measure.

'Just the one glass for me, otherwise I'll regret it in the morning when I have to get Josh up for school.'

'Where is he tonight?'

'He's upstairs in his bedroom. I suspect he's on his phone with his mates, but he's a good boy, so I have to trust him. How's Lara doing?'

'You worry about her, don't you?'

'Is it that obvious? To be honest, I'm not sure how I feel about this sudden interest in her dad. She's writing a blog.'

Heidi sips her wine. 'Yes, she told me about that.' She puts her glass down. 'Are you sure you want to talk about this stuff?'

'Yes,' Rachel says. Have they been messaging each other?

'OK. She told me about the diary she's writing, but I haven't seen it. Apart from the first post, because she asked me if it sounded OK. Actually, I should still have it on my phone.' Heidi locates the message and hands her phone over.

Hey! I'm Lara, I'm almost thirteen and I've decided to write this to tell you about my dad. Who knows, somebody out there might have answers. Because my dad is a mystery, you see. He went missing when I was five and nobody has seen him since. I refuse to believe anything sinister has happened to him until I can prove otherwise. In this blog I'm going to tell you everything I know about him. If anybody out there knows anything, please leave your comments. And I warn you, it's kind of complicated.

'I thought it was harmless enough, and she said she'd told you about it.'

'Yes, she did. What else has she been asking you?'

'It bugs her that she can't remember much, and she wants to know what Tom was like with her. Reading between the lines, I think she wants to be reassured that it wasn't anything she did that drove him away.'

'That's ridiculous.'

'I know. But she's grappling for answers in the same way that we are, I guess.' Heidi finishes her wine. 'That's my limit. I have an early-morning yoga class tomorrow. Are you still convinced Tom is alive?'

'Yes,' Rachel says.

'So you've decided the note is genuine?'

'That I'm not sure about; it's more that my gut tells me he's still around. Stupid most likely, but I'm sure I would know if he was dead.'

'If he's not shacked up with another family somewhere, where do you think he might have gone? If he just wanted to run away from his problems.'

'If I had to guess, I'd say Scotland. He used to talk about how much he loved it there – he had Scottish relatives and used to go on holiday with his family there. Somewhere in the High-lands. He loved the Isle of Skye, too, and said there were loads of other islands he'd like to explore.'

'He raved about Italy to me, how much he loved it there. He never took me on a holiday, though.' Heidi looks disgruntled.

'But if you didn't want to be found, you'd surely go some-where to which you had no connection, somewhere you'd never expressed a wish to go. Not back to a place everyone knows you like. That's what I would do. Poland, for example.'

'How do you mean?'

'I've never thought about going to Poland and have no connection to the country.'

'I think Tom had a friend who was Polish,' Heidi says.

'That would be a link to him, too much of a giveaway. It would have to be somewhere like... Azerbaijan – assuming he doesn't know anyone there.'

She laughs. 'I don't even know where that is.'

'Seriously, though,' Rachel says. 'What would be the point of tracking him down? He obviously doesn't want to be found. I'd love to tell him exactly what I think of him, but after all this time, I'd rather just forget I ever knew him.' She sighs. 'Not as easy as it sounds when Lara is asking me to remember stuff about him. I'm worried she's invited people to comment.'

'I'd look at the site if I were you.'

The landline rings in the hall.

'That made me jump,' Heidi says. 'I don't know anyone who has a landline any more.'

'Excuse me a minute,' Rachel says. 'I have to get that in case it's about one of the kids.'

It's Mrs Andrews on the line, Toby's mum.

'I'm so sorry to do this to you,' she says, after preliminary niceties have been dispensed with. 'I've had a family emergency and I have to travel to Yorkshire early tomorrow morning. Obviously I won't be able to collect Josh from rehearsal after school. I'm so sorry about this – I'm aware it's extremely short notice.'

'It's fine, please don't worry. I'm sorry to hear your news. Leave it with me and I'll sort something out. Is Toby going with you?'

'Yes, he'll just have to miss the rehearsal. I really do apologise.'

'Please, you don't have to. These things happen. I hope everything goes as well as it can for you.'

Rachel goes back into the kitchen to get her phone. Heidi is looking at the noticeboard. 'Problem?' she asks.

'Nothing major. The person who was collecting Josh from rehearsal after school tomorrow can't make it, and I've got an appointment that I don't want to reschedule. I'll need to call my mum. I've had to ask her to help out so often lately. She's supposed to be enjoying her retirement.'

'What time does he need picking up?'

'Five thirty.'

'I'll do it,' Heidi says.

'No, you can't do that.'

'Honestly, let me. I want to.'

'I'll think about it. Excuse me a minute, I need the loo.'

Rachel takes her phone upstairs with her and locks herself in the bathroom. She texts her mother, willing her to see the message and reply instantly. She waits a few minutes, then flushes the toilet. Her mother replies.

Sorry, I'm out with Pat tomorrow evening. Hope you find someone.

Rachel sighs. She washes her hands, kneading the soap into her skin, trying to make up her mind. She'd prefer not to take Heidi up on her offer, but she can't think of anyone else to ask. She stares into the mirror. Her fringe needs cutting. The reality is that Heidi is downstairs now. She's helped Lara. Rachel needs to make a decision. Either she puts a stop to this and cuts ties with Heidi, or she accepts her help. She studies her reflection and makes up her mind.

Heidi is still sitting at the table where she left her.

'It would be a big help if you could collect him, just this once,' Rachel says. 'If you're sure.'

'Of course.'

'Thanks.' Rachel feels a whoosh of relief. Any interruptions to her scheduled plans cause her anxiety to spike. 'I'll text you the address. It's not far from here.'

'No worries. What time will you be back? Or do you want me to take him to mine?'

'No, here is fine. I'll be back by six. See you tomorrow. And thanks so much.'

As she waves Heidi off and closes the door, she's thoughtful. Has she done the right thing?

Josh bursts through the front door just after six the next day, Heidi behind him, cheeks flushed, carrying his bag. She collapses into the nearest armchair.

'I'm exhausted,' she says. 'Does he ever stop talking?'

'Josh, what have you done to Heidi?' Rachel asks.

Josh is taking a carton of orange juice from the fridge. 'Do you want some, Heidi?'

'Yes please, I need the energy.'

He pours two glasses. 'Heidi's car is so cool,' he says, his eyes sparkling.

Rachel smiles. Josh drinks his juice in one go.

'Thanks for collecting me,' he says. He wanders into the living area and switches the television on.

Rachel makes a pot of tea. Despite her earlier reservations, she's beginning to enjoy Heidi's company.

They're still chatting when Lara arrives home, her hair slightly damp.

'Heidi,' she says, her face lighting up, swinging her bag onto the sofa. 'I didn't know you were coming.'

'I didn't have time to tell you this morning.' Rachel turns to Heidi. 'She leaves the house super early to go to the library before school.'

'Have you been swimming again?' Heidi asks.

'Yes. I'm starving, Mum, what's for tea?'

'I can make beans on toast?'

'Are you hungry, Heidi?' Lara asks. 'You can join us.'

'Well...' Heidi looks at Rachel.

'It's fine,' Rachel says. 'If you want to, you're very welcome. It's the least I can do. But I'll try and rustle up something better than beans on toast for us adults.'

'Fantastic!' Lara says, beaming at Heidi.

'You can tell me how you got on with the maths test,' Heidi says.

Josh eats his beans on toast at a furious pace, anxious to get back to the television.

'It's like his batteries are fully charged,' Heidi says later, when the three of them sit down to eat. Lara is content with beans on toast. Rachel has rustled up a tomato sauce with pasta for her and Heidi.

'Try living with him,' Lara says. 'He's a nightmare.'

'He has his moments,' Rachel says.

'Tell us about your investigation, Lara,' Heidi says, as Rachel opens a bottle of wine.

'It's like I'm writing a story about someone else,' Lara says. 'I was stuck at the beginning and didn't know how to start, so I talked to my teacher about it and she suggested that a good way to get into it would be to share my story on social media, detailing my journey. That sounds so corny, but you know what I mean. So I started writing what I was doing, explaining about Dad and how I was so little at the time, I don't remember anything about it, and Josh even less, and detailing my plan. I added a link to the case with a couple of newspaper articles from that time. Loads of people posted comments, which really helped. I've just gone on from there really. Talking about me and Josh spending time with Dad and writing down what we used to do – that bit I couldn't have done without you,' she says to Heidi. 'But it's like they were other children living that experience. It's such a weird feeling, I can't explain it.'

'No, I understand what you mean,' Heidi says.

'Has anyone commented who has a connection to the case?' Rachel asks. 'You have to be careful online.'

'I know that, Mum.' Lara looks at Heidi for agreement. 'Besides, you gave me permission to have Instagram as long as you could look at my page. And you can. Don't treat me like a little kid. I'm not five any more.'

'Of course you're not, don't be silly.'

'Now she calls me silly,' Lara says to Heidi.

'That's not what your mum means; this is a delicate subject, after all. Especially since she received that note. We all have to be extra careful. Who knows what kind of crazy people are out there.'

Lara puts her knife and fork down, no longer listening to Heidi.

'What note?'

Rachel squirms in her seat. How could Heidi have been so indiscreet?

'I'm sorry,' Heidi says. 'I thought you'd told her.'

'What note, Mum?' Lara's voice has risen an octave.

'I received an anonymous note through the door. Supposedly from your father.' The last word stings her tongue; she's always reluctant to assign him that role, given his deliberate betrayal of his family.

'And you didn't tell me? That proves you think I'm still a baby.'

'Not at all. I didn't tell you because it's not to be taken seriously. It's just from somebody wanting to stir up trouble.'

'You told Heidi about it. You've only just become friends with her. This is exactly the kind of material I need for my blog. What if it really is from Dad? Josh and I have a right to know about this. You can't stop him getting in touch with us if he wants to.'

'It's not from your dad, and I don't want you to say anything to Josh.'

'Show me.'

Rachel is thinking fast. She can't show Lara the note in front of Heidi.

'Not now. I'm thinking about giving it to the police.'

'That proves you think it's real,' Lara says.

'Not necessarily, especially after the documentary has brought the case back to public attention. People like to air their opinions. So many people are stalkers these days, trolls, whatever you want to call them. This one happens to use old-fashioned techniques. I'm just trying to protect us all. Especially now that we're almost at the stage where we can put this behind us.'

'By saying he's dead, you mean? You don't want him found, do you? Do you know what it's like not to be able to remember him?' Lara's face is red and her voice catches as if she's on the verge of tears. 'Why do you always have to spoil everything?' She pushes back her chair, causing it to topple to the floor, and runs out of the room.

'Are you OK?' Heidi asks, picking up the chair.

'I wish you'd checked with me before mentioning the note. I deliberately kept it from her. I'll leave her for a while, let her calm down. She's like a different child lately.'

'I hadn't realised,' Heidi says.

Rachel suppresses the urge to shake her.

'She's becoming a young woman.'

'Exactly, that's the problem. I want to support her with this project, but it scares me too.'

'That's understandable. Do you want me to go and speak to her?'

'No, it's fine, but thanks. I need to think about it.'

'I'll go then, leave you guys to sort it out. It's time I was getting off anyway. Oh, and Lara's asked me for an extra lesson tomorrow as she has another test coming up. I said I'd check with you first. Is that OK?'

'Sure. As long as you're happy to face a temperamental teenager.'

'She's good as gold with me.'

Rachel sees Heidi out and is stacking the dishwasher when the doorbell rings. It's Deborah from next door.

'Hi, Deborah. Everything OK?'

'Yes, fine. Remember the other day when you asked me if I'd seen anyone dropping something off at your door?'

'Yes.'

'I should have thought of it myself, but I was telling Simon and he suggested looking at our CCTV. Honestly, why I didn't think of that – talk about obvious. I forget we've got it most of the time.'

'I've been wondering about having it installed myself.'

'We were burgled a few years back. Simon had it installed after that. I can find out the details of the people we used if you like.'

'Thanks. Did he see who left that package for me?'

'Yes. It's funny, I was planning on popping round to tell you today anyway, but I've just seen her.'

'Her?'

'The woman who dropped it off. Your friend. The pretty blonde who just left your house.'

Rachel is glad she's leaning against the door, because otherwise she feels as if she'd fall down. Heidi sent that note? But she's had one too. It doesn't make any sense.

'Are you absolutely sure?'

'Well, ninety per cent, I guess. Come and take a look later if you like.'

A pressure is building in Rachel's head. She's let this woman into her life, she's been seeing her daughter and she even let her collect Josh from school. Her heart pounds at the implications of what might have happened. But it didn't. They're all still safe. What is Heidi planning? What does she want?

'I'd better get back,' Deborah says. 'Simon's cooking tonight and I want to make the most of it. I hope that helps, though you probably knew already that it was your friend.'

'Yes,' Rachel says. 'Yes, of course. Thanks, Deborah.'

If only she had.

SEVENTEEN

TOM

SEVEN YEARS EARLIER

Heidi's flat is a studio. Despite the minimalist industrial look, there's no way of disguising the fact that this is one room. Heidi is five foot and petite and looks as if she's been designed to fit in this space, with its gleaming appliances and few but expensive pieces of furniture. Tom is a large man. From the bed, he can see every area, except inside the bathroom that nestles behind the wall.

Heidi is in the kitchen area making coffee and singing to herself. She's wearing his T-shirt, which comes almost to her knees. Rachel is a lot taller than Heidi; his previous girlfriends – not that there were many – were also tall, and he likes the way Heidi fits into his arms when he spoons her. He's keeping her safe, protecting her from the enemies outside. *His* enemies.

Tom saw himself as a man under siege in those first few weeks after leaving the family home and settling into Heidi's flat. Although 'settling' isn't an accurate depiction. He's anything but settled. His children are never far from his mind, and he misses those precious hours when he'd get home from work and read them stories while Rachel soaked in the bath and had a window of respite from her day. Almost as difficult are the times when he wakes up at night, his body clock maddeningly regular, waiting for Josh to cry out for him, to need him. He misses his boy most of all, although he'd never admit that to anyone. Those moments were just about the two of them, pacing around in the half-light, the room occasionally lit up by the headlights of a car passing, the light picking out wisps of Josh's baby hair, his tiny button nose. Now when he wakes in the middle of the night, he crosses the room in three paces and sits by the window, staring at the closed curtains, unfamiliar with the street behind them.

He knows they can't stay here; already he wants to move, to get them a bigger place, but first he needs to discuss the house with Rachel. Hopefully they can do this face to face, otherwise it'll have to be through a solicitor. It still feels too early and too confrontational to take such a step, though. Whatever happens, he has to stay close to the children, which means Heidi and Rachel will no doubt have contact. He has to find a way to make this work, but it will be expensive.

He's also under siege from Freddie, once so familiar, now a stranger, with his new matter-of-fact attitude to Tom. To an outsider, nothing will have changed – they are polite to one another and work as well as they always have. But they are both taking on more individual clients now, instead of team projects.

He's also a little suspicious of Freddie. Last week, he went into Freddie's office when he wasn't there, looking for a document on his untidy desk. He nudged the mouse with his hand, and when the screen came to light, he saw that Freddie was looking at the accounts, in particular the transactions Tom had made with the supplier the week before. He felt a chill creep down his spine. Freddie couldn't suspect, surely? He told himself not to worry, that he had a good explanation, although his pulse was faster than it should have been and his chest felt tight.

He has started leaving the office early and going to the pub. The small flat is too oppressive, and he needs air and normality around him. Nothing about his situation is remotely normal, even though he chose it himself. It will get better, but that will involve a move, which means more financial pressure, and that means... Tom's pulse races even faster. What if it isn't his love life that is making Freddie pull away from him, but something far worse? What if Freddie knows what he has done?

Tom engaged a solicitor because he likes to have clarity; that way he can take control of at least some parts of his life. It's a relief to have no mortgage, having unexpectedly inherited the house from his parents early in his twenties. He'd rather they were still with him, spending their hard-earned savings on cruises and holidays, or on spoiling their grandchildren as he knows they would have done, instead of having their lives ripped away from them in the car accident that ended his swimming career. Swimming was his father's dream, and something they had always shared, and Tom couldn't go near a pool for over a year after his death. Besides, he wasn't as talented as his father had believed, and he'd never have won an Olympic medal – he'd known that for a long time. He hopes his boy will inherit his talent for swimming.

He could offer to help Rachel financially to get her out of the house, although that would mean uprooting the children and seeing them having to lower their standard of living. He wouldn't stop paying for them, of course, but she can't continue living in the house indefinitely without paying him some sort of rent. Realistically, she'll need to get a job, otherwise she will have to downsize and possibly move away. The area they live in is expensive. Everything in her life will change, and he's not sure he can put her through that. But without selling the house, he won't be able to buy a place for himself and Heidi, and that is his number one priority right now. Her flat was OK when it was used for the odd sleepover, but not for them both to live in. Already he feels like a caged animal, prowling around a tiny space, peering through the bars at the outside world that he no longer feels part of. All his money has gone on the family expenses; his earnings are no longer enough to live comfortably on. He'll have to apply for a mortgage, or a loan, and there are always his credit cards.

He hasn't discussed any of this with Heidi; he doesn't want to burst the bubble of their early days together. But the truth is, he's finding it difficult to keep it from her.

He wishes he hadn't more or less promised Rachel that she wouldn't have to leave the house, though the relief he saw on her face told him he'd made the right decision. Afterwards, he cried, sitting in the car in a car park where nobody he knew was likely to see him, making him feel like a criminal.

EIGHTEEN

RACHEL

Present day

Rachel phones Deborah after half an hour of pacing the floor and wondering what all this means. Never mind that Simon is cooking, she can't leave this unverified. There must be hundreds of women with blonde hair, and Deborah often forgets to put her glasses on. She asks if she can see the footage. Immediately. Deborah tells her to come round.

The smell of lamb and spices fills the kitchen. Deborah pours them each a glass of wine and puts the footage on. They both watch the blonde woman coming up the path, looking around her before slipping an envelope through Rachel's letter box. Her face fills the camera as she reaches the door. A pretty, heart-shaped face. Definitely Heidi. She scurries back down the path and disappears from view.

'It's her, isn't it?' Deborah asks.

One hundred per cent. No doubt whatsoever.

'Yes, thank you. I wanted to be sure.' Rachel drinks her wine, wanting to drown out this new knowledge.

'You look like you needed that,' Deborah says. 'I can't drink quickly. I'm so out of practice these days.'

Rachel wants to down the glass in one, but restrains herself.

'Stay for a bit. We're not eating until later. The boys were on a school trip today and they exhausted themselves. Went out like lights, both of them.' Deborah moves some pieces of Lego from the sofa and Rachel sinks into the soft cushion. Something digs into her thigh and she removes the offending yellow piece.

'Whoops.'

'Have you noticed my friend from the tape around here before?'

'Never. First time was on that recording. Although I was away at the weekend.'

'Where did you go?'

Deborah launches into an account of her recent mini break in a countryside cottage, letting off steam with her girlfriends, leaving Simon at home with the children. Rachel half listens as she replays the image of Heidi delivering the letter, and how she has invited her into her house. She envisages Heidi and Lara with bowed heads at the table. Lara is on her own looking after Josh next door. What is she thinking? She jumps to her feet.

'I'm so sorry. I've just remembered something I have to do. Thanks for the wine, and the chat. And for showing me the footage.'

'You'll be able to thank your friend now, won't you?'

'Thank? Oh yes, of course I will. See you soon. Sorry, I have to dash.'

Back next door, everything is as normal, the children in their rooms. Rachel heads upstairs and knocks at Lara's door. Lara is sitting on her bed listening to music through headphones.

'Can I come in?'

Lara nods and removes the headphones.

'I wish you'd told me about the letter,' she says. 'You made me feel silly in front of Heidi.'

'I'm sorry I upset you, love, but I thought it was for the best. I'm sure it's a hoax. I haven't even shown the police, that's how unimportant I think it is.'

'But you said—'

'I only said that because Heidi was there.'

'Promise?'

'Yes. I don't want her knowing my business; we have to be careful of her.'

'Where have you been?'

'Only next door. Nothing happened while I was away?'

'Like what?'

'Phone calls, visitors?'

'No. You've only been gone ten minutes.'

'It was longer than that.'

'Why were you next door anyway? I didn't know you and Deborah were mates.'

'Just being neighbourly.'

'So, can I have that extra lesson with Heidi tomorrow?'

'No.'

'Please, Mum, she's helping me so much.'

'It's not fair of us to keep asking her. I shouldn't have let her collect Josh.'

'But she doesn't mind, I know she doesn't.'

'That's not the point. *I* mind, and I'm saying no for tomorrow.'

'I really like Heidi, Mum.'

More's the pity.

'I know you do. Trust me, we'll only push her away if we keep imposing on her. You're not to contact her without checking with me first. '

· · ·

Rachel sits on the patio and calls Freddie. The children are in bed, and she likes the quiet outside at this time of the evening, before the pub at the end of the street closes and people make their way home past the house. Josh will be asleep and Lara drops off listening to audio books, so there's no danger of the conversation being overheard; plus their windows are closed.

'You were right,' she says.

'I usually am.' She likes the way they slip into conversation as if they've only just left off. She tells him about the camera footage.

'I didn't expect that,' he says. 'Are you OK? Do you want me to come over?'

'No, I'm fine, just shaken up. The kids are in bed and I will be too after this. I'm puzzled. Why would she do it?'

'She obviously wants to make you think he's alive. I don't know why she would want that.'

'To worm her way into my family. That's what she's done. Successfully. Lara thinks everything she does is amazing. The note she said she received – that must be a lie too, to bring us together. But no, it can't have been her. The second note told me things only Tom would know.'

'Like what?'

'Haven't I shown you?' She's pacing in circles now; something is warning her not to trust anyone. 'I'd rather not think about it now.'

'Without knowing, I can't really comment, but are you sure Heidi couldn't have written it?'

Tom wouldn't have told her, would he?

'I'm sure.'

'Did you check the time on the recording? Could she have been delivering something else?'

Rachel groans. 'I didn't, but... I can't bother Deborah again. I've already interrupted her evening meal. She'll think I'm crazy. I bolted out earlier when she'd settled in for a chat. I'm so furious and confused about Heidi. I was even starting to like her, for God's sake.'

'You contacted her initially, didn't you?'

'Yes. And it was me who suggested meeting up. So it's not like she was doing the chasing. And the maths thing was a coincidence, she just happened to be there when Lara was doing her homework. Although she chose to call round that day.'

'I wonder if it's to do with the time frame. The seven-year period you have to wait for. That's coming up. If Tom were to turn up now, it would ruin your intention to take control of your finances in the way you want, at least straight away. Given that it's unlikely he has any intention of reappearing, perhaps she wants you to pause your plans. Or maybe it's just jealousy? You're making improvements to the house – she most likely saw the scaffolding, as she's still in the area.'

'I thought she'd have moved on years ago. She's young and attractive still; I thought she'd have her own family by now, or at least a partner. She didn't need to stick around for the children; they were nothing to do with her really. I'll just have to ask her.'

'I wouldn't challenge her. She might be unstable.'

'I told Lara she won't be coming for a lesson tomorrow. I can't have her in the house.'

'Will you tell Lara what she's done?'

'I don't want to worry her. Lara gets so anxious about things.' She tells him about the letter scenario earlier. 'She's already getting attached to Heidi. I'll think of something. Sorry to bother you with this, I bet you're regretting asking me out now.'

'Never. Which reminds me, when do you want to cook me dinner?'

'Friday night? I'm hoping the builders will be finished by then.'

'Suits me. I'm looking forward to seeing you again.'

'Me too. Thanks again for listening.'

'No problem. Don't do anything rash.'

'I won't.'

Rachel sits outside for a while longer, thinking. The temporary euphoria she felt after speaking to Freddie has evaporated as reality sinks in. The notes aren't from Tom.

They have caused such disarray mainly because of the timing. If Tom were to walk in now, aside from her emotional turmoil, it would put a halt to the moment she has been looking forward to for the last few years. Ever since she forced herself to accept that, for whatever reason, he had gone, and that she had two children who were more important than anything else in the world and they had to be her focus. She's been marking a calendar for the last three years, counting off the days until he will have been missing for seven years and can officially be declared dead. If he were to turn up now, the chaos would commence all over again, and she could never forgive him for that.

She walks down to the bottom of the garden and looks back at the house. Josh's room has a dim glow behind the blind. He'll be asleep now, her happy little boy who is so full of fun, as yet unpreoccupied by the absent father he barely remembers. If only the innocence of childhood could cocoon him forever. She doesn't want anything to happen that will make that babble of non-stop conversation stop. A brighter light glows in Lara's room, and this picture is more difficult for her to create. She wants her to be sleeping on her back, as is her habit, hands resting together as if in prayer on her chest. She fears the reality will reveal her hunched over her laptop, writing out questions and hoping for answers to the essential mystery that now figures all too large in her life.

It would be so much easier for everyone if Tom was dead.

Causing her lesser angst is the dilemma of Heidi. She has

caught Rachel unawares; how foolish she's been, how easily Heidi has slipped into her life. The same goes for Freddie – he asked how well she really knows Heidi, but how well does she really know *him*? Emma touched on this in one of their recent phone conversations, remarking how strange it is the way he's come back into her life, hinting that he could be after her share of the company.

Behind her, the bushes rustle as the wind blows across, and she hurries back to the house, goosebumps breaking out on her arms. How can she have been so trusting? Everyone has to be approached with caution, and that includes Freddie.

She bolts the back door behind her and draws the curtains to shut out the darkness of the garden, shivering now. Freddie's friendly face and warm smile loom in front of her. She forces herself to imagine him with Heidi, cooking up a plan to frighten her. Another picture flashes into her mind. The documentary, the shot of the two of them together. She shivers. It makes no sense. She has proof that Heidi sent the note, but Freddie barely knows her. She's shattered from a combination of anxiety and lack of sleep, and her mind is playing tricks. He's shown her nothing but kindness, and one day they'll laugh together about her fantasies. He'll understand that she has to be like this because of her children. She'll do anything to protect them. She will fight to the death for them.

But these thoughts are overshadowed by the bigger chasm that has opened up in her. She has dared to hope. Never mind the seven-year scenario. Hope has resulted from her thinking with her heart over her head.

She's been unable to admit to herself until this moment that part of her wants Tom's note to be genuine, to put an end to the years of not knowing – no one can ever imagine how that slices you apart unless you've experienced it for yourself. And for him to say he wants to come back to her. That's where her heart got involved. Not that she would have necessarily taken him back –

she hasn't got that far in her thought processes – but she longs for him to explain where he has been all this time and whether he ever loved her. And the children – for he abandoned them too. Imagine if she'd told Lara she thought the note could be from her father, got her hopes up, her interest already piqued by the documentary. Who knows how the thought of him turning up might have screwed her up. For if he's alive, wherever he is and whoever he is now, he abandoned them.

Whereas if he's dead... Ice trickles through her veins. Maybe she should face up to that outcome. After refusing to acknowledge the possibility for so long, maybe now it would be less painful.

But how can she find out the truth?

NINETEEN

Rachel has to stop Heidi coming to the house to give Lara maths lessons. She's just decided to hire a proper tutor when Lara brings home a letter about a new maths programme at school, which is free. Perfect. Confronting Heidi about the note would seem the best idea, although she's conscious of Freddie's reservations and his warning to her to be careful. Does he know something about Heidi she doesn't? If she doesn't tell Heidi she's found out about the note, this gives her the upper hand. But Lara is developing an attachment to the woman, and she needs to let her down gently.

Lara has been glued to her laptop lately. Rachel hovers around the kitchen and waits until her daughter goes to the bathroom, then she scans the screen. Lara is chatting to Heidi.

Lara: *That was a great lesson the other day. You teach so well. I never thought I'd be able to do all those sums. You're good enough to be on Countdown.*

Heidi: *Ha! I'm not that good. You should be proud of yourself.*

Lara: *It's down to you.*

Heidi: *You'll give me a big head. You're the one doing all the hard work.*

Lara: *We've got an exam this term. Last year I did really bad.*

Heidi: *You'll smash it this time.*

Lara: *You're coming next week, aren't you?*

Heidi: *I'll be there.*

Lara: *I can't wait to see you.*

Heidi: *Same here*

'Mum! What are you doing?' Lara slams the laptop closed, almost trapping Rachel's fingers. 'That's private.'

'Why are you messaging Heidi? I specifically asked you not to.'

'It's maths stuff. Not that it's any of your business.'

'I don't want you pestering her.'

'I'm not pestering her. You make it sound as if she doesn't like me.'

Rachel sighs. 'I don't mean that at all. Sit down for a minute, I need to talk to you.'

Lara is scowling, a look Rachel hasn't seen for a while, and she hates having to do this to her. Her mood has been so much better lately – the improvement in her maths has raised her confidence. She slumps into a chair.

'It's the extra maths lessons. Now you're enrolling on the maths programme at school, you won't need the sessions with Heidi.'

'No, Mum. Don't cancel them. It's the first time I've ever understood maths. I wouldn't have got onto the maths programme if it hadn't been for Heidi. The school programme won't help me in the same way she does.'

'They have excellent results and the teachers are really good. They're external, not from your school, so it will be like a fresh start.'

Lara bursts into tears. 'But it's at school, and I hate school, you know that. I don't fit in and I never will. Heidi makes me feel good about myself and she's more like a friend. You like her too, you said so. Please don't make me do this, Mum. I won't go, and you'll be wasting your money.' Tears slide down her face and she sweeps them away with the back of her hand.

Rachel's chest tightens. She hates to see her daughter like this and to know that she has caused it. She reaches for her hand, but Lara snatches it away.

'The school aren't charging anything for it.'

'I don't care. I wish I'd never told you about the maths programme at school. I never would have jeopardised my lessons with Heidi.'

'Even if you don't go on the school programme, I won't be able to continue your lessons. I can't afford it, love. The building work is taking all my money.'

'You told me you were using the money Granny gave you for that.'

'Yes, I am, but it doesn't change our day-to-day scenario. Your dad left me in an impossible situation.'

'That was forever ago.'

'I know, but I've been unable to move forward. I had to make a lot of difficult decisions when he left, and I chose not to go back to work because I wanted to look after you two properly, given the circumstances. The extra lessons were only meant to be a temporary thing.'

'You never said that. You got my hopes up. Finally I find something I enjoy, and you want to take it away from me.'

'Are we talking about maths? You're saying you *enjoying* it now?'

'Yes... no... I mean I like seeing Heidi. She makes me feel better in myself, not just about the maths. She's so positive – she's like a mentor. Some girls have them at school. They give you advice and stuff.'

'What is Heidi giving you advice about?'

'What to wear, how to believe in myself. She really helps me, Mum. Even if the maths stops, she'll still want to see me. You can't stop me.'

Rachel freezes. Apart from that one time Heidi turned up unexpectedly, she's sure they haven't actually seen each other without her. Lara must have been messaging her more than she realised. She grips the table and tries not to show her alarm. Just what has this woman been saying to her daughter?

'I don't think it's a good idea for you to stay in contact with her. I made a mistake inviting her here.'

'How can you say that? Mistake for you maybe, Heidi has shown me the kind of mum I would like. Why can't you be more like her?'

Lara's words are painful to hear. If Tom hadn't gone missing, Heidi would have been Lara's stepmother for years by now, and she'd be a proper rival. Or would she? Who knows how things would have played out and how Rachel would have reacted. For now, though, her suspicions are confirmed. Lara is far too attached to Heidi and it needs to stop.

'I've told Heidi and she understands. She wishes you well.'

'She wouldn't just abandon me. Not without saying goodbye.' Lara's lips are wobbling and she jumps to her feet. 'I hate you. Heidi understands me and she treats me like a grown-up. You can't keep us apart, you just can't.'

Rachel hears her daughter's feet as they pound up the stairs, followed by the slamming of her bedroom door. Music follows, a loud, insistent beat. She rubs at her forehead, a headache threatening. She suspected Lara was forming an unhealthy attachment to Heidi, and now she has proof. Lara's angry outbursts don't usually last long, but when her children are in pain, Rachel suffers too.

Josh touches her arm and she jumps.

'I didn't hear you come in,' she says, putting her arm around him as he snuggles up against her.

'What's up with Lara?'

'She's fine, just a bad day.'

'Toby said his teenage sister is always in a bad mood. He said that's what teenage girls are like. They go all weird when they start growing and they go all silly when they're around boys. It's called puberty.'

Rachel bites her lip to stop herself from laughing.

'That's a bit simplistic, and that's not what this is about for Lara, but yes, it can be a difficult time when you become an adult. It will happen to you too, you know.'

'Toby says we get hair sprouting out in all kinds of weird places.'

Rachel smiles, brushing his hair away from his face. 'Kind of.'

'Why are so many men bald, then? That doesn't make sense.'

'I feel a bit like that too. Nothing makes sense tonight. Be nice to your sister.'

'I'll try. She's been a lot nicer to me lately. I hope that doesn't change back; she was so moody before.'

'Do you remember Uncle Freddie?'

'Of course. He worked with Dad.' Rachel still talks to the children a lot about their father, to try and keep his memory included in their lives so that they get a sense of who he was. 'And we bumped into him in the park once. You talked to him for ages and me and Lara got bored. Did he tell you I saw him?'

'When?'

'After school, when Heidi picked me up. I saw him near school and I waved but he didn't see me.'

'Are you sure it was him?'

He scrunches up his face. 'Eighty per cent.'

'Did he speak to Heidi?'

He shrugs. 'I don't know.'

'He's coming to dinner on Friday night.'

'You can ask him yourself then. Hang on, what about Scouts?'

'Grandma will take you, and you can stay at her house afterwards if you promise to be good.'

'Cool.'

Eighty per cent. Josh must be mistaken. The park meeting was years ago.

She rings Freddie later to check he is still on for Friday.

'Of course, I'm looking forward to it. I'll bring some wine. How was your day?'

She hesitates, wondering whether to challenge him about seeing Heidi.

'Terrible.' She tells him about Lara and her strop over the cancellation of her maths lessons. 'I haven't seen her since she ate her supper. She's been holed up in her bedroom since then.'

'She'll get over it.'

'I hope so. I think she's got a bit of a crush on Heidi.'

'Oh dear.'

'She got very attached to one of her teaching assistants once and I was quite worried about her. I had to involve the school in the end and she had some counselling. I should have been more careful, but taking Heidi on as a tutor just sort of happened organically.'

'Did it, though?'

'What do you mean?'

'You know I don't trust her. It's too convenient the way she just appeared in your life. I'm sure the timing is significant.'

'How well do you know her exactly?'

'Barely. Most of what I know is gleaned from what Tom told me about her, and then from getting to know you after he went missing. Why are you asking?'

She hesitates. 'Josh said he saw you when he was with her.'

'When was this?'

'One day last week. She picked him up from school.'

He sighs. 'I'm sorry, I should have told you, but I wasn't sure how you'd react. I've been suspicious of her ever since you told me about her coming over to help Lara. Seeing her the other day was a complete coincidence. I was heading back to work after a meeting and I saw her outside the school, so I parked up to see what she was doing. I was alarmed when she collected Josh, so I followed her to make sure he got home safely. I thought I was being inconspicuous; I didn't realise Josh had seen me. I don't trust her. Why was she picking Josh up?'

'It wasn't planned. She was here when his usual lift cancelled, so she offered. Right place, right time. And that was before Deborah told me about seeing her deliver the note. I don't need you to protect me, Freddie.'

'I'm sorry. I overstepped the mark.'

'It's OK, I know you mean well. I'm driving myself mad trying to work out what she's up to.'

'Does she know you know she sent the note?'

'Of course not. I'm keeping her on side, but I'm not sure I'm clever enough to pull it off. I'm going to pretend to stay friends, because I want to find out what she's after. I need to know what I'm up against. At the same time, I have to prevent her from coming to the house. And stop her from seeing Lara.'

'It all sounds a bit messy.'

'I know. I've made a right pig's ear of everything.'

'I didn't mean that. Have you told Heidi the lessons are over?'

'Not yet. I'm not looking forward to it. Lara isn't going to make this easy either.'

'You're thinking of her well-being. She'll understand when she's older. Don't beat yourself up about it. I'm sure it will all work out in the end. Let's chat more about it on Friday. I'm looking forward to seeing you again.'

'Me too.'

Rachel normally feels better after speaking to Freddie, but tonight a sense of unease prevails. She reminds herself of the positive: that he could easily have been driven away by her complicated life. Maybe he is genuinely interested in her. Or does he have an ulterior motive? What secrets is he keeping from her? If she wants the relationship to work, they must start from a position of trust. He's been honest about Tom's thieving from the company. It's time to tell him about what happened that weekend, otherwise it will always be on her conscience. The more they know about Tom, the more they are likely to find out exactly what happened to him seven years ago.

TWENTY

Rachel formulates a plan. Next morning, she texts Heidi.

Can we meet?

Sure. When suits you? I'm free today.

This afternoon? 2 p.m.

Shall I come over?

No, let's meet in town

Tea? Proper drink? Or is that too early...

Do you know Le Bistro? That way we can have either.

Great! See you there. Can't wait already...

Rachel may need a large drink to get her through this, but

she has to keep a clear head. For now, she makes a strong coffee to perk her up after the rough night she's had.

'Lara, hurry up. You're going to be late and you need to have breakfast.'

It's unusual for her to have to chase her daughter. Lara insists on having a shower every morning before school, but today she's been in the bathroom far longer than usual. When she finally emerges, she's dressed in her school uniform, neat as ever, hair loose. But something about her looks different.

'Why are you staring at me, Mum?' she says as she helps herself to Weetabix and pours milk over it.

'Not sure,' Rachel says, then she sees what it is. 'Your eyebrows, what have you done to them?'

'Nothing.'

'Yes you have, they look completely different.' Lara's eyebrows, normally a non-descript shade of brown, are dark and sculpted. 'Is that allowed in school?' Closer up, she sees that she's also wearing a light coating of foundation.

'Of course it is. Everyone has them.'

'In your class? You're only twelve.'

'I'm practically thirteen. Don't make such a fuss about it.' Lara cuts her Weetabix into pieces, the spoon clattering against the bowl, then mashes the pieces into crumbs, pressing down hard. 'Nobody else's mum makes a fuss.'

'You don't know that.'

Lara glares at her. 'Because I don't have any friends, you mean.'

'Oh love. That's not what I meant at all.' Rachel wishes she could swallow the words back down. So what if Lara is trying to impress her schoolmates. She wants to fit in, that's all. She can remember her own school days, full of angst at not having the same trainers as everyone else, raging at her mum for refusing to buy her a pair. Her parents couldn't afford it, simple as. 'You've made a good job of your eyebrows. I just think saving make-up for weekends is more appropriate. School has a no-make-up policy.'

'They never bother with that.'

'That's not the point. Rules are there for a reason.' She hates sounding like her mother.

Lara's phone buzzes and she picks it up, smiling as she reads.

'Who's that?' Rachel leans over to look at the screen, but Lara snatches it away, holding it to her chest.

'It's private, Mum.'

Rachel is left wondering as her daughter goes upstairs to clean her teeth.

As Lara sets off for school, she collides with Josh on the stairs.

'Slow down, you moron,' she says.

'Lara!'

'Well he is. He bashed right into me.'

'What have you done to your face?' Josh asks.

'Shut up, you gremlin.'

Josh is getting a lift to school today with his friend so Rachel doesn't have to go out. She waits until the house is empty before sitting down to drink her coffee. She should be pleased her daughter is receiving a text, but her mind works overtime. The sudden desire to wear make-up is ringing alarm bells. It has to be a boy. Or a girl, she corrects herself, although all Lara's childhood crushes have been on good-looking boy-band types and her room is currently covered with posters of male singers. She recalls the way her daughter blushed when she first met Danny; surely it can't be him? He's way older than her. She banishes the thought. It will be to do with school. Rachel went to an all-girls school and can't imagine the hassle of having to cope with boys in the classroom. She remembers her teenage self, the hours spent thinking about the opposite sex and how to present herself to them. What to wear, what to say, how much interest to show, learning the games people play when they enter the dating field. Finishing her coffee, she sighs and heads off to the shower.

Heidi is sitting outside the bistro. Rachel notices her as soon as she rounds the corner; she's wearing a pastel-pink top, which alongside her blonde hair makes Rachel think of an ice cream. She's looking at a menu and hasn't spotted Rachel, who pauses a moment to prepare herself for this potentially awkward conversation. She's decided not to let on that she knows Heidi sent the note. Last night when she was struggling to sleep, it occurred to her that Tom could be alive and colluding with Heidi, that they could have come up with a master plan to get her out of the house – honestly, her thoughts became so ridiculous, she plugged into an audiobook just to stop driving herself mad, and eventually drifted off. If she doesn't get any closer today to finding out why Heidi sent the note, she intends to cut off all communication with her, and stop her contacting her children.

She draws herself up tall before crossing the road, waving to Heidi, who looks up and smiles at her.

Rachel opts for a soft drink, not wanting to muddy her thoughts. Heidi orders a lemonade.

'I've been thinking about the note supposedly from Tom,' Rachel says, watching Heidi's face keenly.

'Oh yes.'

'I don't want to involve the police, but I've been wondering about hiring a private detective.'

Heidi laughs. 'Seriously? Do they actually exist? I thought they were just invented for crime novels.'

'Of course they do. It's just that most of their cases are

pretty uninteresting stuff, like fraud or extramarital affairs.' Rachel realises what she has said. 'I didn't—'

Heidi waves her concerns away with a flick of her hand. 'It's fine. What if we found him? Would we confront him? Together we would be stronger. Can you imagine his face?'

'I hadn't even thought that far. I meant that the detective might be able to track down whoever sent the note.'

'Oh.' Heidi picks up her drink. 'Have you tried to find out yourself?'

'Well, yes, with my limited resources and knowledge of how to go about it. We could ask the neighbours whether they've seen anyone hanging around. There's no CCTV in the street – I checked.' Rachel doesn't want Heidi to know about Deborah's camera. She pauses. 'I've been wondering, do you remember Freddie?'

'Freddie? The guy who worked with Tom?'

'Yes. Are you in touch with him?'

'Hardly. He made it quite clear he disapproved of me. If I ever went into the office, he would go out of his way to avoid me. Tom was upset about it; they had a fight over it.'

'Oh?'

'It got quite nasty. They'd gone out for a drink and both of them had had one too many. Their argument got so heated they were asked to leave the pub.'

'Really? I had no idea. I can't imagine either of them being nasty.'

'Tom said Freddie brought up some really hurtful things. He didn't elaborate, though. He wanted to forget the whole thing.'

'How close to his disappearance was the argument?'

Heidi tries to remember. 'I'd say it was about a month before. He hated going into work even more after that.'

'It must have been difficult,' Rachel says. Heidi shrugs. 'So you haven't seen him since then?'

'Not by choice. He was at the hearing, as you know. I have no idea whether he still works for the business.'

'He does.'

'Hang on, do you think he had something to do with that note?'

'Not really. I'm just going through possibilities – anyone I can think of related to Tom.'

'And say you were to find this person, what would you do?'

'Firstly I'd ask what the purpose of sending the note was. That's the priority. I've got my children to think about. Are we in danger? Plus, I need to make sure they have no genuine knowledge of Tom's whereabouts. And then I'd expose them as a troll.'

'On social media, you mean?' Heidi shifts around on her seat, as if she can't get comfortable.

'Yes, to start with. If it's a criminal offence, I would take it further – depending on the situation. There are so many unknowns in this.'

'It could be harmless – like they didn't realise what they were stirring up.'

'That would mean they had to be pretty stupid.'

Heidi looks past Rachel. 'I have no idea why someone would do such a thing. Just when we were all coming to terms with it.'

Rachel sighs.

'Is everything OK?' Heidi asks.

Rachel fusses with her hair. 'I have something difficult to tell you and I'm not sure how you'll react.'

Heidi picks her drink up, only to realise it's empty.

'Just tell me. I'm a big girl. I'm surprised, though, as I thought we were getting on OK.'

'We are, all things considered,' Rachel says. 'That's why this is difficult. It's just the lessons with Lara. They have to stop.'

'Oh no. Why is that? She's doing so well, and we get on fine...'

'It's nothing to do with you or your teaching. You've done a great job, honestly.' Rachel crosses her fingers under the table, although she's not sure why she bothers, as Heidi is lying to her about the note and goodness knows what else. 'It's to do with the school. They're enrolling Lara and some other children in a maths programme and it involves one-to-one tuition, so there's no need to carry on with the lessons at the same time.' Heidi doesn't need to know the programme isn't costing her anything. 'I'm sorry about that, but I wanted you to know that she's been selected. Especially since you've been helping her. I'm grateful to you – as is Lara, as I'm sure you can tell.'

'What does this mean for us? It's all a bit weird – are you trying to say you don't want us to be friends after all?'

Rachel almost chokes on her drink. *Friends?*

'No, not at all. It's all come out wrong. It's more to do with how I manage Lara and her expectations – nothing to do with you at all.'

She watches Heidi for her reaction. She seems OK about it, but something about her expression is bugging Rachel, and she's no closer to understanding what motivates the woman.

'There's also the issue of the notes arriving, and a couple of other things. I'm getting a bit paranoid about security. Having the builders on site is making me nervous. So please don't take it personally.'

'Shall we get another drink?'

'Sure.'

Heidi calls the waiter over. Rachel watches her flirt, and the way her glance lingers on him as he makes his way back to the counter.

'He likes you,' she says.

'I'm not interested.'

'Are you sure?'

'It's just habit.'

'You're not seeing anyone at the moment, are you?'

'No, not for ages, actually.'

'Has there been anyone since Tom?'

'Of course.' Heidi laughs. 'I couldn't possibly go that long without male attention. How about you? Are you dating?'

'No,' Rachel says, willing herself not to blush. 'I don't have time for any of that.' For now, she wants to keep Freddie to herself. Her days of seeing Heidi in a new light are over; all she has to do is picture the scene on Deborah's camera to remind herself how careful she needs to be.

Heidi's phone buzzes and she smiles at the incoming message, then puts it away in her bag. 'I'll be right back,' she says. 'I need the bathroom. Watch my bag for me.' She disappears inside.

Heidi's phone is sticking out of her bag, the light glinting on the metal. Before Rachel has time to reflect, she grabs it and taps the screen. There is a message on the home screen from a sender called Danny.

I'm at your flat. Don't be too late back. We've got a long night ahead.

She clicks through to more messages from Danny, constantly glancing towards the bistro door, her heartbeat racing. The Ladies is way across the other side of the restaurant and up a flight of stairs. Steep stairs. Heidi is in heels. She'll freshen up her face in the mirror. Rachel scrolls through the messages, fingers on fire. Danny and Heidi are in constant contact. Messages that make her blush; talk of a plan; cryptic texts she doesn't understand. She clicks on Danny's photograph and his face fills the screen.

A familiar face.

It's Danny, the builder's assistant who's spent the last few months in her house. Sullen, silent Danny, who she caught emerging from her bedroom. She puts the phone back in Heidi's bag as if it's burnt her fingers, loosening her collar, over-whelmed by heat.

Heidi emerges from the bistro, heels clicking on the pavement, a smile on her face.

The smile of a traitor.

TWENTY-ONE

TOM

Seven years earlier

It took three months before the situation reached a head. Living in the cramped studio flat, no matter how much they loved each other, was beginning to get to him. Having been used to a spacious three-bedroom house with a garden, he found this tiny space increasingly impossible. This morning he'd bashed his head on the ceiling after his shower and had yelled out loud. Heidi had come running – the few steps it took – and found him sitting on the floor with his head in his hands.

'I can't do this any more.'

He found a two-bedroom flat to rent on a nearby street. The rent was extortionate, but at last he had somewhere for the children to stay, and Rachel grudgingly agreed to split the weeks with him. The children were young enough not to protest about spending time with him, and for Lara it was a bit of an adventure. Heidi was better with them than he had expected, and he began to hope his life might settle down.

The trouble was, Heidi wasn't content with another rental and refused to sign a contract for longer than six months. He wished she wouldn't compare herself to Rachel all the time. She wanted to buy somewhere of her own, with him. If Rachel could have her own home, she wanted the same. Otherwise, in her mind, she felt she was less than Rachel, that Tom wasn't affording her the same privileges. Wasn't she sacrificing a lot of her time for the children?

'I love you, isn't that what's important?'

'Yes.' But she'd scowled and he'd barely got more than a few words out of her that evening.

He wished he could confide in Freddie about it – his friend always gave him some sound advice. But when he asked Freddie if he wanted to go for a drink, Freddie said he was saving money. Like he had the last time Tom asked him to go out. If he didn't have to work with him, Tom would have confronted him. He was so frustrated, he imagined slamming Freddie against the wall and demanding he tell him what the problem was, and why he couldn't cut his supposed mate a bit of slack when he was having the hardest time of his life. He would never do that in reality, but the fantasy helped a bit and made him feel slightly calmer. He went for a drink by himself anyway, and ended up having a decent chat with a guy he'd seen before who was always in there, willing to talk to anybody. Anonymous company was exactly what Tom was looking for.

Heidi was on her laptop when he got home.

'Look at these new houses,' she said. He had to admit they were perfect, exactly the right size, not too far from the children and their schools, plus there was a small garden for them to play in, and the price was good for what they were.

'They're completely energy-efficient,' Heidi said, 'with a small garage across the way for parking. It would save us money in the long run. You like them, don't you?'

'Yes,' he said.

'That's good, because I've set my heart on one. And I've

booked a viewing at the weekend. We need to get in early; they'll be snapped up otherwise.'

That Saturday, they followed Sandra with her clipboard and glossy brochures around the show home. Heidi was ecstatic, discussing the decor and learning how she could influence the design if they put down a deposit now; that way they could start planning the move, as the houses were scheduled to be ready in about six weeks' time.

'Do you have children?' Sandra asked.

'Not yet,' Heidi said briefly, so Tom closed his mouth and swallowed the words he was about to say. That made him feel uncomfortable, like he was denying the two most important people in his life.

On the drive home, Heidi was animated, eyes shining, talking at top speed about the house and her plans. Lara and Josh would have their own rooms there, and would be able to stay with them, she pointed out.

'You haven't asked whether I can afford it yet,' Tom said as he searched for a parking space a couple of streets away from the flat. Parking was getting harder by the day.

'Whether *we* can afford it,' Heidi said. 'And of course we can. You told me you had a lot of money saved for an emergency. Well, if this isn't an emergency, I don't know what is.'

Tom thought of the dwindling balance on his savings account. Having the kids was proving expensive now he had to be out with them all the time; the flat was far too small to entertain them there, and anyway, Rachel would hate that. Who knew activities for children were so expensive? When you factored in food and ice creams and impulse buys, it soon added up.

It was the decision to buy the house that made him do it. He couldn't stop providing Rachel with money for the children, and he had to keep Heidi sweet. What would he be without her after all? Leaving his family would have been for nothing, and he'd feel even more wretched than he did now in those dark moments when he couldn't sleep and everything was getting on top of him.

The business had been an incredible success at the start. Thanks to an old school friend, he'd landed a huge contract for a successful hotel chain, and this had given his fledgling company the kick-start it needed. Money had poured in and he'd stopped obsessing over the accounts, as had been his habit. His new bride and young family had occupied his mind, and it took him a while before he'd realised how little work he'd been bringing in over the last few years. He'd thrown himself back into the job and managed to acquire a few new clients, but now that he was with Heidi, fretting about money had begun to stop him sleeping at night.

Why hadn't he confided in Freddie? Pride, largely, and not wanting to worry him. Enough money was coming into the business to keep them afloat; the problem was, the salary he could afford to pay himself just wasn't enough now that he had to fund Rachel and the children as well as Heidi's grand plans. He needed more disposable income.

The bank manager was friendly but firm. He couldn't lend him any more money, not even as a loyal customer of many years' standing. Rules were rules.

That was when he had the idea. He could borrow a little, just to keep him going. No need to tell Freddie, because obviously, he was going to pay it back.

Wasn't he?

It started with a small overpayment to himself. He'd set up the company after all, and the finances were under his control. They weren't a big enough company to warrant hiring a person to do the accounting, and Freddie had always been happy for him to continue, even after they became equal partners. 'I'm a creative,' he'd say, 'I'm most definitely not a mathematician. I wouldn't know where to start with figures.' It was a one-off, borrowing the money.

The deposit for the house was larger than the amount initially discussed at the show home, and his savings were all but swallowed up. The next time he needed money, he amended an invoice to make it look like less money was coming in for the job. It didn't affect the client at all, and the payment was just a small loan. He wrote down the amounts in the back of his work diary so he could keep track. He would pay it all back as soon as he was in a position to.

He rationalised the house purchase to himself: aside from the deposit, it wasn't going to cost them much more than the current rent. He was sure they'd have enough furniture, and anything they did need, they could pick up from a recycling website. That was the way the world worked now. However, Heidi had other ideas. She spent hours poring over Instagram sites and making mood boards for the look she wanted for her house; a very particular look, she said.

Expensive, he replied, and they had their first argument, but made up shortly afterwards on the bed, which was soon to be replaced by a designer one. Heidi had already ordered it.

TWENTY-TWO

RACHEL

'Why are you ringing me so late?' Emma's voice is thick with sleep. 'What time is it?'

Rachel imagines her sister pulling herself up in bed, switching on the lamp, squinting at her phone.

'It's not that late. I'm sorry. I didn't think you'd be asleep.'

'It's OK. I had a headache and crashed out early, but it feels better now. What's up?'

'I've just had a bit of a shock, and you're the only person I can fully trust.'

'What's happened?'

Rachel runs through the events of the past few days, culminating in meeting Heidi at the bistro this afternoon.

'I'm not surprised at all by her sending the note. I bet she knew you'd contact her, and even if you didn't, saying she'd received one too would be a legitimate reason for her to get in touch with you. Clever. But then she always has been a manipulative bitch. The question is, what is her game plan?'

'She mentioned a plan in the texts with Danny. I was so

scared she was going to come back and catch me with her phone that I didn't have a chance to read anything properly. But he's obviously her lover, and she lied about that.'

'Another lie. But he's been in your house, Rach, this is serious. You have to report it. He could be bugging the place or anything.'

'Oh God, I hadn't thought of that. He's Pete's assistant, though, so he'd have to keep it from him.'

'Unless Pete's in on it too.'

Rachel feels sick.

'How did you find him?'

'One of the mums from school recommended him.'

'Unsolicited?'

'No. I was asking around and I posted a message in our WhatsApp group. I followed up on a few suggestions and chose him. I'm sure he's legit. He's really friendly and his work is great.'

'Friendly doesn't mean anything. Has he known Danny long?'

'I've never asked.'

'You need to speak to him, pronto.'

'First thing tomorrow, I'm on it.'

'Have you wondered about this Danny at all?'

'I hadn't – he's very quiet – until I caught him coming out of my bedroom.' She laughs, a harsh, unhumorous laugh. 'I even thought Lara might have a crush on him. She's suddenly started paying more attention to her appearance. He's very good-looking, and something has put a spring in her step lately, but I'd concluded that was Heidi paying attention to her with the maths lessons.'

'Rach, you should never have let her get close to Lara.'

'Don't, I know how stupid I've been. Since I found out about the note, I've been trying to pretend to be friendly so I could find out what was going on.'

'And now you know you need to report her. Even if she hasn't committed a crime, given your history, the police will have to give her a warning at least. You should have shown them the notes at the time.'

'I know. Stop telling me what I already know. You're right, OK.'

'What about Freddie. Does he know?'

'He knows about the notes, but I haven't spoken to him this evening. I've started to wonder about him too.'

'Look, I need to get some sleep. I'll come over at the weekend and we can talk then. You need to check Lara's phone as well, if she's been communicating with Heidi. God knows what she'll have been filling her head with. It won't be maths-related, I bet you. I'll have a word with Lara at the weekend if you like.'

'Yes, I would. Thanks.'

'Get some sleep yourself. You need a clear head to deal with all this. No point lying awake worrying.'

'I'll try. Thanks, sis.'

The children are in their rooms. Rachel switches everything off and locks up downstairs, but she's unable to sleep. She gets out of bed and climbs the stairs up into the loft extension.

During the daytime, light spills in here from the dormer windows and shines onto the freshly laid flooring, making the room feel large and airy. Now it's dark and barely lit. She switches the light on and looks around, blinking at the sudden contrast. The room smells of paint, and an open stepladder stands in the middle of the floor. Painting paraphernalia and half-used tins of paint are stacked up on sheets of newspaper. Beside them is a large canvas bag, which she's seen Pete carrying around, and a medium-sized sports bag. Each night the builders tidy away any belongings they want to leave on site into these bags. She peers into Pete's bag but can't bring herself to go through it. Her gut tells her Pete is good. It's his assistant she's concerned about. She kneels on the floor and looks into the sports bag, which she's guessing is Danny's. In it she finds a pair of blue overalls, which she's seen him wearing, and an old T-shirt. A faint smell of dried sweat makes her want to heave. An empty water bottle is stashed underneath, along with a notepad and an old copy of a free newspaper. She takes out the notepad and looks inside. Numbers are written on most of the pages; they look like measurements, with scrawled notes alongside. On the most recent page is what looks like a shopping list:

- *Large bottle of white spirit*
- *Replacement paint rollers*
- *Palette knife*
- *Large rubbish bags*
- *String*
- *Strong tape*
- *Protective face coverings*

She uses her phone to take a photo of the list, unsure exactly why she's bothering, then puts everything back in the bag. Unzipping the front pocket, she sticks her hand inside. Various receipts, a pack of chewing gum and a betting slip. She photographs the slip too. She rummages around to make sure there's nothing left behind, finding one last scrap of paper, which she holds to the light to read. Written in red biro in tiny square writing is a series of digits. A phone number. She gasps aloud as she recognises the number.

It belongs to her daughter.

TWENTY-THREE

The first thing she thinks of when she opens her eyes the following morning is Danny. Why would this man who is so much older than her daughter have her number?

She gets out of bed and goes into Lara's room. Lara is fast asleep on her back, face almost completely covered by the duvet. Rachel stands and watches her for a few moments, listening to her steady breathing. A car horn hoots from the street, startling her, and Lara stirs, mumbling, before her breathing settles back into the same rhythm. If only Rachel could see inside her mind, know what was going on in there. She has to tackle her about Danny, make sure nothing improper has happened. Her heart flutters with fear at the thought of harm coming to her children.

Next she looks in on Josh, whose hair is sticking up in a tangle, the duvet half on the floor. She straightens the covers over him and goes downstairs.

Priority number one is speaking to Pete. The builders usually arrive by nine; Pete is always first. It's seven thirty now. She hopes she can speak to him before Danny arrives. She doesn't want Danny in her house. If it delays finishing the job, so be it. She could always complete the decorating herself, if necessary. Just thinking about him prowling around the place makes her skin crawl. She makes a mug of tea and opens the back door to let in some fresh air.

Half an hour later, Josh is chomping on his cornflakes, reading a graphic novel at the same time, and for once she doesn't nag him about eating too fast. Her phone lights up with a text. It's Pete.

I won't be in today due to illness. Sorry.

'No.'

'What is it, Mum?'

She composes herself. 'Nothing to worry about. Pete's not coming in today, that's all. Now go and get your stuff ready or you'll be late for Toby's mum. And tell your sister to hurry up. She's been in the bathroom for ages. She's got ten minutes until her bus leaves.'

Both children are ready in time, but there's not enough time before the bus leaves to take Lara aside to ask her about Danny. The conversation with her daughter will have to wait. She calls Pete's number instead.

'Hello, Pete.'

'Oh no, love, this is Pete's wife. Oh dear.' Rachel can hear a commotion in the background.

'Is Pete OK? I got his message. Is it possible to have a quick word with him? It's important.' She can hear the sounds of a street in the background, traffic, muffled voices.

'I wish you could, love, but they're just getting him into the ambulance.' The woman's voice wobbles. 'We think he's had a heart attack.'

'Oh no.' Rachel sinks to her haunches, back against the wall. 'Is he conscious?'

'Yes, they're doing everything they can.' More voices in the background, a dog barks. 'I have to go.'

'Good luck,' Rachel says, but Pete's wife is gone. She imagines the slam of the ambulance door, the siren, Pete's kindly face covered in an oxygen mask.

Please let him be OK.

The house feels too empty, and she switches the radio on for some background noise. Her immediate worry is Danny. Will he turn up at the house without Pete? Pete normally drives them both in, and they always leave together. She doubts he will, but she doesn't have his phone number. All her communications have been with Pete. Lara might have his number. The thought makes her blood freeze.

She wanders around the kitchen, unable to settle. Despite the sun shining into the kitchen, she shivers. She wishes the children weren't at school, that she could keep them with her, where nobody can get to them. She pictures Lara hearing her phone, answering with that hopeful look she gets on her face of late whenever it rings or beeps. Is she waiting for Danny to call? Rachel can't see how their paths have crossed very much. Most of the time he's at the house, Lara is at school.

Rachel has to speak to her before it's too late. She texts her and asks her to call urgently at break time. At ten forty, she's holding her phone. Break lasts for twenty minutes. Lara will have to go down to the reception area to make the call, otherwise she risks having her phone confiscated. She calls at ten fifty.

'Sorry to bother you at school, love, but there's a bit of a situation with the builders.' Rachel explains about Pete. 'This is a wild shot, but you don't have Danny's number, do you?' She's clenching the phone so hard her nails are digging into her palms.

'Are you being serious, Mum? Why would I have his number? He's creepy.'

She relaxes her grip. 'I didn't think you would.' She almost laughs from relief. 'Never mind. Don't forget Gran is picking you up from school later.'

'I won't. But I wanted to go the cinema with a friend this evening. Do you think Gran will mind?'

'I'm sure she won't. I'm so pleased you're hanging out with Holly again; you two used to go to the cinema all the time.'

'Mum, stop it. I'll be home by nine thirty.' A buzzer sounds in the background. 'Got to go or I'll be late for English. Bye.'

That afternoon, Rachel heads to the park for a walk. She spends a couple of hours out of the house to clear her head, and treats herself to a coffee in the park café. Freddie is due for dinner later, and normally when she has anyone over to eat she'd spend the afternoon cleaning and cooking before taking time to have a bath and get dressed up. But given everything that's been going on over the past few days, she's finding it hard to be in the house on her own, and with the children going straight to her mother's after school, a long afternoon stretches ahead. Talking through her problems with Freddie always helps, though she can't quite stifle that niggle of doubt that lingers. But he genuinely likes her, she can tell, and the attraction she feels for him is so strong it's hard to ignore.

It's late afternoon when she gets back to the house, and she switches the kettle on before heading up to her bedroom to sort out an outfit for the evening. Freddie texts to say he's looking forward to it, and she replies that she is too. As soon as she reaches the top of the stairs, though, she knows that something is wrong. The wooden staircase to the loft extension hasn't been painted yet, but a thin stripe of red paint leads up it, roughly in the middle, as if a trail has been left for her to follow.

'Hello,' she calls, clutching her mobile, ready to dial the emergency services if she hears as much as a sound. Deathly silence greets her. She crouches down to touch the paint. It's dry. How long does paint take to dry? One hour? Two? Pete would know. The thought of Pete in a hospital bed adds to her panic. Everything is crumbling around her. She thinks of Danny, who has been a fixture in her house, spying on her for the past few weeks. He has to be behind this. She won't be scared of him.

She heads upstairs, following the trail into her new bedroom, and stops short. A can of red paint has been poured over the floor, making the wood look bloodstained. She leans against the wall, hands over her mouth, unable to believe what she is seeing. Paint has been spattered over the walls, too, completely ruining the work here. The only paint being used for this room and the en suite is pale in colour, and those cans are still stacked on the newspaper. This lurid red paint has been brought in specifically for this task. To frighten her. Pete's bag is still stashed with the paint, but Danny's is no longer here. Pete who now lies in hospital. A coincidence? She can't help wonder. Did something frighten him? How well does he know his assistant?

Danny has to be behind this. He must have let himself in with the key Rachel gave him. Did he know she would be out; was he watching the house? Is there a camera installed somewhere? She photographs the room, then makes sure all the windows are secure and locks the door behind her. She needs to get the front-door locks changed as a priority.

She checks her phone. Freddie's due in a couple of hours. She can't speak to the police alone. She'll wait until he arrives, and together they can decide what to do.

TWENTY-FOUR

Freddie stands on the doorstep, his arms full of yellow roses and a bottle of Merlot. He's wearing a short-sleeved pale pink shirt and dark blue chinos. He leans in to kiss Rachel on each cheek, and she inhales a hint of the sweetness of the roses, which is quickly overwhelmed by his spicy aftershave. She made an effort and put a dress on, but she feels sick.

She found it hard to settle after discovering the paint. She called a locksmith straight away, and she's comforted by the new set of keys hanging up in the hall. Pete's wife rang to say he was stable in hospital, and Rachel asked her to contact Danny and tell him to hold off on coming to work on Monday, while Pete is out of action. She'd made a casserole and stuck it in the oven on a low heat.

'Thanks,' she says, taking the flowers, the covering of crinkly paper rustling as she goes into the kitchen. The table is laid for two; she's opened the back doors, and lamps glow in the garden, casting shadows over the small pond, which is lit by the silvery light. 'Such beautiful roses.'

'You're shaking,' Freddie says.

'Something terrible's happened,' she says. 'Come upstairs and I'll show you.'

He follows her upstairs into the loft extension and gasps when he sees the violent red splashes. In the half-light, it looks like a crime scene. He pulls Rachel to him and hugs her. 'Who would do this?'

If only she could melt into his arms and enjoy the warmth she feels through his shirt, but she can't stop shaking and she can't trust anyone. She pulls away.

'Come downstairs. I can't stand to be up here.'

'Have you called the police?' he asks as they return to the kitchen.

'Not yet,' she says, locating a vase. 'There's a bottle of wine on the table if you want to do the honours while I sort these out. Let's try and be normal. I refuse to let whoever is doing this ruin my evening. I've had the locks changed and cancelled the builder. I'm sure he's behind it.'

She updates him about the situation with Pete and Danny while she clips the stems of the roses, strips excess leaves and arranges the flowers in the vase, which she sets in the middle of the table. Freddie hands her a glass and she drinks hungrily, welcoming the hit, anything to calm her anxiety. She smiles tightly, wishing she could forget the comments both Heidi and Emma made about Freddie. She can't imagine this relaxed, friendly man fighting with Tom, but she holds back the discovery she's made about Heidi and Danny, wanting to keep something to herself just in case.

'I've made a casserole,' she says. 'It's in the oven.'

'You needn't have cooked,' he tells her, 'not after that intrusion. Are the kids eating with us?'

'No, Josh is at Scouts and Lara's gone to the cinema. Josh will most likely stay over at my mum's afterwards.'

'That's good about Lara, isn't it? Weren't you worried about her not having any social life?'

'Yes. It's her friend Holly from school, I think, though I didn't want to ask her too many questions. After the row we had yesterday, I didn't want to upset her again. She promised to be back by nine thirty.' It occurs to her she didn't ask how Lara was getting back from the cinema.

'Do you want me to stay? We can do this another time if you prefer.'

'I'd rather not be alone. Let's park all the horrible stuff for now and try and enjoy ourselves. I'm going to take advantage of the kids not being here and put some music on. They hate my music. Why don't you choose something?'

Freddie chooses a compilation of world music.

'Good choice,' Rachel says. 'It reminds me of holidays I've been on.'

They talk for a while about travelling, and find they both like the same kind of holidays. Rachel has a sensation of watching herself go through the motions. Chat flows easily and they move on to the food, which she hardly touches, and eventually to coffee. Afterwards, they make themselves comfortable on the sofa. Rachel has barely drunk anything more; she needs to keep her wits about her. She glances at the time. Lara should be back soon. If she's going to speak to Freddie as originally planned, she needs to get on with it.

Emma's warning flashes again in her mind. What would her sister say if she knew she was alone in the house with Freddie? What if he's the one behind the notes after all? Anxiety rises and she pushes it away. Freddie has been nothing but support-ive. If he'd wanted to hurt her, he could have done it up there in the loft. If she's honest and upfront with him, then he's likely to reciprocate. On no account must he sense that her fear has anything to do with him.

'What's up?' he says.

'There's something I need to talk to you about.' She smiles

wryly. 'That's exactly what I said to Lara yesterday, and look how that went.'

'I'm sure I'll cope if you tell me I can't see Heidi again. That suits me just fine.'

'Idiot.'

They laugh, although Rachel's stomach is fluttering at what she's about to reveal. She clutches her wine glass to her chest.

'I don't know how you're going to take this, but I want to be honest with you. I like you, Freddie, and I want us to have a chance. My relationship with Tom was ruined because of his secrets, and I don't want to make the same mistake again. If you can't deal with it, I'd rather know now.' She risks a glance at Freddie, who is watching her intently. She swallows hard, dives in. 'I didn't tell anybody at the time, but two weekends before Tom disappeared, we slept together.' She runs through an account of exactly what happened that evening.

'Why didn't you want anyone to know?'

'I suppose I was hoping he might come back to me. That night, it was how it used to be before he met Heidi; we were close and he spoke honestly. He told me he had made a mistake leaving me and the children. Plus I didn't want it to get back to her. I thought it would make things more difficult between me and her; as it was, we were barely speaking, and we were bound to encounter one another occasionally because of the children.'

'Have you told her now?'

She shakes her head. 'No.'

Freddie puts his wine glass down and takes her hand. 'It doesn't affect how I feel about you,' he says. 'I didn't tell you everything about the finances either, did I? And you were right not to tell Heidi.'

'It probably wouldn't matter to her now. I have no idea. I'm not sure any of us would know what to do if he were to come back. I wouldn't go back to him, though. It's funny, I've only recently realised that, become so sure of it. I've finally started looking to the future. Are you sure you're not bothered by what I've told you?'

'Of course not.'

Rachel's phone rings.

'Hi, Mum.' She listens as her mother confirms that Josh wants to stay the night. 'Sure, as long as you don't mind.' She laughs. 'I know you do. Thanks, Mum, see you tomorrow. Yes, any time.'

Freddie has taken their glasses into the kitchen.

'Lara should be back any minute,' Rachel says. 'Do you want something else to drink?'

'Another coffee would be good. Let me make it. You put your feet up.'

Rachel keeps an eye on the time as they chat over coffee and talk about music, finding they were into the same kind of bands as teenagers. Freddie selects another album to play her, and she notices it's five minutes past the time Lara was due home. She sends her a text.

'Lara,' she tells Freddie. 'She was due back at nine thirty. It's not like her to be late – or not to be in touch, actually.'

'How is she getting home?'

'I'm guessing she's walking back with her friend. The cinema complex isn't far away – fifteen minutes at most. Holly lives just round the corner. At least, I assume she meant Holly.'

'It's not even dark yet,' Freddie says.

'I suppose I'll have to start getting used to this as she gets older. Sitting up fretting, waiting for her to come home. Then the same with Josh. You're lucky not to have to deal with that.'

'I don't know,' Freddie says. 'I haven't ruled out children in my life. Even if they are somebody else's. I'm sure she'll be back any minute.'

Rachel nods. 'You're right. I'll just call Mum, just in case she's heard from her.'

But her mum has no word from Lara. Although it's hard to

concentrate on Freddie's conversation, she is comforted by his presence. Every now and then, an image of the room upstairs with its bloody-looking walls flashes through her mind, and she's relieved not to be on her own. She'd no doubt have worked herself up into a state.

At nine forty-five, she calls Lara's phone.

'Voicemail,' she says. She types out a text.

Are you on your way home?

Nothing.

'She'll be fine,' Freddie says. 'Do you want me to go out and look for her?'

'Would you mind?'

'No, of course not. Point me in the right direction.'

Rachel shivers on the doorstep, the light properly faded now and the street lights illuminating the length of the street. She explains the route to him and he sets off. She leans against the doorpost watching him, her eyes straining to pick out a figure walking towards him, but there's nobody in the street apart from Freddie, who now turns the corner out of sight. She closes the door, tries to ring Lara again. Voicemail. She scrolls through her phone and looks for Holly's number. Thank goodness she had the foresight to make a note of it. She also has the girl's landline.

Holly's mobile rings out, and then an extremely young-sounding voice invites her to leave a message.

'Holly, this is Mrs Webb. Lara isn't back from the cinema yet. I'm sure she's fine, but could you give me a call when you get this message.'

She closes the doors leading out to the patio, as she's properly shivering now, before running upstairs to grab a sweatshirt, no longer caring about her appearance.

Suddenly her phone rings: Freddie. Hope soars. *He's found*

her, he's ringing to let me know everything's OK, that I'm being stupid as ever, of course she's fine...

'Is she back?' he asks.

'No.' Rachel's heart takes a nosedive.

'I haven't seen her and I'm outside the cinema now. I'll go inside and check she's not still hanging around the foyer.' He rings off.

Rachel paces the wooden floorboards, her fingers crossed, knowing how futile the superstitious gesture is, knowing the unlikelihood of Lara being spotted by a cinema attendant amongst the hordes of youngsters streaming out of a viewing at the most popular showing time of the evening. It's not as if she has purple hair or anything that would make her stand out from the crowd. She's ordinary and... special.

She lets out a sob and tries to call her again. Texts again. Her bedroom! She runs upstairs, in such a rush that she trips over a step and lands on her knees mid staircase, just managing to break her fall by grabbing the banister, but grazing her knee. The wood is cold to touch. Her heart is hammering fast and panic threatens to engulf her at the thought of her daughter coming to harm out in the dark night. Why didn't she insist on meeting her from the cinema? How could she have put a date with a man before her daughter?

Her knee throbs where she landed, and she reaches down and feels blood. She limps into the bathroom and turns on the light, the brightness making her gasp. Holding on to the edge of the sink, she tries to compose herself. She catches sight of herself in the mirror and is aghast at her image, her face pale, her eyes wide and terrified, blood streaked across her cheek. Her knee stings. She grabs some tissue to stem the bleeding. Freddie will turn up any moment with Lara in tow.

Her phone rings again, giving her such a start she almost loses her balance. She grips it as if her life depends on it.

'Have you found her?'

'No,' he says, and she slides to the floor against the side of the bath. 'I'll be back in a minute. I'm sure she's fine.'

Rachel gets to her feet and runs downstairs, keeping a hand on the banister. She locates the pad where Holly's landline number is written down.

'Hello?' An adult voice, female.

'Susan?'

'Yes. Who is this?'

'It's Rachel Webb, Lara's mum. Is Holly back from the cinema?'

'Cinema? Holly's here, she hasn't been to the cinema.'

Rachel puts her hand to her mouth to stop herself screaming, a million thoughts jumping into her head. 'Sorry, I thought she went with Lara this evening to the Pixar film.' She only *assumed* it was Holly. 'Please can you ask her if she knows who Lara might have gone with? I'm really worried.'

'Of course.' Rachel hears footsteps and Susan calling her daughter's name, followed by a muffled exchange. She imagines Lara in Holly's room, Susan's surprise at seeing her there, Rachel's panic unfounded...

'Rachel, Holly's here with me now, would you like to speak to her?'

'Yes please,' she says, gripping the phone so hard her knuckles turn white.

'Mrs Webb, it's Holly. I haven't been to the cinema this evening and I haven't seen Lara. Um... we don't hang out much any more. We had an argument a few months back. I asked her about her dad and she got really mad and stopped speaking to me. I didn't really understand what I'd done wrong.'

'When did you last see her?'

'This afternoon, we had double geography. But we weren't sitting together and I came straight home after school.'

Holly lives so close, their routes to school are identical; Lara just has a little bit further to go once Holly has reached her house. They used to take the journey together in Year 7, but lately Rachel gets the bus on her own.

'Did you see her leave the classroom? Her gran was picking her up today.' She hopes to jog Holly's memory.

She hears Holly breathing as she thinks. 'No,' she says eventually, 'but I had to speak to the teacher after class, so I wasn't paying attention.'

'Do you know if any of your classmates were going to the cinema? I assumed she was going with you.'

Holly hesitates. 'Lara doesn't talk to anybody much at school. I can't imagine her going to the cinema with any of our class. I'm sorry I don't know anything, Mrs Webb.'

'Don't be silly, you have nothing to be sorry for.'

Susan comes back on the phone. 'What time did you expect her?' she asks.

'Nine thirty.' Forty-five minutes ago.

'Let me know when she gets home,' Susan says. 'I'm sure there's a simple explanation.'

The doorbell rings, and Rachel sees Freddie's tall shadow through the glass. She opens the door and he shakes his head.

'I asked at the box office and they checked all the screens she could have been in, but it was empty.' He shrugs. 'There were so many people...'

'I don't think she went to the cinema,' she says, and bursts into tears. Freddie puts his arms around her and she sobs for a few seconds and then pulls away.

'Tell me why you don't think she was at the cinema.'

Rachel recounts the phone conversation with Holly's mother. 'Lara was lying. Why would she do that? Where has she gone?'

'Has she been acting differently lately? Is there anything out of the ordinary you can think of?'

'The only difference is seeing Heidi, the growing attachment. Which I tried to put a stop to. And she's started wearing make-up.' She pictures Lara's face, her new look, suddenly real-ising that it's familiar. Lara's eyebrows are exactly the same shape as Heidi's – she's copied them.

'Heidi, I'd better check with her, just in case.' She calls Heidi, all disinclination to contact her abandoned. But Heidi can't help and her heart sinks.

She shakes her head at Freddie, in answer to his enquiring expression, ending the call.

'She hasn't seen her.'

'What about the internet? Do you know her online passwords?'

'No, but it's worth seeing if I can log straight in – I'll get her laptop.' She fetches it from the coffee table and opens it. Imme-diately she's asked for a password. She tries a few obvious ones, but to no avail. 'If I try again I'll get locked out.'

'Let's check her room.'

Rachel runs upstairs again, cold air following her from the open front door. Lara's pencil case is on her bed, the pink unicorn sticker making her want to howl. Her baby. Getting older, growing away from her. Where is she? She looks around the room, searching for any evidence of where she might be, trying to see if anything is missing. When she left for school this morning, her hair was tied back into a high ponytail. Pretty. She looked pretty. She stifles a sob. She opens the wardrobe and flicks through the carefully hung clothes. Jeans and a red sweat-shirt are missing. It looks emptier than usual; something normally fills the floor space, but she can't think what it is.

Freddie comes into the room. 'Anything?'

'No, but...' She scans the room again, goes to the dressing table, where Lara's school books are piled up. A folded piece of paper sits on top of the stack, one word written on it: *Mum*.

'Oh no.' Freddie is at her side. Her hands shake as she opens the note.

Don't worry about me, Mum, I'm out with a friend.

She collapses against Freddie.

'At least we know she hasn't been taken against her will,' he says.

'But where is she, what friend? Holly's the only person she talks about from school.' A pang of fear rises to her throat. Could it be Heidi? No, she wouldn't. Rachel has had the odd missed call, a few texts from her since she ended the lessons, but nothing excessive.

'What about a boyfriend? Is it a mixed school?'

She stares at him. 'It's mixed. I'll ring Holly back and ask.'

Holly tells her she hasn't seen Lara show any interest in any of the boys at school. 'She keeps to herself most of the time. I've never seen her chatting to any boys, if that helps. She always used to say the boys in our year were childish and idiotic.'

Rachel hangs up and turns to Freddie, the note clutched to her chest. 'We should call the police. They might say she hasn't been gone long enough, but she has, it's too long. She's a young girl on her own. She might have met someone on the internet, a man pretending to be a boy.' Panic rises as terrifying scenarios crowd her mind. 'They have to take notice; she's only twelve.' Tears pour down her face. She can't bear to put the thought about Heidi into words.

'They will. Is anything missing from her room? Does she have a bag, a purse? They'll be able to track her phone.'

'Bag, that's it.' Rachel lurches back to the wardrobe, indicating the empty space. 'Her large sports bag. It was there.' She turns to look at him. 'It's gone.'

TWENTY-FIVE

TOM

SEVEN YEARS EARLIER

Now that he had time to look back, it was easy to see that the new romance was a distraction. All those endorphins whooshing through his body swamped the little niggles that had started creeping into his mind with increasing frequency. They enabled him to focus on the new object of his attention – Heidi – and push any uncomfortable thoughts back into the filing cabinet to look at later. A drawer he hoped would stay firmly locked.

Inevitably the gloss wore off his new infatuation – as was perfectly normal – and once he'd made the decision to set up home with Heidi, he was forced to confront reality. He was in serious financial straits.

He opened the window near his desk; he wasn't cold, but the atmosphere in the office was thick with the tension between him and Freddie. How could it have got this bad? Long gone were the days when they'd break for coffee and banter, laughing at each other's jokes, feeding off ideas each would spark in the other, their vision for the company growing. Not only was the business faltering, Tom's personal life was also causing angst between the two of them.

Freddie looked up from his computer as if sensing Tom was thinking about him, glancing away quickly when their eyes met. Tom stood up, taking a deep breath.

'We need to talk,' he said. 'Pub after work?'

'I can't.'

'I won't put this off any longer. You're not happy, I can see that. If we're going to continue working together, something has to change. I can't stand this atmosphere. One quick drink, that's all.'

'Fine.'

Three hours later, they were in a booth in their preferred pub, both grateful for the babble of conversation and the background thrum of music, the convivial atmosphere a complete contrast to the cold office they'd left behind. Tom paid for two pints and downed a huge mouthful before carrying them back to the table.

'What do you want to say to me?' Freddie asked. He was holding himself awkwardly, as though awaiting an interview.

'I miss you.'

'I'm still here. It's not me that's changed.'

'I know you don't approve of me leaving Rachel for Heidi, but it's happened. Do you think you'll ever be able to forgive me? If we can't move on from this, then we have a problem. I dread going to work at the moment, and you don't look too thrilled to be there either.'

'How could you do it to Rachel? She's in bits, and the children need so much looking after at that age. Are you really sure about Heidi? I'm worried you're caught up in this passion and it will fizzle out and you'll be left regretting what you've given up.'

Tom holds his head in his hands. 'I hate what I've done to

Rachel.' He sips at his beer. 'But I've fallen in love. I didn't ask for it. Hasn't that ever happened to you? Hit you out of the blue and kicked your legs from under you?' He picks up the beer mat and squeezes it in his palm. 'I tried to fight it, honestly I did.'

Freddie sighs. 'It's just such a mess. I've always been great friends with both of you, and I can't stand seeing Rachel look so unhappy. And you're right, work is not a great place to be at the moment and I've no right to be so judgemental. You're still my mate, I just don't like your behaviour. Let me buy you another pint.'

Things improved slightly for a while, but their relationship wasn't the same. Lara had mentioned 'Uncle Freddie' on one of their visits, and he suspected his partner was being more of a friend to his wife than to him. Weirdly, he was grateful that she had someone to lean on, even though he himself had nobody to confide in.

The Freddie problem became dwarfed by his desire to appease Heidi, not wanting to be a failure in both his relationships. The way he'd found the deposit for the new house she had set her heart on had been keeping him awake for weeks, weighing on his mind. Paying the business back was going to take a lot longer than he'd first thought, and the auditors could pay a surprise visit at any time. He'd had a shock too when he opened his credit card statement. Heidi had been ordering furniture for the new house and the card was almost at its limit. The minimum repayments were a considerable amount. Last time he'd suggested she was being too extravagant, she'd gone into a sulk for days, answering him in monosyllables and turning her back on him in bed. Rachel had concerns about Lara, who'd been having nightmares since he left, and Josh was impossible to settle at night. Something had to give, but he couldn't decide what, his feet sinking deeper and deeper into the mud.

Late at night, he'd begun to imagine a scenario. He'd pack up his suitcase, just the essentials he needed, plus his driving licence and his passport. He'd borrow one last instalment from the safe, enough to hire a car. Then he'd get on the motorway and drive, see where he ended up. Each night his imagination grew more vivid, adding details: changing his name, a different career, a whole new life. What about his children, though? The thought of leaving them was a physical pain, and he doubted he could go through with the plan.

But what if he had no choice?

TWENTY-SIX

HEIDI

Two months earlier

Heidi stands on the corner of the street and looks at the house. She couldn't miss it even if she wanted to, with the scaffolding erected around the building, the vulgar advertising board and the company name emblazoned on it for all to see. She ignores the fact that she didn't need to return to her flat this way, needn't have passed by the street where her nemesis lives.

Rachel.

It's as if she's a magnet, being dragged towards the scaffolding poles against her will. If she *were* a magnet, she'd run far away, dragging the poles away from the building so that they'd stop supporting the house and it would all fall down, like in the story of the little pigs. Rachel makes her feel like the littlest pig, the unwanted runt of the litter who was left with nothing when the family silver was handed out, skulking back to her poky flat when she should be the one living in that house, having expensive improvements done to make it even more desirable, with two healthy children and a fulfilled life. Instead, she is left lurking on the street corner, wondering what progress the builders have made and wishing she could have a peek inside. Scratching the itch, making it worse. That's what she always does.

She's about to turn away when a blue Mini pulls up at the house and Josh and some fat woman with frizzy hair get out. He's laughing at something she's said. He's grown since she last saw him. He must be eight now. Would he even remember his father? And what about her? Her fingers curl into fists as the thought enrages her, and she turns abruptly on her heel, unable to bear the sight of the domestic scene playing out in front of her any longer.

On an impulse, she stops off on her way home at the DIY store and loses herself amongst the paint charts, the choice of colour becoming more important every moment. Anything to make her flat look better. She settles on a shade of grey that is featured on the cover of the glossy paint brochure and named as the colour of the year. Do people vote on paint colours? She wants to be the kind of person who has time to devote to trivia like this, instead of the person who trudges to an office every day. The thought brings a sharp pain in her chest; no matter how much she hated the windowless office and the endless tapping at the keyboard and headache-inducing staring at a screen, being made redundant was not a life event she had planned. She needs money to pay her rent and bills; she shouldn't be buying paint. But the images posted around the home decor aisles of desirable houses and beautiful people living enviable lifestyles lure her in. A few tins of paint won't hurt, and if it makes her feel better about the wrong that has been done to her, then it's a necessity for her mental health.

At the till, she taps her card and baulks at the amount, imagining Danny sneering at her extravagance, saying she always has to go that one better. After all these years, Danny shouldn't be in her life any more, but somehow they can't help hooking up, even if months have passed without their paths crossing. He managed to stay away for a year once, and then one drink in a pub ended up with them in bed together. That was when she was with Tom – she doesn't need to be reminded of the domino effect that had.

The woman behind her in the queue coughs in a deliberate way and Heidi hoists the bags of paint off the floor, wincing at the unexpected weight. Maybe the decision for a feature wall was a step too far, but the contrasting green and grey in the brochure look so classy. Perhaps Danny will help her with the decorating, but that would mean seeing him, and after last time, she isn't sure that's a good idea – as if seeing Danny was ever a good idea.

She avoids opening a bottle of wine when she gets home – that way memories of Tom lie; sharing a bottle of wine over dinner was their routine. She's never been one of those women who fall to pieces after a break-up, spending the evening drinking and playing sad music to evoke memories. After all, she didn't actually break up with Tom. Officially, in her eyes, they are still together. Not officially enough for the authorities, however. Heidi prefers action. She likes to be in control. She keeps Rachel's number in her phone; it's a link to him in a strange sort of way, that lure as strong as the pull of his house. Not his house any more, but *hers*. When it should be Heidi's.

One glass of wine would loosen her resolve, and Rachel is only a message away. Not something Heidi has considered doing during the past few years, but now, with the seven-year deadline approaching, Tom has been on her mind a lot. The alternative to the wine is beans on toast, a strong cup of tea and a night in front of the television. That way she won't be in danger of doing any harm. She'd like to know whether everyone is afraid of their own selves and what they might do. It's something she'd love to know but never dared ask anyone. Apart from Danny, of course, always Danny. He isn't afraid of what he might do; he just does it and relishes it afterwards, leaving others with the angst.

She won't see him again.

She's watching a drama set in a hospital and at first doesn't notice that her phone is flashing with an incoming call.

Danny.

She won't pick up.

She picks up.

'Where are you?' he asks in his gravelly smoker's voice. Danny isn't one to worry about his health. Danny doesn't worry about anything.

'Why?' She's stalling – if she says she's at home, he'll want to come round.

'If you're at home, switch the television on.'

'I'm already watching.'

'BBC2, I've just seen a trailer for a new documentary, it's about him.'

Heidi's pulse shoots into overdrive and she's unable to move.

'What do you mean?'

'It's about him and a few others in the same situation. It's going to be shown in a few months' time. Thought you might be interested. It's because of that Maria woman who's just gone missing. Some girl who's looking for her mother. Tearjerker kind of thing.'

Heidi knows about Maria Jennings, as does everyone who isn't living under a rock. The nineteen-year-old student who set off for a lecture in chemical engineering and never arrived. Long fair hair and freckles, a dazzling smile. Clever as well as beautiful, and a lovely person according to anyone who'd ever met her. People would probably say that about Rachel, until they found out what she was really like. But would they say it if she actually died...

'Did you know about it?' Danny snaps a lighter and she

hears the inhale, imagines the satisfied look on his face as he sucks in his angular cheekbones before exhaling a dirty cloud of smoke.

'No,' she says. 'And I'm not interested. My mate's due round any minute.'

She chucks her mobile onto the sofa and frowns at the screen. Danny should know she can't watch anything about Tom. The hospital drama is reaching its peak, but she no longer cares whether the protagonist survives. Her mind is a tangle of possibilities.

Why now?

Whatever the reason for airing the documentary, it has nothing to do with Tom's case. But it serves a purpose; it gives her an idea. Remembering the scaffolding being erected around the house, the house that she has spent so much time thinking about, reminds her that Danny is in the building trade. Her resolve not to see him evaporates. She invites him round to discuss her plans, and he's in – Danny could never resist a little illicit behaviour. It's the thrills that keep him going. Within a week, he's made the right contacts and got himself some extra work.

Which is only the beginning of their plan. If they can pull this off, then Heidi will get everything that rightfully belongs to her.

And about time.

TWENTY-SEVEN

She wakes with a jolt, immediately recalling the activities of the previous night. Writing a note. Walking down the road, skulking out of sight behind a car.

The full scenario plays in her head now, and she lets it unreel, wanting to know exactly what lengths she went to in case she hasn't got every detail right and needs a contingency plan. Walking through the park, which hadn't yet closed, so it must have been before seven, and she remembers wishing she'd waited until it was dark, welcoming the cloak of anonymity it would have covered her with. Seeing the scaffolding as soon as she turned the corner, the bars catching the rays of the late afternoon sun as if signalling to her where to come. As if she needs reminding. Friends ask how she can bear to live in the same area, why she didn't make a fresh start after it happened, wipe it from her mind. How naive people can be. They've forgotten that she lost everything when she'd been about to gain it all. The house she'd set her heart on was snapped up by another couple. Thinking about it makes her seethe even now.

When these thoughts plague her, she reminds herself that that house was a mere stepping stone; now she's got her heart set on the real prize. The reason she stays is because she won't settle for second best. She knows what is hers by right, and she's ready to claim it back.

Hence the note.

Danny put the idea into her head. Of course he did. She wishes she'd come up with it herself, but he won't let her forget they are in this together. Just in case. The timing is crucial, he reminded her, otherwise Rachel might take action and snatch the house from under her nose, and then it will be too late. If she doesn't pitch in and delay the inevitable, she'll have lost it forever. All she needs to do is ingratiate herself with Rachel in order to get access to the house. That way, if Danny doesn't get a chance to hide it somewhere, she can do it herself.

She switches on the kettle and adds two heaped spoons of dark grains to her cafetière, then goes to the coffee table where the evidence lies. If she hadn't already remembered what she'd done, she would have found out as soon as she'd come in here, as the floor is covered in balls of crumpled-up paper, and her black pen lies with the lid off, dried up and useless. She unfolds one of the paper balls and sees an attempt at his writing. She smooths each page out and compares them. Any one of these would have passed the test; she perfected Tom's writing a long time ago. Copying handwriting is a particular talent of hers, thanks to years of forging notes to the school to get out of PE lessons and other unnecessary indignities that were demanded of her when she was a child. She sweeps the whole lot together and puts them all in the waste-paper basket.

The coffee revives her, and she mulls over what she has done. Was it stupid? Rachel will have no idea the note is from her, but what will she do? Will she think it's a joke and throw it away? Heidi thinks this is unlikely. Rachel, although very different from her, has suffered the same indignity, and Heidi knows that if their roles were reversed, there is no way she couldn't take it seriously. Because if there was the slightest chance that Tom was alive, she would be all over it.

She doesn't want to, but she rings Danny. Heidi is used to doing things she doesn't want to do. He doesn't pick up. She pictures him on the scaffolding, moving carefully in case of a wrong step that would send him hurtling to the ground. She imagines him skulking around the house, relaying every detail back to her. She likes knowing exactly how much the fancy extension is costing, how much value is being added to the property, all the more for her to take from Rachel.

For the first couple of days, every time she thinks about the note, her heart hammers and she breaks out in a sweat. It happens in the supermarket, in the bank, but it mostly happens in her bedroom, at night, when she should be asleep. Danny laughs when she tells him, offers to come over, but she's determined not to see him again in that way. He reminds her of everything that is bad about her; he's like the Dorian Gray portrait in the bedroom – though one of those would be preferable, because at least she could lock it out of sight. Every time she thinks he is out of her life, he reappears. At least this time he is serving a purpose. Shame he wasn't in the house when the note arrived; she'd have loved to see Rachel's reaction.

Four days later, the inevitable happens. Rachel phones.

Heidi's mother always said she should have been an actress. She'd be proud of her now as she sucks up to Rachel, the bitch she last saw when she fleeced her in court. Heidi has been licking her wounds ever since. Today she's friendly and concerned, but what starts as an act dissolves as Rachel surprises her by being friendly, and talking about Tom. This impossible connection between them is refreshing and enables her to drop her guard.

And Rachel hasn't told the police.

'I don't suppose you want to meet, do you?'

Rachel is silent for what seems like ages, and Heidi almost laughs to think she even dared suggest it. But her mouth runs away with her as she can't stop herself from filling the awkward silence, and what she says about them both having had this unique experience reaches its target. They arrange to meet for coffee the next day.

Rachel lies about the note. Heidi wrote *I want to come back to you*, but Rachel omits the final two words in the telling. *Interesting*. For a moment she regrets dropping her guard, but she doesn't want to break the connection they are making. Rachel thinks Tom is alive, although she's undecided about the note.

The big surprise is that Lara has no memory of her, after all the effort she put in to win the girl round. The Lara she first met was very hesitant; she clung to her dad and asked for her mother. Heidi tried so hard to get the little girl to like her; every time they came to stay with Tom, she'd give both children a present, a small toy or an edible treat – she thought children liked anything shiny or sparkly. Lara soon came round; she was always excited with whatever Heidi gave her and would wrap her chubby arms around her, and Heidi would scoop her up and hold her close. With Josh, it was hard to form any kind of bond. He yelled a lot at night and grizzled when she picked him up. Tom comforted her by saying that he was going through an unsettling time. Heidi gave up with Josh, but by the time of Tom's disappearance, she had formed a tight bond with Lara.

The Lara she meets when she drops by Rachel's house is a quiet pre-teen who is trying to understand herself. Heidi couldn't have planned it better, for Lara to be stuck on her maths homework, which is Heidi's forte after years working in accounts. She still experiences a bitter taste in her mouth when she recalls the moment she learned of her impending redundancy from the accountancy firm, so unexpected when she innocently clicked on the email. Who fires someone by email? Her manager explained that she wasn't getting the sack, but couldn't argue with her when she branded it a redundancy. Heidi cringes as she does whenever she hears the word. Whatever was she thinking of, blowing all that money on a luxury holiday? All she has left to show for it is a fading tan.

Lara is in need of help and not just with mathematical calculations. The girl is lost, anyone can see that; she's quick and intelligent, and Heidi enjoys showing her a better way of working out her sums. Even though Lara doesn't remember her, she's friendly enough, almost eager for attention. As for Josh – she can't imagine this happy-go-lucky boy being 'the devil child', as she used to think of him. She made the mistake of calling him that in front of Tom and she thought she'd lost him that night. Those children meant the world to him.

TWENTY-EIGHT

HEIDI

Every time Heidi enters the new flat, she stands in the communal hall and wrinkles her nose at the smell of tobacco wafting down from the upstairs apartment, the peeling paper on the walls, and reminds herself this is only a temporary move. Inside, the flat isn't so bad; it's much larger than her studio, and has plenty of room for when the children stay. Tom has promised they'll be able to put a deposit down on the house she's set her heart on in the new year.

She sensed a reluctance from him when she pushed him on the subject, but he assures her this is what he wants; he's just being mindful about expenses as he still has his old house to run. His older, grander house. Heidi has learnt to squash those envious feelings – she knew he was married, and having to play second-best for a while is a process she has to go through. His reluctance has nothing to do with her, or the house.

Yet still it grates.

She leaves her bag on the kitchen table and wanders into the living room, then out onto the small square of decking surrounded by Astroturf. The look is ruined by the plastic toys left on the lawn from the children's visit this weekend. She gathers them all up, cursing as she scrapes her leg against the wheel of a tricycle. She throws the toys into the small shed and pulls the door shut. More debris is left on the floor in the living room, and she feels her temper rising at the sight. She is learning to love the children, but it's hard when they leave so much mess behind, spoiling the look of her new home.

Tom is due home in an hour and she decides to cook something special. He was in a strange mood at the weekend when he returned from running the children back to Rachel. Heidi hates the fact that they are forever going to be linked with Rachel due to the sharing arrangement they've agreed on. She's made it quite clear that she doesn't want anything to do with the woman, so Tom does all the fetching and collecting himself.

She showers and changes and freshens up her make-up. The mirror reflects her pretty twenty-four-year-old face back at her. No Botox for her – starting too early is not recommended – so she takes good care of her skin with specialist treatments, making sure she's using the most advanced skin creams and make-up. Her youth is the best advantage she has against Tom's wife, and she intends to preserve her looks. She fetches a bottle of water from the fridge and takes her book outside to read while she waits for Tom.

'What's the matter, Tom?'

Heidi puts down the paperback she's attempting to read – an impulse buy from WHSmith, the number two in the top ten latest must-reads display; apparently it's a heart-warming love story but she can't get past the first page. Her own love story isn't running as smoothly as she would like. Tom barely spoke during dinner and she knows something's bothering him. It's bothering her too, and has been for the last few weeks. This week has been on a different scale altogether. He's been off with her since Sunday, and she still feels the sting from when he removed her hand from his thigh and turned his back on her last night in bed. 'Too tired,' he mumbled.

Never mind that this evening, when she came in exhausted from work, she had to spend an hour clearing up after the children. *His* children. Not hers, not yet. Little Lara is melting her heart and she loved her the moment she set eyes on her. Josh has taken longer to win over, but there's been a recent breakthrough. She'll get there, no matter how long it takes.

Tom looks up from his phone. 'Nothing. Why do you ask?'

'You've changed. I thought moving here would make you happy – look how successful the weekend was, the children loved it. Even Josh, I knew he'd come round in the end.'

'I'm just busy, that's all. I've got a lot on my mind.'

Heidi wants to ask about Saturday. She felt hurt when he said he wanted to take the children out for the day without her. They went for a picnic in the park, where the kids paddled in a stream. Heidi admits she isn't a great fan of roughing it, but she'd bought a pair of outdoor boots especially, determined to make their new family work. Saying she couldn't come was like a slap on the face, and it's still smarting, as if a red stripe is visible on her cheek. It might as well be. Living in her new home isn't meant to be like this.

She didn't want to be *that* woman, the one who gripes and nags, so she bit back her displeasure and spent the day arranging the bedroom with the new furnishings she'd purchased. Dressing the flat made her feel better, and she cooked a nice dinner for when Tom returned; she knew he'd be hungry. But he didn't get back until ten, texting her to say he and Rachel had to discuss some legal documents to do with the divorce, and they might as well get it over with. She didn't like to imagine the two of them in the cosy living room in their house, snug on the sofa with the lamps down low, discussing papers over a glass of wine.

'You haven't told me about your conversation with Rachel.'

Tom looks puzzled.

'Saturday night? You can't have forgotten; you were with her for ages.' Without details, her imagination runs riot.

A shadow flickers across Tom's face. 'There's nothing to tell. We had a conversation about the kids, the usual stuff. There's nothing you need to worry about.'

'I'm worried about *you*. You haven't been yourself for a while now.'

'Leave it, Heidi. I've had a hard day at work and I don't need this when I get home.'

'You're regretting it already, aren't you? Agreeing to buy the house – admit it, you've been reluctant all along.'

'Now you're imagining things. Just leave it.'

Heidi wants to tell him how hurt she was on Saturday when she had to stay at home, especially as she's made this breakthrough with Lara. The previous night, after Tom had read the children their stories and tucked them into bed, he crashed out on the sofa during the film they were supposedly watching, and Heidi snuck upstairs and stood in the doorway watching the two of them sleep. Stars glowed on the ceiling; Lara lay on her back, as if she'd fallen asleep gazing at them, her eyelashes fluttering. Josh was on his side, head turned towards the dim lamp that glowed in the corner of the room. This room had taken Heidi the longest to decorate, as she wanted to get it exactly right. Watching the children, she experienced a rush of love so strong and unexpected she had to grip hold of the door frame to keep herself steady. Everything was coming together. The man, the first step on the property ladder, and now the children. She almost had everything she wanted.

TWENTY-NINE

HEIDI

PRESENT DAY

The smell from the bakery makes Heidi stop walking and look in the window. Buttery croissants are heaped on a plate. Usually after yoga she stops at the juice bar for a smoothie and some overnight oats; today she decides to be impulsive. A thought jumps into her head: she could buy one for Rachel and take it round; they could sit out in the pretty garden and try to ignore the sound of the builders on the scaffolding above. She decides against it.

She buys a croissant and a large coffee and takes them over to a bench under some trees. Flakes of pastry fall on her lap as she savours the taste and watches people go by. Three girls in school uniform walk past the bakery, stopping at the window display, laughing and pushing one another before they carry on down the road. The bottle-green uniform is the one Lara wears, belonging to the high school in town. Heidi is furious that Rachel has cancelled the lessons and wonders if she's done something to upset her. She thought they were getting on well.

As if in response to her thoughts, her phone buzzes and she

wipes her greasy fingers on a serviette before reading the message. It's from Rachel. Shame she's missed out on a croissant.

> *Apologies again that I had to cancel the maths lessons for the foreseeable. Thanks so much for everything you've done for Lara. We appreciate it. :)*

Heidi wants to erase the smiley-face emoji, the inane grin tormenting her. The text that has an ominous air of finality about it. She clicks the button to call Rachel back. The phone rings until it switches to voicemail.

She picks up the paper bag from the bakery and crushes it in her fist. The satisfied fullness she felt after the croissant is replaced with the frustration she feels at not being able to visit the house again, chatting with Rachel, helping Lara, seeing the girl's delight. She clicks on Lara's name and reads through their WhatsApp messages, pictures the way Lara lights up when she sees Heidi, when Heidi pays her attention and shows an interest in her. She's begun confiding in her, and she's at such a vulnerable age that Heidi withdrawing her support won't be good for her. She won't understand.

She abandons the trip into town, where she was planning to drop her CV off, instead heading back home. She's overreacting. Even if the lessons are cancelled, it doesn't mean their friendship is over, or that she can't continue seeing Lara. Persuading Lara to keep it from her mother could be tricky, but if it works, Heidi can be her surrogate auntie. The thought perks her up.

Heidi decides to wait for Rachel to get back to her, but she doesn't. Rachel has never not answered her texts before. The suspicion that she's being rebuffed grows. She wonders if

Rachel suspects she's behind the notes. Receiving a call from Danny doesn't help.

'Pete's had a bloody heart attack.'

'No. That doesn't stop you going round, surely? She'll want the work finished.'

'That's what Pete's wife told me. Down tools, instructions from the boss. It's best anyway, she almost caught me the other day. That's why I haven't managed to hide the will yet as we planned.'

'What do you mean?'

'I was coming out of her bedroom and she came up behind me. Frightened the life out of me.'

'What about the daughter? Have you got anywhere with her?'

'Not yet, but I've had an idea. Text me her number.'

'What for? What are you going to do?'

'Maybe it's time for us to give Rachel more of a scare. Shall I come over later?'

'No, not tonight. I'll be in touch.'

Maybe Rachel has sent the notes to the police. Is this why she's keeping her distance? Heidi empties the waste-paper basket in her sitting room and flattens out the failed attempts at the forgery she's discarded. Then she runs them through her paper shredder, her decision to buy an extra-secure model justified, crossing and slicing through the offending writing. Once it's done, she jumps in her car and takes the bag of shreddings to the nearby dump, hurling it into a container along with tons of rubbish deposited there.

Back home, she checks her calendar where she writes down reminders to herself. Only the cancelled lesson with Lara is marked for this evening. She takes a black pen and scrawls a cross through it, pressing down hard. She can't help picturing the scene as it would have been – should have been. Lara next to her at the end of the table, her brow furrowed as she deliber-

ates the maths puzzle, Heidi feeling comfortable in the large
kitchen that smells of coffee and cooking and makes her feel like
she's sitting in her family home – a family she hasn't managed to
create for herself yet. Self-pity and frustration at her circumstances put her in a bad mood. When Rachel asked her
yesterday about dating and relationships she'd had since Tom,
she laughed it off, implying she wasn't short of admirers, but the
truth is, the only man who's stuck around in her life is Danny,
and thinking about him raises many conflicting emotions in her,
few of them good.

When Rachel's name lights up the screen of her phone later
that evening, she's relieved both to hear from her and to be
taken away from the dreadful sitcom that isn't making her
laugh. Relieved that Rachel isn't shunning her and cutting her
out of her life.

'Hey, Rachel.'

'Have you seen Lara since we spoke yesterday?' Rachel's
voice is breathy, as if she's been exercising.

'No.' The cross on the calendar taunts her from the wall.
'I'm not teaching her any more, so I wasn't expecting to see her.'

'Have you heard from her at all? She hasn't come home yet
and I'm worried.'

Heidi checks the time. It's past ten o'clock. Late for a
twelve-year-old, she imagines, although she's no expert on
teenagers and their domestic habits.

'Where did she go?'

'I thought she'd gone to the cinema, but...'

'I'm sure she'll be fine. You must be so worried. Shall I come
over?'

'No. Look, I've got to go.' She hangs up.

Heidi wants to know details. Was Lara on her own? Has she
disappeared walking home? The cinema isn't far from a path
through a wooded area. People use it as a shortcut all the time.
But a young girl, late at night... Lara isn't streetwise, she's not

even a teenager, and she's young for her age. Heidi is tempted to grab her coat and go out looking for her.

She's being absurd.

She tries to call Rachel back, but the phone is engaged. No doubt she's ringing anyone who might possibly know where Lara might have gone. Has she called the police, invited them into her home, told them that a second person in her life has gone missing? Heidi thinks of Danny. He's the sort of man you want in a situation like this, strong and hands-on; he'd drive his van around, lead a search of volunteers, because that's what he did last time, after Tom vanished. But Heidi can't involve Danny. She doesn't want Rachel to know about the connection between them.

She's pacing about, only now realising how fond she has become of Lara. As a little girl, it took her a while to warm to Heidi, but once she did, she grabbed hold of her and wouldn't let go until her mother prised her away and made her forget. The twelve-year-old Lara is old enough to make up her own mind, and she knows Heidi is important to her; she's the mother figure she's never had. Anyone can see Rachel doesn't understand her daughter.

Heidi scrolls through her messages with Lara. Initially solely about maths, they developed into Lara asking questions about make-up and clothes and Instagram, trying to understand social media. Heidi was educating her on the pitfalls, the traps young people can fall into. She was advising her on her blog about her father, which was strangely satisfying, keeping his memory alive for her. She can't help feeling angry that Rachel couldn't see that she was good for Lara, she was helping her. Everyone knows teenagers don't want to confide in their mothers.

But there's no evidence in the messages that Lara is unhappy, or thinking of running away, which Heidi would find more acceptable than the alternative of being snatched from the street or causing harm to herself. She opens her emails to check that Lara hasn't been in touch, and sees one from an unknown sender that has gone directly into her spam account. She opens the email and her pulse speeds up as she realises it's from Lara.

Mum doesn't know I'm sending this. I'm furious because she says I can't have lessons with you any more. She knows I hate school and I can't learn maths there and I want you to keep helping me. Can you change her mind for me? She also says not to contact you, but she can't tell me that – it's not as if you've done anything wrong and that's why she doesn't want you teaching me. It doesn't make sense. She should be pleased I'm making such good progress. Even Mr Graham said I might be able to move up a group next year. Please can you try and ask her to change her mind? I've got some pocket money I can use if you need paying.

Also Heidi I like seeing you. You get me in a way that none of my teachers do. Plus you have a connection to my dad. I like the chats we have. I don't have many friends and I want to keep talking to you. Please Heidi.

Lara

P.S. My mum is so annoying. She doesn't understand me and all she cares about is my stupid grades. She doesn't like me trying to find out about what happened to my dad either. There was a piece of news today. Have a look at my blog post where I've written about it. I've been listening to what you said and adding to it regularly. After the programme about missing people they did a piece on Crimewatch *and somebody phoned in and said they'd seen a person acting suspiciously near where my dad was last seen. It was someone driving a blue car. I know there must be millions of blue cars driving around, but I want to follow*

*this lead. You could help me and Mum doesn't need to
know.*

Heidi checks to see when the email was sent. Two days ago.
She's annoyed with herself for not seeing it earlier. If she'd
reached out to Lara... She wonders about calling Rachel again to
see if there has been any news, but there's nothing in the email
that could have any bearing on Lara's whereabouts. Next, she
goes to Lara's blog, which she's added quite a bit to since she
first showed it to Heidi. She clicks on the *Crimewatch* link and
reads the report. She was hoping that somehow Lara had got her
information wrong, but she hasn't. A man called while the
programme was on air to report the suspicious car.

Heidi wonders about the caller and how you could possibly
remember a detail like that so many years later. Unless an event
of significance happens to make a day stand out, nobody really
remembers what happens from one day to the next. She imagines a sad little man, trying to make himself feel important by
getting a mention on television before he returns to his frozen
meal for one and wonders what other stories he can tell, whose
lives he can meddle in. She imagines him hitching up his too-big
trousers as he stares out of the window, half listening to the
programme while watching a blue car go by. Imagining a
fantasy in his head. Then picking up the phone and trying to
make it real.

Blue cars are everywhere, and it will be an impossible task
to track down that car: the make, the age, the registration
number.

The owner.

At least that's what Heidi hopes. She hasn't thought for
years about the blue Nissan Micra she was driving on the day
Tom vanished.

THIRTY

Heidi returns her attention to Lara's email. There is no mention of the maths course at school, the reason Rachel gave for cancelling the lessons. She doesn't buy into the money excuse; besides, she offered to teach the classes for free and Rachel turned her down. If she was a real friend, she wouldn't have done that. There's a reason she wants to keep Heidi away from Lara, and Heidi is now convinced she must know about the notes. That would make far more sense. What if she's come up with some kind of evidence? If she knows Heidi is behind the notes, she will be wondering what she is going to do next. If she goes to the police and the notes are proved to be a forgery, she'll assume that Tom really is dead and the house will finally be hers. Danny is right: it's time to act before it's too late, and for that she needs him, but not tonight – she can't face the inevitable guilt that seeing him sets off in her.

Another night of television on her own beckons, and she flicks through the channels, unable to decide what she's in the mood for. It's so hard to settle not knowing whether Lara has come home. She decides on a drama, but the first scene, set in a cosy kitchen with a happy two-adult two-children family, has her switching over. She can't help picturing Rachel's kitchen, Lara's seat empty, the agony she must be going through not knowing where she is.

She hates to think of Lara out there on the streets, needing help but not daring to reach out to anyone. Perhaps Rachel should know about her email after all. It shows Lara's frame of mind, and anything that might help shed light on her recent thought processes will be important. She knows that much from the investigation into Tom's disappearance. But what if Rachel refuses to take her call? The way she cut her off earlier when she offered to go round reinforces her belief that Rachel wants to keep her at a distance, away from the children. Maybe she's jealous of Lara's obvious attachment to Heidi, and that's why she's cut her off – nothing to do with the anonymous notes at all. Heidi has a spike of adrenaline at these thoughts; this is far more plausible a solution. But the most important thing is Rachel needing to know about Lara's emotional state. She reaches for her mobile.

The doorbell rings and she freezes. It's the police, come to question her about Lara. Or the notes. Or it's Danny, though he never turns up without warning, he always texts her first. It rings again, less forcefully this time, and she goes to open the door.

Lara stands on the doorstep, her shoulders damp with rain-drops, a hood over her head, a holdall at her side. Heidi didn't realise it was raining, she's been so absorbed by her thoughts. Lara's face is pale against the dark of the night. Heidi reaches out her arm to bring her in and Lara bursts into tears, reminding Heidi that she is still a child.

'Come in, let's get you into the warm.' She guides Lara into the living room. 'I'll get you something dry to wear and make you a hot drink, and you can tell me what's going on.'

Lara sits in the armchair and Heidi runs to her bedroom to grab a sweatshirt. She helps Lara out of her wet hoodie and makes her some hot chocolate while Lara puts the sweatshirt on. She wants to make sure she's OK before she rings Rachel, and she also doesn't want to scare Lara away by immediately mentioning her mother.

'Are you hurt?' she asks, pulling up a chair so their knees are almost touching. Lara's legs are shaking, and Heidi fetches a blanket to wrap around them. 'Drink this,' she says, handing her the mug. 'It will warm you up.'

Lara shakes her head. 'I didn't know whether you would let me in,' she says. She's stretching the sleeves of the sweatshirt over her hands, as if to protect her.

'Of course I would. What are you doing out so late? Your mum is worried, she rang me.'

Lara's expression darkens. 'I don't want to go home.'

'I won't make you do anything right away, but I will have to call your mother and let her know where you are.'

'Please don't call her. She'll make me go home and I don't want to. She'll force me to go back to that school, and I can't do it any more.' She's crying now, wiping tears away from her face, which are immediately replaced by a fresh set. 'You helped me understand maths, and now she says you can't teach me and she's taking away the one thing that was good in my life. And she doesn't like me asking questions about Dad or anything I do. It would be so much better for her if I wasn't there any more. Then she can just have Josh, who does everything right and is going to be a star. I love him, but he makes me look even worse and I'm supposed to be the eldest, and I'm just useless and...' She breaks down into sobs and Heidi puts her arms around her.

'Shh, you must never say that. You're a wonderful human being. I was gutted about the lessons too and I'm going to do my best to make your mother change her mind.'

Lara listens, her eyelids drooping with tiredness.

'You're exhausted, and it's late. I think you should go and have a sleep in the spare room – I'll make up a bed for you.

Then I'll ring your mum and tell her you're fine and you're staying the night, and we'll talk again in the morning. OK? You know I have to tell her; you're an intelligent girl and it would be wrong of me not to put her out of her misery. She'll be going out of her mind with worry. Whatever you think, she loves you, anyone can see that. We can talk to her together when you're in a better frame of mind.'

'OK,' Lara says, sniffing.

'Drink your hot chocolate and I'll sort the bed out. I'll leave out a pair of pyjamas you can sleep in.'

Heidi prepares the room and pops back in to see Lara when she's ready for bed.

'How did you know where I lived?' she asks her. Lara is lying in the same position she did as a small child, and Heidi feels the same tender feeling she used to get then at how vulnerable she looks. When she plotted to get access to the house, she didn't expect the added bonus of rekindling her affection for Tom's daughter.

'Mum's ancient address book. This is the flat I came to, isn't it?'

'Yes, a few times. We never got to move into the house as we'd planned.' Heidi strokes her hair. 'Get some sleep. You'll feel much better in the morning, and we'll have a proper talk then.'

'Thanks, Heidi.' Lara's eyes brim with tears.

Heidi kisses her on the forehead. 'Shall I leave the hall light on?'

'You remembered?'

'Yes. Sweet dreams.'

Heidi is sitting in the kitchen wondering what exactly she will say to Rachel when her phone buzzes with a text. It's from Danny.

I'm outside your flat.

She gets up and peers out of the window. A cigarette tip glows in the darkness, and as her eyes adjust, she makes out Danny's tall figure on the path, his car parked on the street behind him. She goes into the communal area and opens the front door, shivering at the cold, damp air. Light from the hall makes the rain from earlier glisten.

'Danny! What are you doing here?' She's whispering.

'I need to speak to you – it's urgent.'

She bristles at how loud his voice is, carrying through the night air. Most of the houses are already in darkness, the street is quiet, and she doesn't want to wake Lara.

'What's with all the secret squirrel stuff?' he asks, taking his jacket off and leaving it in the hall. 'Got a job as a librarian?' He chuckles as he goes into the living room, and she closes the door. He looks surprised. 'Am I interrupting something?'

'No, but keep your voice down. You know what the neighbours are like around here.'

He goes through to the kitchen and helps himself to a beer. 'Want one?'

She shakes her head. 'Help yourself, why don't you.'

'What's up with you? You're not normally like this. You seem edgy.'

'It's late and I need some sleep. I've had a busy evening.'

'You're seeing someone, aren't you?' He looks at the door. 'Have you got a bloke here?'

'No, but so what if I had. We're not exactly exclusive.'

'Fair point,' he says. 'Sit down, will you, you're making me nervous.'

'What's so urgent?' Heidi sits on the armchair, avoiding the spot he indicates next to him on the sofa.

'I need some money.'

'How much?'

'A thousand.'

'I haven't got that kind of money. I lost my job.'

'You got the sack?'

'No, of course not. I was made redundant.'

'Same result.'

'Come on, Danny, I'm tired and I want to go to bed. You can't just turn up demanding money.'

'But we both know that I can.'

'I don't have it.'

'Then find it.' He tips the bottle and drains it, then belches. Heidi flinches. Whatever did she see in him? 'You'd be very stupid if you were trying to double-cross me. I don't see how you can, though, because I know you'll never tell her about our little deal. Get me the money and there won't be any need for me to pay her a visit.'

'You mean...'

'Stop playing dumb. You know exactly what I mean. If you've got no money, then we need to proceed with the plan. Get rid of her and you've got more chance of getting the house.'

'You wouldn't.'

He stares at her unblinking. 'I thought this was what you wanted. You can't back out now; you're involved just as much as I am.'

'But we haven't had time to plant the will yet. That's crucial.' Maybe when she takes Lara back, she'll get a chance then.

'We'll think of something.'

As he puts his hands on the arm of the chair to lever himself up, there's a crash from the spare room. He jumps to his feet.

'I knew there was someone here.'

'Danny, wait.' Heidi grabs his arm.

THIRTY-ONE

Heidi can feel Danny's muscles tightening under her hand where she's gripping his forearm. He could shake her off like a fly should he so wish. Possibilities of what she could tell him flit through her head, but time is not on her side and she can't have Danny frightening Lara. Besides, he knows too much about her recent movements. She decides to tell him the truth.

'Sit down, it's not what you think.' A floorboard creaks, Lara returning from the bathroom, she guesses. She holds her breath, willing her not to come into the living room.

'Who is it?'

'It's not a man. It's Tom and Rachel's daughter. Lara.'

Danny ignores her instruction to sit and paces the floor, shaking his head.

'What? What are you up to? Have I got this all wrong? I thought we were in this together. We agreed we were going to make her pay. Look at you, you've got no money, while she's building a new extension on a house that should be yours. What's going on?'

'This isn't how it looks. I've been helping Lara with some homework. She got into an argument with her mother and turned up here unexpectedly. It was late and I thought it was best if she stayed the night. That's all this is; there's nothing sinister going on. I need to let Rachel know where she is, she'll be going frantic by now.'

'I'm impressed you got friendly with her so quickly.'

'Your plan is working. It's much better if we both have access to the house.'

Danny is nodding now. He leans back in the chair and stretches his legs out.

'As long as you're not getting too friendly; I don't want you double-crossing me, getting too pally with her, maybe spilling our secrets.'

'I would never do that.'

'I know you wouldn't. You know what would happen to you if you did.' He holds her gaze and his cold eyes cause her to shiver. 'Let me think.' He steeples his hands together, flexing his fingers. 'I've got it. We use the kid.'

The chill Heidi is experiencing spreads through her body. No matter what she's done, she doesn't want anything to happen to Lara. Lara needs her, and Heidi hasn't been needed by another person in such a long time. Apart from Danny, but he only needs her silence.

'No.'

'Hear me out. We won't hurt her, but we can use her to put our plan into action.'

'What do you mean?'

'This is what we'll do. We'll text the mother, tell her we've got her daughter. Then we'll tell her our demands.'

'It's too risky. Why can't we let it lie? This way everything might come out into the open. The police will be all over the hunt for Lara.' She can't believe she's saying these words aloud.

'You've lost your focus. Remember what he did to you, and what happened to you afterwards. How *she* got everything. If we play this right, warn her what will happen to the girl if she goes to the police, she'll give in immediately, give you back what is rightfully yours.'

Heidi bites down on her lip; she doesn't know what to do. But he's right, she has lost her focus, allowing Rachel and her children to get under her skin. The injustice of her situation spurs her on to make a decision.

'You're right, let's do it.'

'Good girl. Listen to my instructions and do exactly as I say. Text Rachel from my burner phone, tell her we've got her daughter and that she's not to go to the police or else the kid gets hurt, and that we'll be in touch in the morning. You have to act normal with the kid, everything depends on that. I've got some-where in mind to take her, but you'll need to get her phone off her. That should be easy enough while she's asleep. And slip a couple of these sleeping tablets in her drink before we leave so she sleeps in the car.' He takes a blister pack of tablets out of his pocket. 'Got that?'

Heidi nods.

'Come and sit here,' he says. 'You look like you need a little reassurance.' He takes her wrist and pulls her down next to him, puts his hand on the back of her neck, looks into her eyes. He kisses her, hard. 'Don't look so worried.'

'I'm scared, Danny. So much could go wrong. Promise me you won't hurt Lara.'

'She's got to you, hasn't she?'

She shrugs. 'I'm human, aren't I? She hasn't done anything wrong.'

'And as long as the mother plays ball, she'll be fine. Best go and get the phone while she's asleep.'

'OK.' Heidi sighs and gets to her feet. 'Don't worry, Danny, I'm just tired. I know what I'm doing.'

'I know, babe. You don't have a choice after all, do you?'

THIRTY-TWO

RACHEL

'Are you absolutely sure?' Freddie has his phone poised, a call away from setting a whole machine in motion, questioning, searching, waiting. They're in the bedroom, Lara's wardrobe door open, only a shoebox on the floor.

'Yes, look, it's normally here.' Rachel pushes the clothes to one side, metal coat hangers banging against wood, releasing the smell of washing powder and something indefinable that is her daughter. Dust surrounds a rectangular shape where the bag has been stored. She inhales deeply and closes her eyes.

'Call the police.'

Freddie is about to dial when Rachel's phone beeps with a text.

'Wait, it might be her.' She reads the message and sinks onto the bed, the phone slipping from her hands.

'Who is it?' Freddie asks.

'I don't recognise the number.'

His face pales when he reads the message.

We have Lara. If you go to the police her life will be in danger.
Keep quiet and she will be unhurt.

Rachel can't stop shaking, as if a current of electricity has taken hold in her body, causing her to vibrate. Freddie kneels in front of her and holds her hands.

'Breathe,' he says. 'Deep breaths in and out. You've had a terrible shock.'

Rachel grips hold of his hands and never wants to let go. She can't imagine life without her daughter. The thought of her being harmed, in pain, is a physical hurt, and she lets out a cry that turns into sobs.

'Don't call the police,' she says. 'We can't risk it. I will never forgive myself if she comes to harm.'

'The police will be used to this scenario, they'll know what to do. We could be getting ourselves into danger.'

'I don't care about that, I only care about Lara.'

'These are dangerous people. I'm not sure we can deal with them on our own. Taking this on by ourselves is a risky thing to do. You must have seen those television dramas where avoiding the police causes everything to go wrong further down the line.'

'This isn't drama, it's real life. *My* life.' Rachel looks at Freddie and holds his gaze. 'I am not going to call the police. This is my daughter, my decision.'

A flicker of hurt runs through his eyes, followed by a nod.

'I understand. OK, whatever you decide, it's up to you. But let's keep reviewing it. Every minute will count.'

'Which is why we must stop talking about the police. I need to reply to this text.' She opens the message and they both look at the screen. 'Should I try calling?'

'Yes.'

She presses the call button and holds her breath as the tone rings out over and over. Eventually she hears that *the caller is not available at this time.*

'Send a text message instead,' Freddie says. 'Let them know you're complying with their demands.'

Rachel hesitates, then types: *I won't go to the police. Tell me what you want.*

She looks to Freddie for confirmation and he nods. She presses send, then stares at the phone, willing it to light up with a message, a call, anything to let her know what is happening to Lara. Her baby.

Images haunt her mind. Her daughter locked in a cellar, chained to a bed, being dragged off the street and into a car. Or she arranged to meet someone online only to find they weren't who they said they were, and now she's been taken somewhere against her will, or worse... She won't let her mind go there, can't bear to comprehend her little girl being assaulted. She should have asked more questions when Lara said she was going to the cinema.

'Rachel, you're shaking again.' Freddie strips off his sweatshirt and wraps it around her shoulders, pulling her to him, trying to stop her body from juddering.

'They're not going to reply, are they? What if they don't? What can we do? I can't bear this.' She pushes him away and shrugs the sweatshirt from her shoulders. 'I can't just sit here wrapped up like an old woman, I have to do something.' She paces around in circles, then stops.

'Money, they're going to ask for money, aren't they?' Her eyes fill with tears. 'I'm not going to have enough, I'm not a millionaire. I have a bit left that was for the builders, but what if it's not enough?'

'Try not to second-guess them. It will just make you more stressed. All we can do is wait.'

'No, we have to be prepared. If they're going to make a sudden demand for cash, then I need to get it ready for them.'

'They'll know you'll need time to get it out – nobody has huge sums of cash lying around. If it comes to it, I have some money, and we'll see what we can do. Are you sure you don't want to ring the police, though? They'll know exactly what we should do, and—'

He's interrupted by the sound of the phone, alerting them to a text message. Rachel snatches it up.

'It's them.' She reads it first, and then shows it to Freddie.

Drive in the direction of Underdale Hill. Come alone. You are being watched. If you bring anyone, Lara will not be safe. Tell no one. Further instructions will arrive by text when you are nearer your destination.

She swallows down the lump that has lodged in her throat and draws on her inner strength. She has to step up for Lara. She will get in her car alone, and she will go and save her daughter. She will do whatever it takes to keep her safe.

'I'm coming with you,' Freddie says.

'No.' She finds her car keys and puts on a jacket. He watches her in silence.

'You can't do this alone; you could be walking into a trap. Let me drive behind you. I'll be discreet, I promise. These are dangerous people.'

'Do you know who they are?'

'No!' His shoulders slump. 'How could you ask that? Nobody takes a child without being dangerous or disturbed. It's an unpredictable situation you're heading into, and that scares me. I'm frightened for you as well as Lara.'

'I can look after myself.'

Her phone beeps with another message, and she jumps before opening it with trembling fingers.

Leave the house and get in the car now.

She gasps. 'They really are watching. They know I haven't left yet.'

'We don't know that for sure. Please let me come with you.'

'No. Don't try and stop me, Freddie, and don't follow me. If you do, I will never speak to you again.'

THIRTY-THREE

The car radio blares out when Rachel turns the key in the ignition, and she snaps the dial to off. She doesn't need that interfering with all the other horrors that are swirling around in her head. She programmes the satnav for Underdale Hill. She knows roughly where it is, but it's not an area she's familiar with. It's at the far edge of the town, where the roads become narrower and darker as the trees loom up on either side, as if pressing down on you and making you feel small beneath them.

She drives through streets that are still busy with people streaming out of pubs and restaurants. She wishes she was one of them, able to relax and enjoy eating out with friends. It's hard to believe it was only a few days ago that she was doing that very thing with Freddie. Automatically she glances in her mirror, to check he isn't following, but the road is empty behind her. She hates herself for the way she was forced to speak to him, pushing him away when she's been dreaming of something happening between them. His concern for her shows he cares, and she's relieved that at least he knows where she's heading, should she fail to come back.

Drive to Blackberry Farm.

Her stomach drops when she sees the message. She has no idea how far away this farm is. Her mind is scrambled and she forces herself to focus. She pulls over in a lay-by to enter the address into the satnav, not trusting herself to do it while she's driving. She's shaking as if all the windows are open, blowing the cold night air in. Something raps on the back window and she lets out a cry, twisting her neck awkwardly as she swivels round to see what it is. A branch is knocking against the glass, and she lets out a breath of relief. A car drives past in the other direction, the headlamps lighting up the inside of her own vehicle momentarily before she is plunged back into semi-darkness.

She sets off again, driving faster now, anxious to get off this lonely road. What lies ahead may not be any better, but she has to get to her daughter, find a way to save her. As she follows the twisty lane, she tries to make sense of the motivation behind this kidnapping, given that she hasn't been asked for any ransom money. What else can they be after? The sense of unease she has felt since the notes arrived through the letter box is magnified, and she can't help wondering whether the two are related somehow. Her life was ordinary until Tom met Heidi.

Heidi. Is she somehow involved? She banishes this suggestion immediately. Heidi likes Lara, she can tell from the way she interacts with her, the disappointment when she told her she was cancelling the lessons. She wouldn't hurt Lara.

In the mirror, she sees the glow of headlights a long way behind. It's the first car she's seen since she stopped. She presses down harder on the accelerator. The satnav makes her jump.

At the next junction, take the first left, then after fifty yards take the first right.

She cuts her speed and slows down as she comes to a small junction. The final turn is barely a road, more of a track, with scarcely any room for another vehicle to pass, and the car bumps along over the uneven terrain. Feeling exposed, she switches off the headlights. She needs the advantage of surprise; any help needs to be grabbed with both hands. She continues along the track for a few minutes, her anxiety growing.

Destination reached.

She switches off the engine, and peers ahead. In front of her is a five-bar gate. The track continues beyond the gate and disappears into blackness. She checks her phone: no more messages. She's loath to get out of the car, as this will mean facing whatever's out there. As her eyes adjust to the darkness, she notices a white wooden signpost behind the gate. She undoes her seat belt and gets out, closing the door softly. She leaves it unlocked, just in case she needs to get away fast. She can't help thinking she's acting like a character in a television drama, but that's exactly how she feels. This kind of thing doesn't happen to people like her. If only Freddie were with her. Thinking of him gives her strength, though, and she walks towards the gate. She is doing this for Lara, and the sooner she gets it over with, the sooner she can take her home. If it's not too late.

THIRTY-FOUR

The sign says *Public Footpath*. As Rachel unlatches the gate, a loud creak startles her. She waits until she has composed herself, and walks ahead. Another sign appears as she follows the path round to the left: *Blackberry Farm*. An arrow indicates a left turning. The wind is blowing through the trees and the damp seeps through her thin jacket. She follows the path until she sees a building take shape ahead. It is in darkness and looks too small to be a farm; it's more like a barn from what she can make out. A loud cracking sound makes her whip round: a twig under her foot. She can see the white gate looming in the dark.

It suddenly hits her that she's alone with no idea what she's heading into. She runs back to the car and opens the boot. Her gym bag is stored there, and she takes out one of the weights she uses when she exercises in the park. She empties everything else out, puts the weight back in the drawstring bag and tests it on her shoulder. Not too heavy, but heavy enough. At least she won't feel so exposed. She closes the boot softly, even though there is nobody else around, goes back through the gate and follows the path signposted to the cottage. As she nears the building, she sees that it is indeed a barn, or some kind of outbuilding. She walks around to the front of it and comes to a halt. A car is parked here, lights off. A white Fiat 500. Heidi's car.

She gasps out loud. So Heidi *is* behind all this. The realisation gives her a shot of confidence. Heidi wouldn't harm Lara, she's sure of it. And Rachel can get the better of her. She's a lioness, fighting for her cub. She grips the bag for strength to remind her she has a weapon, and looks towards the farmhouse that she can now see across from the barn. But as she does so, she becomes aware of a light shining out from the barn door, which is ajar. She hesitates – should she go to the farmhouse first? If only she knew where Lara was. Deciding that she's far more likely to be in the barn, she steps towards the open door, pulling the bag to her, slackening her shoulder so it doesn't look as if she's carrying anything heavy.

Outside the door, though, she hesitates. Should she text Freddie, let him know where she is? She slinks round to the side of the barn and types two words: *Blackberry Farm.*

'I wouldn't do that if I were you.'

Heidi's voice cuts through the darkness, and Rachel lets out a cry.

'OK, OK, I won't, I promise.' She sounds manic, trying to get the words out. She drops the phone into her pocket without pressing send and forces herself to calm down, changing the tone of her voice to sound firm. Heidi has her hands on her hips. She's dressed in jeans and a black hoodie top. She looks slight, insubstantial.

'What are you playing at, Heidi?'

'I just want to talk to you.'

Rachel laughs. 'And you thought you'd scare me out of my wits by luring me out here. Where's Lara? That's all that matters.'

'Lara is safe.'

'Let me see her.'

'She's in here.'

Heidi's feet crunch across the stony ground and Rachel follows her, eager to see her daughter, still conscious of the weight of the bag at her side. Heidi pushes the door open to reveal piles of old petrol cans, bits of wood and various items of broken furniture. Rachel's pulse is racing at the thought of seeing Lara; she just needs to know she's unhurt and not traumatised.

Inside the barn, she swivels around. She can see immediately that Lara isn't in there, and a trickle of fear creeps down her spine.

'Where is she, Heidi? What's going on?' As she speaks, she slides the bag from her shoulder, gripping it in her fist.

'She's safe, I promise you. You'll see her very soon, but first we need to talk.'

'Talk? We've been talking for the past couple of weeks. You tricked me into letting you into my house, getting close to my children. Why couldn't you say whatever it is you need to get off your chest then? This is madness. You're scaring me.' She's holding the weight in an uncomfortable position but tries not to wriggle.

Heidi has a wild look in her eyes, but as Rachel watches, her expression changes and she moves her attention to something behind her. Rachel turns to see a man standing there, and the trickle of fear turns into a wave. She's walked into a trap, and she still has no idea where Lara is.

THIRTY-FIVE

Danny is wearing black skinny jeans and a Nike jacket, a baseball cap on his head.

'I knew it.' Rachel controls her voice to stop it from shaking.

'Have you told her how well we know each other?' he asks Heidi, who scowls, dismissing him with a shake of the head. He walks to her side and slides his arm around her, all the while keeping his gaze on Rachel. 'Me and Heidi go back a long way, since well before you ever met your husband, before he became Heidi's.'

'He wasn't her husband.'

He sniggers. 'That was most probably down to me. Tom wasn't too happy when he found you'd been cheating on him, was he, babe? He should have kept quiet.'

'Shut up, Danny,' Heidi says, shrugging his arm off and stepping away from him.

Rachel is watching the pair closely. Heidi's antagonism towards him has to work in her favour. If only she'd allowed Freddie to come. The unsent text is on her phone screen, in her pocket, if only she could somehow send it. Her mind is working furiously as she wills herself to come up with a strategy to get out of this situation. If she's hurt, or worse, she won't be able to get to her daughter.

'Where's Lara?' She focuses her attention on Heidi, who is shifting around, watching Danny. She's afraid of him too. 'What's going on? Is this to do with Tom? I know you sent the notes. My neighbour's CCTV caught you on camera.'

Heidi looks off balance. 'That's why you cancelled the lessons. I knew something was up. It didn't work. Lara came to my flat. She's beginning to remember being there, I can tell, and even if she can't remember, she has an innate sense of the bond we once had; she knows we were close and she still feels it. You won't cut me out of her life, Rachel. Tom wouldn't have wanted that.'

'What do you know about Tom? Are you still in love with him, is that what this is?'

'Put her out of her misery,' Danny says. His voice is loud in the barn and Rachel shivers. If he's unstable, who knows what he will do to Lara. It's hard to focus on Tom when her daughter could be in danger. Heidi has deceived her, proved she's a liar; how can she believe anything she says? But if Tom is behind all this, she needs to know what she's dealing with.

'Is he alive? Have you been pretending all this time? You have to tell me. Did you force him to write those notes to me?' Her legs feel unsteady at the thought of finally knowing what happened to her husband. The thought is so enormous, it's hard to comprehend it's really happening. 'Tell me first, though – is Lara safe? Is she here?'

'Yes,' Heidi says, 'of course she is. She's fine. I wouldn't hurt her. She's a great kid. Josh is too. *They* haven't done anything wrong. The notes were just a little teaser, to unsettle you. Tom's handwriting is something I've had loads of practice at – did you think I was going to let you get away with getting the guardianship and Tom double-crossing me over the new will?'

'There never was a new will,' Rachel says. 'You know that. Just the wills Tom and I made together when Lara was born.'

'I know. He went back on his promise to rewrite the will and leave everything to me. He drafted it up and then changed his mind. The bastard. He promised me the house. I should be the one living there, making those alterations, not you.'

'I can't believe you're still harping on about that.'

'It's what I deserve. It must be hidden in the house somewhere. I bet you haven't even looked.'

'My solicitor told you there was no evidence of one. Is that what all this is about?'

'I know it exists. The house should be mine. Can't you see that?'

'No. It's always been mine, mine and the children's. You took my husband from me, surely that's enough?'

'He was going to leave me, though, wasn't he?' Heidi laughs, a chilling sound. 'I know you were stealing him back from me. Tom told me all about it. How he was having doubts about *us*.' She kicks her foot against the ground.

Her sudden movement alarms Rachel. Heidi sounds deranged; who knows what she is capable of?

'I want to see my daughter. Where is she? I need to know she's safe. Please let me see her.' Lara is her priority. Heidi's grievances can wait.

'Stop bleating. We'll take you to her when we're ready,' Danny says.

A scream pierces the night.

THIRTY-SIX

The three of them freeze.

'A fox,' Danny says. 'I'll go and check on the kid.'

'Lara,' Rachel says, her heart still knocking. 'What have you done to her?'

She may have lost her husband, but she won't lose her daughter. Her fingers curl around the weight through the thin nylon of the bag. She raises her arm. Fast action is required, before Danny returns. If she can just get away from Heidi...

Something heavy thumps into her back and she stumbles forward, landing on the floor. The weight drops from her hand. A foot is pressing down on her back, and she struggles to breathe, looking up to see Danny standing over her.

'That was a stupid move,' he says.

She tries to sit up, but he is too strong for her.

'I can't breathe,' she gasps.

He lifts the pressure of his foot and she heaves herself into a sitting position. He keeps his foot on her hip and she daren't try and get up.

'You made a mistake there, going for Heidi. We go back a long, long way, me and Heidi. Nobody hurts my girl.'

'I need to see Lara. Why have you got her phone number? What have you done to her? I don't care what you do to me, but I have to know she isn't hurt.' Despite Heidi's earlier assurances, Rachel no longer trusts her. She will say anything to calm the situation, but there's no way she is giving up while her daughter is still in danger.

'Get up,' Danny says, digging his foot into her ribs, making her cry out in pain. 'The phone number was just to wind you up, put you off the scent of what Heidi was up to. First you need to see your husband.'

She struggles to her feet. 'He's here?'

Danny ignores her question. 'And then, if you do what I say, we'll take you to your daughter. She's in the farmhouse.'

Silver flecks dance around Rachel's eyes as the blood rushes to her head at the sudden movement. She lurches towards Danny, who grips her arm and drags her out of the barn.

Outside, it's windy and her jacket blows around her. Danny pulls her along and she can hear Heidi's footsteps following them. Ahead, the farmhouse is lit up. Rachel prays that Danny is telling the truth and that Lara is safe in the kitchen, drinking a cup of tea at the table. This image is obliterated by one of her tied up on the floor, struggling and crying, and she lets out an involuntary sob. Her phone is in her pocket with the pre-typed message for Freddie, but she can't get it without drawing attention to herself, and Danny is dragging her along so fast, it's hard to stay upright, let alone anything else.

'Hurry up,' he says, leading her past the farmhouse towards a piece of land that backs onto a forest. He is walking even faster now and Heidi's footsteps behind them quicken too. Suddenly he stops.

'I forgot the spade,' he says to Heidi. 'Can you fetch it from the car?'

Rachel freezes. Are they going to kill her, here in the forest? Or Tom? Have they been keeping him captive? Would they reunite her with him only to snatch him away from her? Or is the spade for Lara? Lara's face swims into her vision – she won't let them hurt her without seeing her daughter again.

She pulls against Danny's hold.

'Heidi, please, help me. Don't let him do this. I'm sure we can work something out.'

Danny pushes her forward. 'Shut up. You're making this worse for yourself. Get the spade, Heidi, and hurry up. Rachel's been waiting a long time for this.'

Heidi turns and walks back towards the car.

'Heidi,' Rachel calls out again, desperate not to be left alone with Danny. Her arm is smarting from the tightness of his grip. But Heidi's footsteps fade away, and she disappears around the side of the barn.

Danny pulls at her, and she gives in, concentrating on keeping her balance as she stumbles along at his side.

'You're going to be doing some digging,' he says. 'We've got some treasure buried in the forest, and you're going to find it.'

THIRTY-SEVEN

HEIDI

Present day

Heidi looks back over her shoulder and watches Danny drag Rachel towards the woods. Satisfied that he's got control of the situation, she hurries to the car. She can't help glancing up at the spare room window as she passes the farmhouse, where a chink of light slides under the blind. Lara was fast asleep when they arrived, after Heidi had slipped a sleeping tablet into her milk, and Danny carried her up into the bedroom. Heidi was uncomfortable with the idea of locking her in the room, but he insisted it was the safest option. She wouldn't come to any harm, and they didn't want her interrupting proceedings while they were in the woods.

Heidi feels energised after having lost it with Rachel. Putting into words the resentments that have built up over the past seven years was a cathartic experience. The sooner they get this over with, the better. She opens the boot and extracts the spade, placing it on the ground before slamming the boot shut. As she turns round, she screams at the sight of a man in front of her. He puts his hand over her mouth.

'Be quiet. I won't hurt you.'

He looks familiar, and Heidi's mind is racing as she tries to place him. Tom, something to do with Tom, and then she recognises him as Freddie, Tom's business partner.

'Let me go.' She wriggles, and he removes his hand from her mouth but puts his foot on the spade.

'Where's Rachel?'

'I don't know what you're talking about.'

'Yes you do. I know she's here because I followed her.'

Heidi hesitates.

'Heidi.' Danny's voice rings out like a shot in the darkness. 'Hurry up.'

'Who's that?' Freddie asks.

Heidi doesn't say anything. Freddie picks up the spade and points it at her face. 'Take me to him. I want to know where you're going with this spade and what you plan to do with it.'

'Stay out of this, you don't want to get involved.'

'It's too late for that. I care about Rachel and Lara. Besides, I've called the police and they're on their way. You can put a stop to this before they get here. I knew Rachel was walking into a trap, and I've been warning her against you. People don't change, not fundamentally. I saw how you got your claws into Tom and refused to let go, I just wish he'd listened to me. Now move.'

Heidi has no choice but to lead him to Danny. She doubts Freddie will be a match for him.

THIRTY-EIGHT

RACHEL

Present day

Rachel's body is shaking and there is nothing she can do about it. Light disappears as they get further into the wood, and terror clutches at her throat. Her arm throbs and she almost loses her shoe as Danny pulls her along. She can't decide whether she's better off with or without Heidi's presence. Is Heidi really capable of keeping Tom captive? Is Rachel about to see her husband again after seven years? Her legs feel like jelly.

Danny comes to a halt. Rachel looks behind her to make sure she can recognise the path they took; she's determined to get away from this man. The farmhouse is pulling her like a magnet, she's so convinced Lara is inside. If only she'd let Freddie come with her. She could have hidden him in the back seat and she wouldn't be so helpless now, failing her daughter.

Danny has stopped near two sturdy trees. Something dark lies between the two thick trunks, and as they get close, Rachel realises it's a hole, recently dug, the black earth piled up around the sides.

'No,' she cries, pulling against Danny's grip as hard as she can. Her left foot slides from under her, her ankle twists with a sickening pain and she's on the floor.

Danny stands over her, his face menacing; above him, the branches of a huge horse chestnut obscure the sky and cut out the dim light.

'Get up.' He pulls at her, and she cries out as she tries to put weight on her damaged ankle.

'Why have you brought me here?'

He laughs. 'I'm showing you where your husband is. Underneath the soil.'

Rachel looks as he points at the recently dug hole.

'You killed him?'

'I didn't kill him, it was Heidi. She panicked, and I came over and helped her sort out the mess she'd made. We had to get rid of him. She'd intended all along to get her hands on the house, but becoming fond of the children took her by surprise. It wasn't part of the original plan. It made perfect sense, though, what with her not being able to have children herself.'

'I didn't know that. But let me go, please, we can work something out.'

He laughs again. 'You're not going anywhere, not now you know where Tom is. You'll go running straight to the police. Heidi should have moved into that house years ago, and all this time she's had to sit back and watch you getting all the benefits. The only way for her to feel secure is if you disappear. This hole is for you. We thought you'd want to be together with your husband. Seeing as how you double-crossed Heidi by trying to get him back. Nobody hurts my girl, ever.' He shakes her arm as he says this, and she stumbles again, her weak ankle unable to support her, and teeters on the edge of the hole. She screams, her cry ringing through the night as the depths of the earth sway in front of her. Then Danny pushes her, and with a cry she tumbles towards the freshly dug pit.

· · ·

'Rachel.' Strong hands grab her from behind, and she's suspended in mid-air. Then she's being pulled backwards, just as Danny lets out a cry and crashes down into the hole. He lands awkwardly on his face and goes still. Freddie stands over the pit, brandishing a large shovel. Heidi, white-faced, is just behind him, and she screams when she sees Danny lying motionless. It's too dark to see whether there is any blood around his head.

Rachel collapses to her knees and sobs. 'You've killed him,' she says. She manages to gasp out a few more words, her lungs constricted. 'What are you doing here?'

'I followed you. Breathe slowly,' Freddie says, and after a few minutes, she is calmer. 'Did you really think I'd let you go off into a dangerous situation like this? I love you, Rachel.'

She's too stunned to take his words in. The situation is surreal. Heidi has crumpled to the floor, a ball that's lost its air.

'What happened? Did you push him? Has he knocked himself out?'

'I hit him with the shovel. I doubt he's dead.'

They both stare at Danny's lifeless body. Freddie's face is ghostly in the dark.

Rachel is crying. 'He said Tom is buried here. I think he's telling the truth.' She can't bear to think of her husband lying out here undiscovered for all this time. As if nobody cared.

'He is.' Heidi raises her head to look at Rachel. 'I killed him. I've lost everything, so you might as well know the truth.'

THIRTY-NINE

HEIDI

Everything had begun to unravel after that dreadful row over the will. Just the previous month she thought she'd finally done it: their relationship was solid, they'd put down the deposit on the house, and she was winning the children over. She couldn't pinpoint the exact moment he had started to withdraw from her, because it was so gradual, but after a while he had become less attentive, more preoccupied – with his work, she presumed – and unable to give her the attention he'd lavished on her before.

That night they went out for dinner, she could never have predicted what was to come. He'd made the booking, wanting to talk to her, telling her he was sorry for the way he'd been behaving and that he wanted to make it up to her. Lots of wine had been drunk, but it had been necessary in order for them to lower their barriers and get them really talking about their deepest desires. He told her how much he loved her. That was when she made the mistake, the biggest mistake of her life.

They got back to the flat and he poured them both a whisky, and she opened up with her secret longing for them to get full custody of his children and move into the big house together.

She'd judged it so badly. At first, he didn't react, but simply stared into his drink. Heidi hated the silence and had to fill it with words, foolish words, words she couldn't get back once spoken. She confessed how much she hated Rachel, how Rachel had everything she herself wanted in life: the man, the house, the children.

When Tom finally spoke, his voice was cold. 'That's what this has all been about, hasn't it? That's why you wanted me to change my will. You don't love me, you just want my money. You want Rachel's life.' He had promised her the previous month that he would rewrite his will, finally giving in to her pressure to make her feel included.

She managed to reassure him that she loved him, that that was the only thing that mattered, but it was soon after that conversation that his attitude towards her changed drastically, especially once he found texts from Danny on her phone, and she had to confess that she'd seen him a couple of times since she and Tom had got together.

She'd never wanted to hurt him. This she told herself in the days, weeks, months, years afterwards. They'd driven that Monday night to Heidi's friend's place out in the country, a chance for the two of them to talk in different surroundings. She'd been on about taking him there for ages. It was cute and rural, with woodland behind the garden; it would be a complete change of scene.

The evening started so well, until once again alcohol was drunk and he lost it with her, telling her he'd never actually signed a new will; he'd had it drawn up but had changed his mind at the last minute. Thank God he'd stopped himself from actually signing it, he said. When children were involved, these were complicated decisions, he added, as if she was a child herself who had no comprehension of how the adult world worked. And he couldn't resist blurting out about sleeping with Rachel and admitting to still having feelings for her and was thinking about going back to her. The admission drove her to grab hold of the ornate candlestick and whack him over the head, causing him to fall face forward into the Georgian fireplace, sustaining a further blow to the temple. Either one of them would probably have killed him. With two blows, he didn't stand a chance.

Heidi did what she always did in a crisis: she called Danny. Danny, who'd been her on-off lover since they were teenagers. Danny, who'd grown into a small-time villain with a lot of shady contacts who would do the jobs nobody else wanted to do as long as the money was right. She'd called him once before when an ex-boyfriend wouldn't leave her alone – a quick word from Danny and she'd never heard from him again. She'd never asked him how he'd achieved this minor miracle.

This time was no different.

He came straight over and took charge of the situation. He wrapped the body in tarpaulin and brought his car round to the back of the house so they could get it in without being seen. Heidi stayed in the house to clean up any traces of the accident while Danny first got rid of Tom's car by calling one of his dodgy friends who owed him a favour. The friend collected the car and that was the last they saw of it. After that Danny drove to the woods near Blackberry Farm, the once derelict farmhouse he used to play in as a boy, and dug the grave.

She owed Danny big-time and he'd never let her forget it. One word from him and she'd be incarcerated, her life would be over, while Rachel got to keep the house that Heidi had tried so hard to get for herself. With Tom missing – and incredibly, more and more days passing without his body being discovered – she found herself becoming obsessed with the woman who was living the life she herself deserved.

When her attempt to get the guardianship failed, though, Heidi had given up and tried to concentrate on her own life. But that was before she took a chance stroll past the house and saw the scaffolding with the name of the expensive builder Rachel was using. She knew that the seven years were almost up – Tom could be declared officially dead and Rachel would get her hands on his assets once and for all. She called Danny and they came up with her plan.

The draft of the old will could still be somewhere in that house. The plan was to find it. Danny would be able to look for it while he was on the job. She'd gain access too, and if they couldn't find it, she'd plant her own, for Rachel to find.

He contacted the builder through his mate who owed him a favour, and requested some casual building work.

And she wrote Rachel a letter.

FORTY

RACHEL

'The police are on their way,' Freddie says, putting his phone back in his pocket.

'I'm not waiting for the police. I've got to find Lara. Where is she, Heidi?' Rachel shakes Heidi by the shoulders. 'Get up and tell me where she is.'

'She's in the farmhouse, in the bedroom upstairs.'

'I'm going to get her,' Rachel tells Freddie.

'Be careful. I'll stay here and wait for the police. They should be here any minute.'

Rachel wants to run as fast as she can towards the farmhouse, but her ankle is seriously painful and she hobbles along the path towards the illuminated windows. Heidi's car is still parked outside; the boot is open, as if waiting to swallow her whole. She approaches the front door and pushes, only to find it locked. She walks around to the back of the house, peering in at each window she passes, but can only make out that the kitchen is empty. The back door is locked too, so she finds a heavy rock in the garden, stands back and hurls it through the window. The sound of glass shattering splits the silence of the night, and a fragment hits her cheek. She puts her hand through the broken window and turns the safety catch on the inside. The door opens and she steps into the house.

She's in a small utility room, which leads into the country-style kitchen. She switches the light on and calls her daughter's name. Her face is stinging and she wipes away a trace of blood as she heads for the stairs.

'Lara,' she calls again, wincing as the wooden floorboards creak under her tread. The house feels empty; she doesn't get the sense that anyone is here. Panic rises at the thought of not finding her. Danny and Heidi are perfectly capable of lying to her, that she knows.

Upstairs, she checks first the bathroom, then the main bedroom. The remaining door has a key protruding from the keyhole. Inside, there is a single bed, a chest of drawers and an overturned coffee table. The bed cover is rumpled, as if someone has been lying on it, and a familiar smell fills the air. She sniffs. Apples – Lara's favourite shampoo. She switches the light on and gazes around the room, her attention coming to rest on something blue in the corner. She pounces on it, a sense of dread overtaking her. It's an item she'd recognise anywhere: Lara's beanie hat.

'Lara!' she yells.

'Mum?'

Her heart thuds at hearing her voice. She swivels round. Lara is standing behind the door. She falls into her mother's arms. They are both sobbing.

'Are you hurt?' Rachel asks. Lara shakes her head, which is buried in Rachel's chest. 'You're safe,' Rachel says. 'I love you.'

Lara holds her tight.

FORTY-ONE

Rachel calls Freddie.

'Lara's safe, they didn't hurt her.'

'Thank God.'

'Have the police arrived?' As she poses the question, she hears a siren approaching and lets out a sigh of relief. 'Thank goodness. I'm coming back.'

As she leads Lara out of the farmhouse, a police car is parking adjacent to Heidi's Fiat. Three officers emerge.

'My daughter was kidnapped,' Rachel says. 'She's unhurt but in shock.'

A female officer takes care of Lara, radioing for an ambulance.

'Try and keep calm, madam,' one of the others says. 'We're here now to help you. Was it you that called us?'

'No, that was Freddie, my friend, he's in the woods. He needs help.'

'Can you take us to him? We need to check he's not in immediate danger.' Rachel looks back towards Lara. 'Your daughter is in safe hands now. An ambulance will be here in five minutes.'

'You need to come this way,' she says, running towards the woods, suddenly terrified that Danny might rise up and pull Freddie into the pit. The police hurry to keep up, radios crackling, feet crunching over the ground beneath their feet.

The police go into feverish action, making lots of phone calls, and it's only when they're taping off the area that Rachel realises Danny is dead. Rachel and Freddie are escorted back to the farmhouse. Lara has already left in the ambulance. Heidi too is taken to the hospital, as she needs to be treated for shock.

Rachel calls her mother to let her know where she is.

'And Josh, is he OK?'

'Fast asleep upstairs,' her mother says. 'Have you been out looking for Lara all this time?'

'Something like that. I'll call you tomorrow, Mum, I don't know when we'll be home.'

She ends the call, energy draining from her body. She should have told her mother about Tom, only she can't bear to, not tonight. The policewoman has explained that the site will be guarded overnight and dug up in the morning as soon as it's light.

Rachel and Freddie snatch two hours' sleep once they are finally released from the police station, neither of them bothering to undress. Rachel sleeps with Lara, who has been released from hospital. She stares at the ceiling and digests everything that has happened on this longest night of her life. She thinks of Freddie, his comforting presence in Josh's room. incredulous that she suspected him, smiling when she remembers him saying he loves her. Then she thinks about Tom, her tears soaking into the bedclothes.

She shakes Freddie awake when the alarm shrieks into the

silence, and they drive back to the woods without speaking, dropping Lara off at her gran's on the way. A uniformed officer guards the scene, and ghostly people in white suits move around the clearing where last night's revelations played out. Blood rushes to Rachel's head as she is back on the edge of the hole, teetering forward. She grips Freddie's hand in an attempt to stay upright.

The white-suited forensic team make slow, careful movements, the detectives who have taken control of the case standing to one side drinking coffee from cardboard cups and talking into their phones. Rachel and Freddie are asked to move away from the scene. They sit in the car, waiting. After half an hour that seems to stretch out forever, a ghost raises an arm and people move in, the detectives bark commands and a white tent is erected. Rachel is about to discover what happened to her husband seven years ago.

Freddie comforts her as the day becomes lighter and the truth is revealed. Tom's remains are found at eight thirty. Rachel collapses and Freddie fetches a paramedic, who wants to take her to hospital and treat her for shock, but she insists on being taken to her mother's house, to her children, to the people who matter to her. Yes, she is in shock, but the difference is she knows the truth at last, and her life is no longer in limbo. She can finally grieve for Tom, a man she loved. Freddie is by her side and a new life is possible.

FORTY-TWO

TOM

What a mess. Tom sits in the dark corner of the pub, hoping nobody can see him. He's never been any good at hiding his feelings, and he has no doubt that the despair is written all over his face. He's made huge decisions over the past few months that have totally overhauled his life, convinced he was doing the right thing. But today, everything he thought he knew has turned upside down and he wants to be able to push the pieces from the board and rearrange them for a fresh start. Undo every crazy thing he has done, then shake the dice to begin. And this time he wouldn't choose Heidi.

He still loves his wife. He loves her, is in love with her, and he's done her a terrible injustice. Last week his world came crashing down when he realised that the woman he had thrown everything away for would never be satisfied and would always want more. And worse, she'd been unfaithful to him. Oh, the irony.

Some might accuse him of what subsequently happened with his wife as revenge, an inevitable lashing-out. Tit for tat.

But the truth is, he'd seen through the dark clouds and realised that what he wanted was already there: his wife and his children and the life they had embarked on. Is he too late to get her back?

Heidi wants a ring. A simple enough request for a woman, getting engaged, but the month before, she wanted a house. He's scrimped and saved and eventually stolen to make that happen, but he can see now that the house will never be enough for her. She finally came clean and admitted that what she wanted was the family home, plus the children. Tom realises that the money he's borrowed from work isn't enough; he needs more, and worst of all, he can't pay the original loan back. For he's always thought of it as a loan; it's his company after all, and Freddie is like a brother to him. Wrong, he's lost Freddie too. Another calamitous consequence of his relationship with Heidi.

He realised all this as he drove the children home to Rachel and found himself wishing he could lead them into the house, close the door firmly behind him and take his wife in his arms, safe in the knowledge that this was his family, his home. Forever.

Instead, he returned the children and told Rachel he needed to talk to her. He waited until Lara and Josh were settled into bed, then admitted to her what a terrible mistake he'd made, sobbing like his son did when he fell over in the park. It didn't surprise him when Rachel offered him a comforting hand, their lips met and they responded to each other in the way they always had before. Before Heidi.

They talked until the sky was pitch dark. He'd turned his phone off to stop Heidi's messages from bombarding him, and he promised he would end it with her. He just needed a few days.

They kissed on the doorstep and he held Rachel tight. Her body was more fragile than he remembered, caused by his actions, and he promised never to hurt her again.

FORTY-THREE

RACHEL

Two months later

The estate agent waves as he gets into his car and drives away. Rachel is left with the wooden For Sale sign and a stomach full of hope. She walks back down the path and looks up at the house. The scaffolding was removed last week. Pete had spent a week in hospital undergoing tests, and his wife said the visit from Rachel in which she recounted the events of the past few years was the most intense hospital visit he'd ever had, and that if she'd been there, she'd have put a stop to it in case he had another heart attack. Pete had arranged for a builder friend of his to come in and repair the damage and complete the work on the extension. Freddie had taken over as unofficial project manager and supervised the work. It didn't take long, given that the house was now empty, and as soon as it was ready, the estate agent came in to organise the sale.

This is the first time Rachel has been back here since she hastily packed essentials for her and the children and they all decamped to her mother's, who complains about the noise and mess but is secretly thrilled with the prospect of seeing her grandchildren every day. She knows it won't be for long, though, because Freddie and Rachel have decided to move in together.

Rachel confessed to Freddie that she'd been suspicious of him for a while, and being Freddie, he understood.

'You were under attack,' he said. 'It makes sense to suspect any new person in your life.'

'Emma was warning me to be cautious, as you'd suddenly got in touch. And you telling me about the embezzlement didn't help. She was concerned that you might be after Tom's share of the business. Declaring him dead would mean I could sell out to somebody else and it would be out of your control. I can see where she's coming from.'

They've spent hours analysing Heidi and her behaviour.

'She was desperate to stop me from declaring Tom dead. She made out she didn't know exactly how much time had passed since his disappearance when she knew down to the day. I'm not sure anything she told me was the truth.'

'Sending the notes was a bit desperate, but I can kind of see her logic,' Freddie said. 'If there was any possibility that Tom was alive, you wouldn't be able to declare him dead and inherit the house. And don't forget that Danny was putting pressure on her. He didn't want to let her go, and he had that ultimate power over her: he could reveal that she had killed Tom and then her life would be over. Like it is now.'

Rachel pulled a face.

'She doesn't deserve sympathy, Rach, especially not from you. She wanted the house and your kids, that's what all this was about. She wanted your life. She didn't want you to finally get your hands on the house officially, because that would mean the end of her dream. The fantasy life she'd dreamed of ever since she met Tom. Tom died because he told her he was still in love with you. She never had any intention of being your friend.'

'I'm just relieved she didn't get any closer to the children. To think that her and Lara—'

'Stop. Don't let your mind go there. Think about Lara now and what a change there has been. You're not the only one to have a new lease of life.'

Rachel goes over these conversations with Freddie constantly. Now she looks at her watch. Time to get back. Holly is stopping over tonight. She and Lara have set up a crime channel and are making short films about old cases. At least one good thing has come out of this. And Josh is still Josh.

She smiles, then takes one last look at the house. She hopes whoever buys it will be happy there. She glances up at the loft extension, her bedroom that never was. Images of the red-splattered walls still come to her, but less frequently, and she's learning to shut them out.

Her phone rings. Freddie.

'All sorted?'

'Yes. I'm just leaving.'

'How long will you be?'

'I'm coming right now.'

'I can't wait.'

'Me neither.'

Rachel has spent the last seven years waiting, and she won't wait around for a moment longer. A new life beckons. She closes the gate behind her with a satisfying click and doesn't look back.

FORTY-FOUR

HEIDI

Present day

It was a relief to get the truth out. Danny, Tom, everything. Danny has no hold over me any more, although he wasn't supposed to die for that to happen. His death means he won't have to face the consequences of disposing of Tom's body, kidnapping Lara, and attempting to murder Rachel. Every possible charge is being thrown at me. My lawyer is confident she can get me a reduced sentence, but I'm finding it hard to care.

Getting close to Lara made me more determined to succeed; not only would I get the house I deserved, I'd have won the children over too, a fitting punishment for Rachel's attempt to lure Tom back to her. Now that I've been exposed as responsible for Tom's death, Lara will never believe that I had genuine feelings for her. I wrote her a letter, pored over it for days, deliberating over each word to get my message exactly right. It was returned to my solicitor. Rachel refuses to let me have contact with any of her family again.

The newspapers have homed in on the story; two women

fighting over a man is always a crowd-pleaser, a story that's been played out millions of times before and will continue to do so in years to come. I've read different versions of my story, but none of them get it right. Rachel is made out to be the victim, the hero, and will forever have the sympathy of the people. While I, meanwhile, have to endure the indignity of going to court with a blanket over my head in a vain attempt to keep out the heckling crowds baying threats and abuse. I hear every word thrown at me, every insult; all the blanket does is screen me from the twisted faces spewing out these words. It doesn't even protect my identity. Everyone knows my face, my crime. Never mind that Danny was my conspirator; words can no longer reach him, and the woman is always easier to blame.

One headline stands out amongst the others: *A CRIME OF PASSION*. I know I am greedy, selfish, inhuman; all the accusations thrown at me are true. But only the word *passion* has true resonance for me; everything I did was for love. The tragedy for me is that Tom didn't believe me. He forgot those early days, and when his financial worries took over, everything became about that. He couldn't see past my material desires – who doesn't want a nice house and a family? It's not a crime. It breaks my heart that he didn't realise how much I adored him. I loved him with a passion I have never experienced in the same way either before or since, and I would do it all again.

A LETTER FROM LESLEY

Thank you so much for reading *The Widow's Husband*. I hope you enjoyed reading it as much as I enjoyed writing it.

To keep up to date with my new releases, please sign up to my newsletter at the link below. I promise never to share your email with anyone else.

www.bookouture.com/lesley-sanderson

As with my first five books – *The Orchid Girls*, *The Woman at 46 Heath Street*, *The Leaving Party*, *I Know You Lied* and *Every Little Lie* – I hoped to create an evocative novel about obsession, secrets and the blurred lines between love and lies.

If you enjoyed *The Widow's Husband*, I would love it if you could write a short review. Getting reviews from readers who have enjoyed my writing is my favourite way to persuade other readers to pick up one of my books for the first time.

I'd also love to hear from you via social media: see the links below.

Lesley

facebook.com/lsandersonbooks

twitter.com/LSandersonbooks

instagram.com/lesleysandersonauthor

ACKNOWLEDGEMENTS

So many people have helped me along the way with *The Widow's Husband*.

Thanks to my lovely agent, Hayley Steed, and to everyone else at the fabulous Madeleine Milburn agency. Hayley, I'm so pleased we managed to meet again recently.

To Louise Beere, Ruth Heald, Rona Halsall and Vikki Patis for constant support with my writing.

Several editors were involved with this book due to staff moves at Bookouture. Thanks to Therese Keating, who worked with me initially – it's been great working with you and I wish you well at Viper Books. To Isobel Akenhead, for interim support while I was between editors: it was lovely to get to know you and learn from your expertise. To my new editor, Susannah Hamilton, I'm already enjoying working with you – plotting is such fun! Also to Eve Hall, thanks for the fabulous line edit you did on this book; it was really enjoyable to work with you and I appreciate your know-how. To Becca Allen and Jane Selley, for enduring and spotting any errors in the proof-reads and copy edits you have now done on several of my books. To Emily Boyce and Alex Holmes for final edits. I'd like to thank all the staff at Bookouture, who are a fabulous, friendly publisher to work with, and I am proud to be one of your authors.

And to everyone else – all the other writers I've met along the way, too many to name but nonetheless important – I'm so happy to be one of such a friendly group of people.

To my family and friends old and new for believing in me, thank you.

And of course, to Paul.

Printed in Great Britain
by Amazon

21258689R00150